Praise for Books by Anna Carey

The Making of Mollie

'I loved Mollie – she is rebellious … thoughtful and funny.'
thetbrpile.com

'A girl's eye view of early feminism … exciting, vivid … with the impulsive and daring Mollie.' *Lovereading4kids.co.uk*

'For junior feminists … a must-read.' *The Irish Times*

'Mollie's struggles are strikingly relevant to the teenagers of today.'
Sunday Business Post

Mollie on the March

'I cannot tell you how much I adore these books. They're funny and clever and Mollie is a BRILLIANT character … I found myself moved by the plight some of these women endured in their struggle to win rights that we take for granted today.' *Louise O'Neill*

'It's wonderful but also brought home how hard the struggle was, how scary, and that's giving me courage to keep on pushing for our rights today.' *Marian Keyes*

'Just as charming as the first … a deeply relatable story and a welcome reminder that Irish history has more to it than nationalist rebellions.'
The Irish Times

The Boldness of Betty

'[Anna Carey's] most substantial and historically enlightening novel yet.'
Evening Echo

The Real Rebecca

'Definite Princess of Teen.' *Books for Keeps*

'The sparkling and spookily accurate diary of a Dublin teenager. I
haven't laughed so much since reading Louise Rennison. Teenage girls
will love Rebecca to bits!'
Sarah Webb, author of the *Ask Amy Green* books

'This book is fantastic! Rebecca is sweet, funny and down-to-earth, and
I adored her friends, her quirky parents, her changeable but ultimately
loving older sister and the swoonworthy Paperboy.' *Chicklish Blog*

'What is it like inside the mind of a teenage girl? It's a strange, confused
and frustrated place. A laugh-out-loud story of a fourteen-year-old girl,
Rebecca Rafferty.' *Hot Press*

Rebecca's Rules

'A gorgeous book! ... So funny, sweet, bright. I loved it.' Marian Keyes

'Amusing from the first page ... better than Adrian Mole!
Highly recommended.' *lovereading4kids.co.uk*

'Sure to be a favourite with fans of authors such as
Sarah Webb and Judi Curtin.' *Children's Books Ireland's
Recommended Reads 2012*

Rebecca Rocks

'The pages in Carey's novel in which her young lesbian character announces her coming out to her friends and in which they give their reactions are superbly written: tone is everything, and it could not be better handled than it is here.' *The Irish Times*

'A hilarious new book. Cleverly written, witty and smart.' *writing.ie*

'Rebecca Rafferty … is something of a Books for Keeps favourite … Honest, real, touching, a terrific piece of writing.' *Books for Keeps*

Rebecca is Always Right

Fun … feisty, off-the-wall individuals and a brisk plot.'
Sunday Independent

'Be warned: don't read this in public because from the first sentence this story is laugh out loud funny … This book is the funniest yet.'
Inis Magazine

'Portrays a world of adolescent ups and downs … Rebecca is at once participant in and observer of, what goes on in her circle, recording it all in a tone of voice in which humour, wryness and irony are shrewdly balanced.'
The Irish Times

ANNA CAREY is a journalist and author from Dublin who
has written for the *Irish Times*, *Irish Independent* and many other
publications. Anna's first book, *The Real Rebecca*, was published in 2011,
and went on to win the Senior Children's Book prize at the Irish
Book Awards. Rebecca returned in the critically acclaimed *Rebecca's
Rules*, *Rebecca Rocks* and *Rebecca is Always Right*. *The Making of Mollie* is
her first historical novel and was shortlisted for the Senior Children's
Book prize at the 2016 Irish Book Awards. *Mollie on the March*, about
more of Mollie's feisty feminist activities, and *The Boldness of Betty*, set
during the 1913 Lockout, are also published by The O'Brien Press.

the MAKING of MOLLIE

Anna Carey

THE O'BRIEN PRESS
DUBLIN

First published 2016 by The O'Brien Press Ltd,
12 Terenure Road East, Rathgar, D06 HD27, Dublin 6, Ireland.
Tel: +353 1 4923333; Fax: +353 1 4922777
E-mail: books@obrien.ie
Website: www.obrien.ie
Reprinted 2017, 2020.
The O'Brien Press is a member of Publishing Ireland.

ISBN: 978-1-84717-847-3

10 9 8 7 6 5 4 3
23 22 21 20

Layout and design: The O'Brien Press Ltd.
Cover illustrations: Lauren O'Neill

Printed and bound by Nørhaven, Denmark.
The paper in this book is produced using pulp from managed forests.

Published in:

DUBLIN
UNESCO
City of Literature

To Jennifer, Louise and Miriam.

If it weren't for Dominican College, we would never have met.

And to Clare Cunniffe, who, in 1918, gave a speech to the same school's Aquinas Debating Society on 'Why Women Should Have The Vote'.

According to the school yearbook, her speech 'gave her full scope to express her rather definite and decided views on that much vexed question.'

Acknowledgements

My heartfelt thanks to the extremely patient Susan Houlden, Emma Byrne and everyone at The O'Brien Press who had faith in Mollie after I abandoned another book and told them I wanted to write about teenage suffragettes instead; Lauren O'Neill, for a cover so perfect it made me cry with happiness; Sarah Webb and Marian Keyes, who gave me much-appreciated advice when I was struggling with post-Rebecca writing; Helen Carr, as ever, for encouraging me (and listening to me whine); everyone on Twitter who cheered me on; and Elizabeth Gilbert, whose book *Big Magic* had a huge effect on me when I was really struggling with starting this book.

This book could not have been written without the generosity of two people. One is Sister Catherine Gibson, who allowed me to spend a fascinating morning in the Dominican Convent on Griffith Avenue eating delicious biscuits and going through the first few years of the Dominican College yearbook, *The Lanthorn*, from 1913 to 1917. The other person is Doctor Senia Paseta of Saint Hugh's College, Oxford, who very patiently answered many, many questions by phone and email about the Irish suffrage movement and provided me with lots of wonderfully useful and inspiring information that I would never have discovered otherwise. Any historical inaccuracies are entirely my own. Thanks also to Ciaran O'Neill, who kindly put me in touch with Doctor Paseta. I hope they all enjoy reading this book.

And thanks as ever to the extended Carey/Freyne family, and to Patrick, for everything.

HISTORICAL NOTE

This book is set in Dublin in 1912. At the time, Ireland was part of the United Kingdom, but there was a big demand in Ireland for what was called Home Rule. This meant that Ireland would be part of the UK, but would have its own parliament in Dublin.

In 1912, the only people who could vote in general elections in the UK were men (and not even all men – only men who owned or lived in property of a certain value). Lots of women, however, were campaigning for the vote, and they were known as suffragists or suffragettes.

25 Lindsay Gardens,
Drumcondra,
Dublin.

25th March, 1912.

Dear Frances,

I hate my brother. I know this isn't a very conventional
way to start a letter and I should be asking you how you
are and whether your house won the last hockey match,
and telling you about my health and what the weather's
like, but I'm so boiling with rage that I can't think of
anything else right now. I know you don't think that
Harry is that bad, but really, Frances, that is just because
you're an only child. If you had a brother like Harry I
know you'd hate him too. He's always been annoying, of
course. He loves lording it over me and acting as if he's
ten years older than me instead of only two, and he loves
the fact that he's allowed to do whatever he wants (well,
practically everything), while I always have to ask for
permission and never get it (well, hardly ever).

But this time he surpassed himself. We were having roast chicken for dinner, which is my very favourite thing to eat as you know, and when Father was carving it I asked if I could have some of the breast, which is my very favourite bit of roast chicken. And as usual Mother said, 'Now, Mollie, wait until your father and Harry have been served.'

Father said, 'Oh don't worry, Rose, I don't mind,' but Harry said, 'I certainly do.'

If Mother and Father hadn't been there I'd have told him to shut up, but as they were there I just made a face at him when they weren't watching. Which clearly wasn't enough to stop him tormenting me, because even when Father had given me and Phyllis a little bit of chicken breast (the rest of my serving was leg, which I do like too, but not as much as the breast), Harry kept going on and on about how good food was just wasted on girls and that as the men of the house he and Father needed to keep their strength up. And even when Mother said, 'Harry, don't tease your sister,' he didn't stop.

I don't know why it made me so angry this evening. It wasn't as though it were something new. Things like this happen at meals every week. Harry is always served before us girls and he always gets the best bits. But for some reason today it was particularly infuriating. Phyllis wasn't impressed either, especially when Harry started on about the 'men of the house'.

'You're hardly a man,' she said dryly. 'You're still in school.'

'And Phyllis is going to be at university next year,' I said. 'While you'll still be stuck in a classroom. Nothing very manly about that.'

Harry looked annoyed at this, but before he could respond, Father said, 'Now, children, do stop bickering,' and Mother started telling us about Aunt Josephine's extremely boring plans to start painting watercolours. Actually, I should probably have been more grateful for this news, because maybe if Aunt Josephine starts spending all her time painting views of Dollymount Strand she'll have no time to call around here every day and tell us exactly what we're doing wrong. If I didn't have such an awful brother myself, I wouldn't believe that someone as essentially decent as Father could have such a dreadful sister. They're not a bit alike.

But I'm getting distracted. The rest of dinner passed peacefully (if boringly), and then Mother played some new songs on the piano, and we all sang (well, me and Phyllis did. Julia only wants to sing hymns at the moment, and Harry just rolled his eyes when Mother got out the sheet music). But then, after we'd sung ourselves hoarse, Mother announced that Phyllis, Julia and I had to help her with some mending. You know how dull mending is, and this evening Father had to go through some documents or other from the Department, so he wasn't even there to entertain us by reading us the latest chapters of that epic novel of his. Which meant that the mending was even more dull than usual.

I don't understand why there's always so much mending to do. It's not as though we all go around ripping up our clothes on purpose. But somehow there's always something to be mended or darned or hemmed or some other fiddly little job, and it's always me and Phyllis who have to do the worst ones (Julia only has to mend things like old tea towels where it doesn't matter so much if the stitches are perfect or not. Even though she's twelve, Mother is convinced that she's a poor little baby, who can only perform the most simple of tasks. She certainly didn't think this about me when I was twelve). Some people send out their mending, but Mother says that's a waste of money.

'I have three perfectly good menders in the house already,' she says, and then laughs as if it were a hilarious joke. I told her that I would gladly go without a hideous new school hat if it would help her afford to get things mended but she said I had to have a new hat for school, and besides, my hat isn't hideous (this is a lie).

So anyway, there we were, sitting by the fire, sewing some buttons that had got loose on my least favourite blouse (me) and fixing a skirt hem that had come down (Phyllis) and a towel that had got a hole torn in it (Julia. I think she might tear them on purpose so she can always have something easy to do on mending evenings and Mother isn't tempted to give her something more complicated, like a lace petticoat). And then Harry marched in with his friend Frank Nugent, who had mysteriously appeared in our house from nowhere as far as I could tell, and THREW A PILE OF SMELLY SOCKS IN MY FACE.

'Go on, darn these,' he said, and sniggered in a particularly enraging way.

Frank didn't snigger. In fact, he looked a bit uncomfortable.

'I say, Harry. That was a bit …' he said, and that was when Mother came in.

'Harry threw these horrible socks at me!' I cried.

'I just told her they need darning,' said Harry calmly. His face was so innocent you would never think he had been gleefully throwing socks around just a few seconds earlier.

'Some of them aren't even clean,' I said furiously. 'They absolutely stink.'

'Harry, you shouldn't throw socks at your sister,' said Mother sternly.

I threw Harry a triumphant look. But my triumph was

short-lived, as Mother then picked up a grey sock and examined the heel. It was practically worn through.

'But Mollie, they do need to be darned,' she said, 'so you might as well do it now. The clean ones anyway.'

Harry smirked at me in a sickening way, and I glared at him as ferociously as I could. Which must have been very ferociously, because Frank looked a little scared. Harry didn't, unfortunately.

'Mother, I'm going to Frank's house,' he said. 'We're going to test each other on French verbs.'

'I'm not sure I should let you go anywhere, after this childish carry on,' said Mother.

'Oh, Mother, I was only teasing,' said Harry plaintively.

'All right,' said Mother. 'But don't be late home.'

If I'd thrown socks in someone's face and then demanded to go to Nora's house, I would definitely not have been allowed to go out.

'I'll try not to be,' said Harry. 'Though we do have so much studying to do.'

And he smirked again at me and Phyllis, and went off.

Frank gave us a sort of apologetic wave as they left. He sometimes seems like he could be quite a nice boy really, but how nice can he be if he's friends with Harry?

Anyway, I knew perfectly well that Harry wasn't going to study French verbs, or anything like it. The two of them were probably going to try smoking Frank's father's pipe again. Nora and I caught them at it in the grounds of the church last week, and very sick they looked too. Which served them right.

But of course, I couldn't say anything about that to Mother. After all, I'm not a sneak, even if some people deserve to be sneaked on. Instead, I had sit there and darn Harry's stupid socks. I should have sewn up the toes so that they'd pinch his feet when he next put them on. But, unlike Harry, I'm not a spiteful, mean-spirited monster. So I just imagined sewing up the toes instead, which wasn't half as much fun.

So that's why I was so angry. Now that I've written it all down I feel much better. Writing sometimes has that effect, I find. I've thought about keeping a diary, but Harry would probably find it and read it, and then make my life a misery teasing me about it. And if he didn't find it, Julia probably would, seeing as we are forced to share a room. It's so unfair that I have to share a room with such a baby who still plays with dolls when I am practically a grown-up (or at least am no longer a Junior at school). And it's not only her babyishness that makes it hard to sleep in the same room with her. Recently she's started to get very religious in an annoying way. She keeps telling us we should all pray more and go to Mass every day, and has started putting up even more holy pictures and scapulars and things next to her bed. And she spends about five years saying her prayers every night.

Of course I say my prayers too, but I'm always finished in about five minutes, and then I have to put up with Julia looking at me reproachfully out of her enormous green eyes while she prays on and on and on. She was even worse than usual tonight. When she finally got into bed she looked across the room where I was sitting in bed reading *Three Men and a Boat* (which is awfully funny, you should see if they have it in your school's library) and said, 'You really should say your prayers properly, you know.'

'How do you know I don't?' I asked, without looking up from the book.

'You rush through them,' she said. 'I looked at the clock tonight. It was only two minutes.'

'What were you doing looking at the clock?' I said. 'I thought you were meant to be praying too.'

And she didn't say anything after that. I sometimes think half of the praying business is just for show, but there's no point in trying to convince some of the grown-ups of that. Aunt Josephine thinks Julia is a perfect little girl. In fact, last week she asked me why I couldn't be more like her, which even Mother thought was a bit much.

'I'm not saying there's not room for improvement,' Mother said, looking at me in a way which showed she was at least partly joking, 'but really, Mollie's a very good girl. Not everyone can be as, well, as devout as Julia is at the moment.'

All the nuns at school love Julia, of course. It doesn't help that she looks so ridiculously angelic with her flowing blonde hair. I never looked like that when I was her age. As you know, the rest of us Carberrys have thick brown hair that looks exactly like a set of wavy brown mops (at least, I presume that's what Aunt Josephine's hair would look like if she ever let it down. Which I doubt she ever does. I bet she even sleeps with it up in that complicated bun). But Father says that when he was a little boy his mother (who died before I was born) had fair hair like Julia's. Honestly, if it wasn't for that, I'd think Julia was somehow swapped at birth with another baby, even though she was born in this very house so I'm not sure who she could have been swapped with. She really isn't like any of the rest of us. Not least because she's so good. Even when she's with her friend Christina, they never seem to do anything interesting.

Years ago, Nora's big brother convinced her that when she was a baby, their maid had left the pram outside a shop and then taken the wrong one home and Nora believed it for nearly a year. She was totally convinced that she wasn't a blood relation to the rest of the Cantwells, even though she has reddish hair and dark blue eyes just like her Aunt Alice. Actually, Nora always says she can't understand how she can look so like Aunt Alice, who is very beautiful (and she really she is; men are always writing poems about her and comparing her to Ireland itself) while not being very beautiful herself. Not that Nora isn't nice-looking – I think she looks very nice indeed – but she is convinced that her nose is too big for her face (it's not that big), her legs are too short and that her hair is always falling out of its hair ribbon. Well, the last bit is definitely true. Anyway, at least you definitely know you're related to your parents. You all have such excellent black curls.

But back to the awfulness of sharing with Julia. The other day, after Julia took all my things off the dressing table that we share and made a little shrine to the Blessed Virgin, I asked Mother if I could take Harry's room if he went away to boarding school. Mother said I was being ridiculous, not least because Harry wasn't going away to school when there was a perfectly good school two miles down the road. Then she said that if he did go to boarding school, he'd still have to have a room at home in the holidays. Which I know is fair enough, or it would be if it applied to anyone but Harry. On a brighter note, she did tell Julia she couldn't turn our dressing table into a shrine, so that's something. Julia put her statues and holy pictures on her bookshelf instead, which is quite all right.

Anyhow, I know it's ages since I got your last letter, and I'm very sorry I haven't written to you sooner, but really my life is so incredibly dull. There's absolutely nothing to say. All I do every day are the following things:

~

Walk to school, usually in the rain, which means by the time I get there I am tired or wet or both.

Sit through hours and hours of boring lessons (well, I suppose some of them are all right, but most are pretty dull).

Talk to Nora about how tedious our lives are. And sometimes other things too.

Try to avoid Grace Molyneaux and Gertie Hayden (which can be tricky because Grace is Nora's cousin and all grown-ups love her and urge us to spend more time with her).

Walk home, usually in the rain (see Number One).

Do my home exercises.

Try to avoid Mother, Father, Phyllis, Harry and Julia, all of whom seem determined to annoy me in different but equally irritating ways.

Listen to Mother play the piano and hear her remind us that she could have been a concert pianist if her parents had had the money to send her to Paris.

Read books about people whose lives are more exciting than mine (Please send me some book recommendations, by the way. I feel as though I've read all the good ones in our house AND the school library).

Listen to Father read from his epic novel (actually, that *is* quite fun).

~

And that's more or less it, apart from Sundays, which don't involve school but which, of course, do involve getting up early to go to Mass. And sometimes there is escaping to Nora's house (or having her come to visit me). But really there is not much variety in my life these days. So you can see that you haven't been missing out on anything due to my lack of letters.

I am trying to think of something more exciting to write about but all I can think of is that I finished knitting quite a nice scarf (blue wool, moss stitch) and that Nora has decided she wants to become a doctor. But she's always coming up with new ambitions. Last year when women were allowed to vote in the council election she said she wanted to be Dublin's first lady mayor, but that only lasted for a few days, so she will probably want to be something totally different soon. Oh, and Phyllis is definitely going to go to University in October, which I suppose means that I will be allowed go there too. But as that won't be for at least four years I can't feel too excited about it at the moment.

And I won't get there at all if I don't work hard at school. It's not that I'm lazy exactly, but I must admit that I don't always work as much as I might. I certainly don't work as hard as Grace Molyneaux, who is absolutely determined to win the Middle Grade Cup. This is a new award that some of the staff at school have created in order to encourage us to work harder. Do you have any prizes like that in your school? I'm not sure they're a good idea if Grace's behaviour is anything to go by. The girl who has received the best marks all term and in the summer exams will win a special little cup, and I haven't mentioned it in my letters before because it is extremely boring, and also I have no chance of winning it. Grace, however, has become obsessed with it and it's made her even more annoying than usual. She's already gloating over what she sure will be her triumphant victory.

Though being Grace, she pretends that she isn't gloating and says things like, 'Oh of course, a silly little girl like me couldn't possibly win that cup! But wouldn't it be awfully nice if I did?'

Meanwhile, Daisy Redmond, who is almost always top of the class, doesn't go on about the cup at all. She works for the love of knowledge and not the supposed glory of a cup. But for Grace it is all about victory and she is always furious whenever Daisy gets better marks than her, even though Daisy doesn't seem bothered either way. Grace is determined to beat her and she (Grace, that is, not Daisy) has got a special notebook in which she takes notes for all the extra study she is doing. I feel exhausted just thinking about all this school-work. All I know is that I hope Daisy wins.

Do write soon and let me know all about your adventures. Your life always seems much more exciting than mine. Maybe it's because you don't have nuns in England (or at least in your school) so it all seems very exotic. Some girls in school think being a nun looks very romantic and important, but I wouldn't want to be one myself. They have to get up practically in the middle of the night and go to Mass every single day and twice on Sundays. Please write soon. Hopefully I will not have died of boredom by then.

Lots of love,
Your fond friend,
Mollie

5th April, 1912.

Dear Frances,

I know my last letter was entirely devoted to how boring
my life is, but something very strange has been
happening in our house, and it involves Phyllis. Yes,
yes, I know what you're thinking: she's generally doing
something odd, and it's never very interesting. We all
remember the summer she decided she was going to be
a poet and went around wearing strange Celtic robes
and going on about Golden Dawns and similar rubbish.
But now she's being even stranger than usual and it's
quite intriguing. I'm not sure whether she's having a
secret love affair or whether she's become some sort of
revolutionary or even a burglar, but you have to admit
that all options sound quite exciting (as long as she
doesn't get arrested).

It started last Wednesday at about half past six. Mother
was in the kitchen talking to Maggie about the next
day's dinner. You remember Maggie, don't you? She's our
cook-general servant. Mother always says she couldn't

do without her, which is perfectly true as Maggie does practically every useful thing in this house, including almost all the unpleasant jobs like cleaning out fires (a woman called Mrs. Carr comes in once a week to do some of the rough work). And Maggie has to get up at half past six and start laying the fires and getting the breakfast ready. Also, she's a much better cook than Mother is. Or Phyllis. Or me, for that matter.

Maggie is almost like one of the family, Mother says (though she *does* sleep in a tiny little bedroom, which none of us do, and she *does* spend all day working for us). Admittedly, she does get much more time off than any other servant I know. Nora's family's maid, Agnes, only gets one half Sunday off a fortnight, but Maggie comes and goes as she pleases as long as all the work is done at the right time. Which it always is.

Anyway, she and Mother were in the kitchen, and Julia was in the drawing room with Aunt Josephine (who I'm sure was telling Julia how wonderful she is – something she will never tell me or Phyllis). Father was still in the office, Harry had gone to his friend Frank's house after school, and I was in the dining room doing my Latin exercises (I still think it's so unfair having to do work at home. Surely the whole point of going to a day school, and not a boarding school, like you, is that you can escape lessons as soon as you leave the place). I was tackling a particularly irritating bit of Virgil when Phyllis came into the room wearing a ridiculous hat and a secretive expression.

'What on earth have you got on your head?' I said.

She nearly jumped out of her skin.

'What are you doing in here?' she said. 'And why are you lurking in the dark?'

The dining room is always dark because it faces north and any daylight that might get in is blocked by the kitchen.

'I live here,' I said. 'And I'm not lurking, I'm just doing my Latin and I hadn't bothered turning the light on yet. It's only just about starting to get dark anyway. In fact, if anyone's lurking around here, it's you. Why didn't YOU turn on a light when you came in? What are you sneaking about for?'

Actually I hadn't turned on a light because I am always slightly nervous about lighting the gas in case it explodes, but I didn't want to admit that to her.

'I didn't turn on a light because it's only half past six and it's terribly wasteful,' said Phyllis. 'And besides, I'm not sneaking.' But she looked away from me and towards the window in a suspicious manner so I knew something was up. She's such a terrible liar.

'Well, if you were sneaking, and you clearly were, you should wear a less dramatic hat,' I said. 'That one looks like you've got half a chicken on your head.'

'I love this hat,' she said indignantly. 'Kathleen trimmed it for me.'

I don't know if you remember Kathleen. She's Phyllis's tall friend with the black hair and the nice long eyelashes. She thinks she's a great artist, even though the only thing she seems to make are hideous hats. She and Phyllis spend all their time together, though not this week as Kathleen has been laid up with a horrid flu and can't have visitors.

'Kathleen? That explains it,' I said. 'Anyway, go on, get out. I've got lots of stupid Latin translation to do and I need to concentrate.'

'You could probably do with a little break,' said Phyllis. 'Go down to Maggie and get a cup of tea. You look like you've been here for hours.'

Now I really knew something was up. Phyllis is not normally concerned about my welfare. Quite the opposite, in fact. So if she wanted me to take a tea break, it was because she wanted me out of the room.

And that was when I had my excellent idea. Frances, I think I might be a natural detective. Remember the Christmas when we read all the Sherlock Holmes stories? They must have rubbed off on me because I suddenly knew exactly what to do.

'All right,' I said. 'Would you like a cup too?'

'What? Oh, no, no,' said Phyllis. 'I think I might ... have a lie down. I don't feel very well. Maybe I've got Kathleen's flu.'

I told you she was a terrible liar.

'You do look a bit pale,' I said, and I left the room. But I didn't close the door fully behind me. And I didn't go to the kitchen. I stayed out in the hall, and I peered back through the door crack. Which is how I saw Phyllis open the dining room window, climb out into the back garden, run across the garden and then gently open the back gate and sneak – yes, sneak is the only word for it – into the lane behind the house. And then off she went, goodness knows where.

Phyllis is not the sort of person who likes climbing and running at the best of times, so if she was leaving the house via the window, it was only because she really, really wanted to get out without Mother knowing about it. But where was she going? That is what I still want to find out. It couldn't have been to Kathleen's house because she wouldn't have needed to sneak off there. Besides, we all knew Kathleen has the flu.

And not only do I not know where Phyllis went, I don't even know what time she came home. She must have come in through the kitchen door because I came into the drawing room at about nine to say goodnight to Mother and Father and she was sitting there reading a book, looking like the sort of well-behaved young lady who would never dream of creeping out a window.

And to make things even more mysterious, on Sunday she went out with Kathleen, who had recovered from her flu, supposedly to spend the day at Kathleen's aunt's house. This aunt was having a visit from some friend from England who is a professional singer and who was going to perform some Thomas Moore songs for a select group of guests. But the next morning I went into Phyllis's room to borrow a hair ribbon (I really did need one. I was NOT sneaking) while she was downstairs finishing her breakfast and I saw the hat she'd been wearing the day before on top of her wardrobe. And amid all the feathers and trimmings I could see what definitely looked like flour mixed up with horrible old cabbage leaves. Which would be a peculiar trimming even by Kathleen's standards, and besides, those leaves definitely hadn't been there the previous morning.

And if that all weren't enough to make any sensible girl suspicious (and I think you'll agree, Frances, that I am always very sensible), this isn't the only mysterious thing she's done recently. There's all the strangeness with Maggie too.

Even though it feels like Maggie has been here all my life, like my parents, she actually only came to work for us when I was about four and she's really closer to

Phyllis's age than my mother's – I think she's about thirty now. And she and Phyllis have always got on well. But recently they seem to have become even closer. Over the last few weeks I keep coming into the kitchen and finding her and Phyllis sitting at the table talking very seriously and quietly, and then as soon as they see me they change the subject. I can't help thinking that this secrecy is probably connected to Phyllis's new habit of climbing out windows and sneaking off down lanes. I mean, it would be a bit of a coincidence if it weren't, wouldn't it? Both of them acting so secretively?

So there you go. Maybe Maggie is helping Phyllis with a secret love affair – like the nurse in *Romeo and Juliet*, although hopefully with less death and poison at the end. Mother and Father would definitely not approve of Phyllis going off to see a young man on her own. Or maybe Phyllis is either a revolutionary or a criminal and she and Maggie are involved in some sort of secret plot. I must admit neither seems very likely to me – especially the secret plot bit, Phyllis has never been the least bit political, but I can't think of anything else Phyllis could be doing that would make her sneak out of the house without our parents knowing about it. And I'm not sure how the cabbage leaves fit in with any of this. They remain the greatest mystery of all.

Maybe I'm thinking too much about it. Nora

definitely thinks I am. She says I'm making a mountain out of a molehill and that the solution is probably something totally ordinary. But Nora always thinks she knows best. I bet if she'd seen Phyllis climb out of that window she'd think very differently. As you know, *she* is never prone to 'wild flights of fancy', which is how she rudely described my perfectly logical ideas about Phyllis.

'Maggie's probably just helping her make a new frock, or something,' said Nora. 'You know how useless Phyllis is with the sewing machine. And she probably just sneaked out because she didn't want to go past the drawing room and be made to talk to your Aunt Josephine. I know I wouldn't.'

Which was a good point, I had to admit. I didn't want to talk to Aunt Josephine either (having Latin translation to do was rather a good excuse to stay out of her way). But why would Phyllis and Maggie be so secretive if they were just making a dress? And I don't think she would climb out of a window (and risk tearing her coat or damaging that dreadful hat, because she really isn't very good at climbing and she could easily have caught her clothes in something) just to avoid Aunt Josephine. Mother isn't the most observant person in the world, and if Aunt Josephine was going on one of her rants about modern young girls (i.e. me and Phyllis) and how awful and shameless and Godless they are, she mightn't even have noticed the front door opening and shutting. But you never know.

Anyway, the gong in the hall has just rung (Mother always tells Maggie she doesn't have to do it, but Maggie says that hitting the gong hard is a great relief after a long day's work), so I suppose tea is ready. I'd better stop writing. The teachers don't read your letters, do they? Or is that just in prison? Boarding school always sounds a bit like prison to me, even though the boarders at our school seem to quite like it. The nuns sometimes take them out to plays and lectures, and the next day they try to make the rest of us jealous by going on and on for years about what a glorious evening they had, though I can't imagine sitting through a lecture about Ancient Greece, especially with all the staff right next to you, could possibly be much fun. Some of the plays sound quite good though.

Have you had any outings recently? I suppose it's harder to go anywhere interesting when you're in the middle of the countryside. At least our boarders can walk to the theatre. I suppose being in a boarding school in the middle of the city has its advantages. Though of course when you *do* get to go on outings you can go to London, which is much more exciting. I'm still awfully jealous of you getting to go to the National Gallery in Trafalgar Square last year, even if you did trip and almost fall right on top of that Raphael painting.

Thanks awfully for the book recommendations. I've read a few of them already. I read *Northanger Abbey* a few months ago. Isn't it terribly good? I do like reading about girls who are our age – well, practically our age. I wish there were more books like that.

Write back soon,
Lots of love,

Mollie

P.S.

I should have told you that I have continued to keep a close eye on Phyllis since that evening, but she doesn't seem to have left the house by any strange means again. In fact, nobody has behaving oddly, or at least no more oddly than usual. Even Harry has been relatively subdued. This evening we all sat in the sitting room while Father read out the latest chapter of his epic story. I do wonder what his superiors in the Department would say if they knew about his literary ambitions. I have a suspicion that he sometimes writes the story in his office when he's meant to be doing whatever civil servants do all day (I am never entirely sure what that is).

'If only I'd found my calling sooner,' he said tonight, 'I would have earned a crust through my pen, instead of becoming a mere cog in the apparatus of government.' This is Father's flowery way of saying 'civil servant'. 'In fact,' Father went on, 'some day I might hand in my notice to Mr. Radley and devote myself to my art.' Mr. Radley is the Department's Permanent Secretary.

'I don't think that's a very good idea,' said Julia. She looked genuinely worried, though the rest of us knew that Father was joking (or at least partly joking).

'Neither do I, especially because you might not be able to earn a very big crust,' I said. 'Nora's uncle James is a writer and you should see his suits. They're practically all patches.'

This was a bit of an exaggeration, but not much. Nora's uncle James is frightfully nice but he's very hard up (and his suits really do look a bit shabby; the cuffs are always worn to shreds). Though I suppose he is a journalist and not a famous novelist, which is what Father wants to be.

'Oh don't worry,' said Father. 'I will continue to slave for the government and keep you all in the style to which you've clearly become accustomed. Now, who wants to hear Chapter Ten?"

And though, as usual, we all groaned and pretended we

didn't want to hear it at all, we did really, because Father's story is actually quite good. To be honest, it's so good that sometimes I wonder if he really COULD earn a decent-sized crust through his pen. It is all about a young man who is falsely accused of stealing some jewels (he says he was inspired by *The Moonstone* by Wilkie Collins, which is also very good and also about stolen jewels). The young man in Father's story, whose name is Peter Fitzgerald, has to go on the run and is pursued by both the forces of the law and a gang of jewel thieves who are convinced he has the jewels on his person (which of course he doesn't, as he never stole them in the first place).

We have now reached a bit in which Peter Fitzgerald is hiding in the cottage of a mysterious old lady. Harry thinks she is going to betray him to the gang 'because women have no sense of loyalty' but I totally disagree. Father is not giving anything away. He says we will have to wait and see. But I wonder if he suspects that there is a mystery going on in his very own house with his very own eldest daughter?

19th April, 1912.

Dear Frances,

Thank you for your letter. I am very relieved to find out
that the teachers don't read your post, though Nora said
I probably should have checked that before I sent you
anything. She said in most schools they actually do read
your post, which I am sure is illegal. But Nora said those
sort of laws didn't count at school, which seems terribly
unfair to me.

And your lovely teachers are taking you to Stratford,
how thrilling! I used to think Shakespeare was awfully
boring, but actually this year we have been reading *Romeo
and Juliet* and he's not bad, really. *As You Like It* is meant to
be jolly good so I'm sure seeing it in Shakespeare's native
land (so to speak) will inspire you when you're putting
on your own drama club play. I agree that you should
write your own play but don't be discouraged if your
classmates want to do something tried and tested (i.e.
old) instead. Genius, as Professor Shields sometimes tells
us in English class, isn't always recognised.

Anyway, you may be interested to hear that Phyllis is now behaving in an even more mysterious fashion. Yes, I thought the cabbage leaves and window-climbing was strange enough, but now she is receiving secret packages. Yesterday I was walking back from school when I noticed her walking ahead of me down Drumcondra Road with a strange woman in a dark green coat. It looked as if they were talking very intensely. And when they reached the corner of Clonliffe Road, the other woman passed Phyllis some sort of bundle. I couldn't see what it was, only that it wasn't very big, because Phyllis immediately shoved it into the bag she was carrying. Then the mysterious women crossed the road and went down Clonliffe Road and Phyllis kept going towards our house.

I caught up with Phyllis before she got there, and she nearly jumped out of her skin when I tapped her on the shoulder.

'It's only me,' I said. 'Who did you think it could be? A policeman?'

I hoped she might turn pale with guilt and reveal her dreadful secrets but she just looked annoyed.

'Don't be ridiculous,' she said. 'I just didn't expect anyone to creep up behind me, that's all.'

'Where have you been?' I said.

'I've been with Kathleen,' said Phyllis. 'We went to a tearoom in town.'

'I thought I saw you talking to someone back there,' I said. 'A strange woman in a green coat.'

And then Phyllis did turn pale. At least, a little paler than usual. But only for a second.

'Oh, I bumped into a friend of Kathleen's,' she said. 'She gave me a book she'd promised to lend her. She can't visit because she doesn't want to catch the flu. Kathleen's sister's come down with it now.' Kathleen's family do seem to be very susceptible to germs.

Anyway, I couldn't prove this wasn't true, because maybe the woman in the coat actually is a friend of Kathleen's with a great fear of germs, and maybe that package was just a book – though it hadn't looked particularly book-shaped – but I absolutely knew Phyllis was lying. I didn't say anything, though.

I told Nora about all this at school today, and even though she has no imagination, she did admit it sounded quite suspicious.

'Maybe she really is becoming a revolutionary,' she said.

But I told her I didn't think Phyllis had any political views at all. 'She's never said anything about that sort of thing,' I said.

'Not to you,' said Nora. 'But that doesn't mean she hasn't got any. She might think you wouldn't understand. And she'd probably be right.'

I couldn't help feeling slightly insulted that she

thought I wasn't the sort of sister someone could confide in about being a revolutionary.

'It's not like I'd tell Mother and Father,' I said. 'Well, I probably wouldn't. Unless I thought she was going to do something dangerous.'

'There you are, then,' said Nora.

'But we're not a very political family,' I said. 'Not like your aunt. Mother and Father are just plain old Home Rulers.'

'That doesn't mean anything,' said Nora. 'People don't always have the same political opinions as their parents. Otherwise nothing would ever change at all.'

You know that Nora can be a bit of a know-it-all, but I must admit that she had a very good point there. It still doesn't mean that Phyllis really was up to any revolutionary activities. I will just have to keep an eye on her.

'You mean spy,' said Nora. Which sounded harsh, but I have to admit that there isn't much of a difference between keeping an eye on Phyllis and spying on her. Though as I told Nora, 'I'm not going to do anything really sneakish and dishonourable like reading her letters or anything. I'm just going to look out for any more mysterious behaviour.' And that is what I will do.

You don't suppose she could have fallen in with jewel thieves like Peter Fitzgerald, do you? It would explain the bundle. But that seems even more unlikely than her being a revolutionary.

Isn't it awful about the *Titanic*? Julia read some of the newspaper reports and had nightmares afterwards. I must admit I kept thinking about it myself. Those poor people! We all prayed for them. Apparently a senior girl's aunt was on the ship but they got a telegram and she is safe.

Well done on winning your hockey match. As my school is in the middle of the city (well, you can walk to Sackville Street from Eccles Street in about fifteen minutes) we don't have as much space as you do out in the English countryside, but we do have a tennis court and a hockey team (there is talk among some of the older girls of starting a girl's hurley team, which is sort of like hockey, but they haven't actually done it yet). Luckily, we're not forced to take part in hockey – as you know I do not enjoy that sort of thing. We *are* forced to take drill and dancing twice a week, however, and I am absolutely terrible at drill, which is basically just marching around doing stupid exercises, though even Nora admits that I am quite good at dancing. Maybe I could become a professional dancer when I leave school? It would be worth saying that's what I want to do just to see the look on Aunt Josephine's face ….

Do write soon,
Fond regards,
Mollie

P.S.

Mother is always telling me off for leaving letters in my writing case for ages before posting them, but for once my bad habit has turned out to be for the best because yesterday evening I made an exciting discovery and luckily I hadn't put your letter in an envelope before I made it, so now I can add this post script and tell you all.

First of all, I knew that package Phyllis had wasn't a book as soon as I saw it and I was right. At least, it wasn't just a book. I think there might have been a book in there too. But anyway, what most of it was was pamphlets. And I know because I saw Phyllis giving them to Maggie. I was slaving away in the dining room at my algebra and I was so caught up in x and y that my head started to hurt so I went to the kitchen to get a glass of water. The door to the kitchen was ajar, and as I went down the steps towards it I realised that Phyllis was in there talking to Maggie. And so, for the second time in just a few weeks, I stayed outside the door and peeked in.

Maggie was stirring something on the range, and Phyllis was leaning against the wall between the range and the big wooden dresser. And in her arms was a familiar bundle. The bundle that the strange woman had given her just a few hours earlier.

'You shouldn't have brought them down here,' said Maggie. 'I told you, we have to stop discussing these things in the house.'

'Oh don't worry, Maggie,' said Phyllis. 'Mother never notices anything.' She paused. 'Mollie did see Mrs. Duffy give me the parcel, though.'

Maggie turned round.

'You've got to be more careful, Phyllis!' she said. 'If your mother finds out, I could lose my place and there'll be no university for you. And you can say goodbye to the cause, too. You'll be packed off to one of those aunts of yours and you won't get near any sort of a meeting if they have anything to do with it.'

'Mollie won't say anything,' said Phyllis. 'She's a good kid. She's not a sneak. Besides, I told her the parcel was a book for Kathleen.'

I must admit I did feel rather sneakish and low when I heard that. There was Phyllis, praising me – she's certainly never said anything so nice about me to my face – and there was me, spying at her through the door. And yet I couldn't bring myself to leave.

'It's still too close,' said Maggie. She sighed. 'How do they look, anyway?'

Phyllis pulled back a corner of the bundle and took out what looked like some sort of leaflet.

'See for yourself,' she said.

Maggie's back was to me as she took the leaflet and I couldn't see what it said. But she seemed to like it.

'Well, I must say they did a fine job,' she said. 'But like I said, we have to stop discussing these things in the house.' She took the bundle and put it in a dresser drawer. 'Anyone could walk in.' And she turned towards the door. I immediately jumped back and then walked very loudly towards it, practically stamping with every step.

'Hello!' I said, pushing the door open. 'Can I have a glass of water, please, Maggie?'

I was worried that my voice sounded a bit too cheerful, but both Maggie and Phyllis looked so rattled by my arrival I don't think they noticed I was a bit nervous myself.

'Of course you can,' said Maggie, and she went into the scullery with a glass.

'I'm going to my room,' said Phyllis. 'I have lots of letters to write.' And without even saying goodbye to Maggie, she walked out of the room. I stayed in the kitchen for a while talking to Maggie and eating one of the delicious biscuits she'd made that morning, but all the time that Maggie was asking me questions about school and I was telling her about Grace Molyneaux and what a monstrous beast she'd been to me and Nora during drill and dancing that afternoon – telling Miss Noren that she was afraid we were talking instead of waving our arms about and how we were missing out on healthy exercise – all I could think of was the bundle of pamphlets just sitting there in the dresser drawer. And even though I knew it was sneaking and spying, I vowed that I would have a look at them later, after everyone had gone to bed.

Except I didn't. I made a very special effort to stay up terribly late. I tried to think of lots of interesting and exciting things so I wouldn't fall asleep, but I was so exhausted after all my earlier spying that my eyelids started to droop, and the next thing I knew it was seven in the morning. I knew Maggie would already be up, dusting the dining room and laying the fire, but I put on my dressing gown and slippers, and made my way as quietly as I could down through the house. When I reached the hall, I could hear the clang of the fire irons in the dining room so at least I knew Maggie would be occupied there for a few more minutes. And then I ran down the steps and into the kitchen.

But when I opened the dresser drawer to look at the pamphlets, they were gone! I should have known Maggie wouldn't just leave them in a place where anyone could find them, not when she was so worried about having them in the house. She must have given them back to Phyllis, or hidden them away somewhere safer. And even

I wasn't going to be so low as to root around in her private things.

I closed the drawer and cut myself a slice of slightly stale bread and butter. I always think better when I'm eating something. Maggie had already made herself a pot of tea and it was still warm so I poured myself a cup and sat down at the kitchen table. I didn't feel entirely happy about spying on Maggie and Phyllis, and as a matter of fact I still don't, but now I've started investigating this mystery it really is very difficult to stop. Could I, I wondered, just drop the whole thing? Or could I just ask Phyllis or Maggie outright what is going on? But even if I did, I thought, chewing the bread and butter, they probably wouldn't tell me. I was just thinking about this when the kitchen door opened and Maggie came in. She nearly dropped the dustpan she was holding when she saw me.

'What on earth are you doing here?' she said. 'It's usually hard enough to get you out of that bed in the morning.'

'I couldn't sleep,' I said. Another lie. 'You don't mind me taking some of your tea, do you?'

'Of course I don't,' said Maggie. 'There's plenty in the pot. But that's yesterday's bread.'

'I don't mind,' I said.

'Well, the baker will be along soon with a fresh loaf,'

she said. 'And if you'll excuse me, early bird, I've got
to sweep the stairs now.' And she headed out the door.
I almost asked her about the pamphlets, but I didn't
dare. She'd know I'd been spying if I did, and I really
did feel guilty about it. But I still do want to find out
what it's all about. It looks like Phyllis and Maggie really
are revolutionaries after all. Why else would they have
pamphlets?

I definitely am going to seal and post this letter now.
I'll write again as soon as something else happens. Surely
I will find out the truth soon?

1st May, 1912.

Dear Frances,

Thanks awfully for your excellent letter. I like the sound
of your new English mistress. She sounds much more
fun than Professor Shields who teaches us English and
French and who has eyes like a hawk and ears like a
bat – I mean as powerful as a bat's; they look perfectly
normal. She's about thirty and quite pretty really, but you
can never get away with talking in class or passing notes.
I must admit that apart from her magical observational
powers, Professor Shields is all right. She's not as bad
as Sister Augustine, who taught us last year and has the
most boring voice in the world. Though it's quite hard
to think about school at all at the moment, when I have
found out the truth about Phyllis and Maggie. Yes, I
know all (or at least, I think I do) and it really is quite
shocking. It turns out they *are* revolutionaries – well, sort
of. They are SUFFRAGETTES!

Yes! Actual suffragettes! At least Phyllis definitely is,
and Maggie supports her. I can't believe I didn't think

of it before (though neither did Nora, so it wasn't just me being dim). But when I look back it all makes sense. Phyllis may not have seemed interested in politics, but she definitely has strong feelings about women being able to do things that men think they shouldn't. Look at how she insisted on going to university. And she got that bicycle a few years ago even though Father Thomas (our uncle who is a priest) told Father that women on bicycles were a shocking disgrace and that the next thing we knew Phyllis would be wearing trousers and smoking a cigar (she has not done either yet, as far as I know, but who knows, maybe she will? It feels as though anything is possible now).

So in a way the news that Phyllis is a suffragette is not surprising. But still, I can't help being a bit stunned by the whole thing. I mean, wanting to go to college doesn't automatically mean you want the vote, and even wanting a vote doesn't automatically mean you're actually going to go to meetings and chalk slogans on pavements and march around wearing a poster-board telling people about it and all those other things that suffragettes seem to do. Lots of people want something and never do anything about it. But Phyllis is definitely doing something about it, and Maggie is helping her. I can hardly take it all in.

Here's how I found out. It was this afternoon –

though it seems like much longer ago. We'd just had tea and I was in the dining room finishing my Latin exercises (Ovid this time, going on about his last night in Rome). Mother was in the drawing room, playing Mozart's *Rondo Alla Turca* at top volume, which is always a sign that she is in a good mood; I could hear it rattling through the wooden doors that divide the drawing room from the dining room. Latin poetry is, as you know, terribly boring, so what with Ovid and the Mozart I couldn't concentrate for more than a few minutes at a time and found myself staring out the window. Which is how I saw Phyllis carefully shutting the back door and making her way stealthily towards the back gate. And instantly I knew what I had to do. Ovid would just have to wait (he can wait forever as far as I'm concerned, though in this case I did have to finish it when I got home).

Now, Frances, you might think that what I did next was very sly and sneakish. And to be honest it probably was. I know I have been behaving in quite a sneakish way recently. But anyway, I did it. I leapt to my feet, ran into the hall, grabbed my coat (which I had left on the bottom of the stairs rather than hanging it on the rack) cried, 'Mother, I'm going to borrow a school book from Nora,' and, before she could say anything (or even let me know that she'd heard me), I raced out the back door

(Maggie was washing up in the scullery, so I didn't have to lie to her, too, about where I was going), through the back gate and ran down the lane. And while I may not be much good at drill and dancing, you might recall that I was always jolly good at races. And so Phyllis hadn't even reached the end of our road by the time I emerged from the lane.

I didn't want her to see me so I kept my distance (actually, I didn't have much choice in the matter because I was so short of breath I could barely walk. I may be good at winning races but only when they are very short ones). Anyway, I could breathe enough to follow Phyllis as she made her way onto the main road. For a moment, I thought she might cross the road and get a tram, which would have scuppered all my plans because I had no money in my pocket for the fare, but she didn't. She started walking towards town.

I'm never, ever allowed walk into town on my own. Father isn't particularly keen on Phyllis doing it, which was probably why she was sneaking out the back door. Of course, I walk to school with Nora, though Maggie collects Julia, who gets off earlier. If Aunt Josephine had her way Maggie would have to go back again to collect me, but Mother says that's ridiculous because it would take up far too much time and that I'm quite all right with Nora.

It's true that between our house and Sackville Street there are a lot of streets that are, as Aunt Josephine would say, 'not at all suitable for girls like you'. But I was so keen to find out what Phyllis was up to, I kept going. It wasn't so terrifying really, although after we passed Eccles Street I saw more and more children (and even some men and women) with no shoes on their feet. A few ragged boys called something rude about my hair ribbons as I went past, but I ignored them.

I followed Phyllis down one side of Rutland Square and onto Sackville Street. The street was full of people, and for a worrying moment I thought I might lose her in the crowd. But, luckily, she was wearing one of Kathleen's ludicrous hats with what looked like the top of a pineapple on it, so she was easy to find in the crowd. She went all the way down the street, through all the flower-sellers and past the pillar, then eventually turned left onto Eden Quay. She went down towards the Custom House, and I started to get a bit nervous then because going into town was one thing, but it was another thing to go towards the docks, which was where Phyllis seemed to be heading now. If I'd stood out walking past the streets where the tenements were, I'd stand out even more now, and so would Phyllis.

Then, when she reached the end of the quay across the road from the Custom House, Phyllis stopped outside a big building with freshly painted letters on it that revealed it was the headquarters of a trade union. I realised that she'd met a lady of about Mother's age, a woman wearing a green coat. She was tall and thin and had a lot of light brown hair piled up under a large straw hat. I wondered if she was the same green-coat-wearer I'd seen giving Phyllis that bundle a few weeks ago; then I was quite sure she was, because she gave Phyllis another bundle of what I could clearly see were newspapers or magazines. Then the two of them crossed the road to the Custom House. Of course I followed them, even though at this stage I felt more than a bit scared AND I nearly got run over by a bus when I was crossing the road.

Just before I scurried out of the way of the bus I could see a small crowd gathered outside the Custom House and at first I thought I might blend in with them. But soon I could see that they were all what Mother and Father would call 'working men' and a fourteen-year-old girl in shiny shoes and a new coat was not going to blend in with them at all. But then, neither would Phyllis (though you could argue that she wouldn't fit in anywhere in that ridiculous hat). What on earth was going on?

As I got nearer, I could see what the men were gathered around. There was a woman standing on some sort of a box, and she was making a speech. She was quite young, in her thirties, I suppose, and was wearing a very nice coat and a pair of spectacles. There was a green, white and orange rosette on the lapel of her coat. I got a few odd looks from the men as I made my way through the small crowd, trying to avoid Phyllis, who was now standing right next to the box. But no one said anything to me until one man turned to his friend and said, 'They've even got young ones out fighting for them now!' But he didn't sound angry or even disapproving. He almost sounded impressed.

Now I could hear what the woman was saying.

'We women are thinking, working creatures just as men are,' she said. 'And yet we are treated like children. If we work, we must pay our taxes, but we get no say in how those taxes are spent. We are told from girlhood to defer to men in all things.'

I suddenly thought of Harry taking all the good bits of chicken.

'But we have our own needs too, and we have our own voice,' cried the woman. 'We are not here to take anything that belongs to men. But to demand what is rightfully ours too – the right to have our say. The right to vote!'

'Bleeding lot of good ladies having the vote,' yelled a man standing near me, 'when a working man like myself doesn't even have a say.' And I remembered that men who don't have a certain amount of property can't vote either.

'We women want the vote on the same terms as men – whatever those terms may be,' said the woman on the chair. I could see that the rosette on her coat was emblazoned with the words 'VOTES FOR WOMEN'. 'And if those terms change with the Home Rule bill, then they should be applied to women too.'

I was in a bit of a daze. Was this the heart of the mystery? Was Phyllis – and Maggie too, I supposed, as they were clearly in it together – not a Fenian revolutionary, but a suffragette?

I don't know how much you know about suffragettes. I must admit that until last night, I had a very different picture of them. Whenever I heard grown-up people talking about them, it always seemed to be in a disapproving way. I remember Father looking at a picture in a magazine and saying that if the women really wanted to prove they deserved the vote they shouldn't be making an exhibition of themselves marching around in poster-boards. Mother hadn't said anything, but she hadn't disagreed with him either. And I do remember hearing Aunt Josephine holding forth to Mother about 'silly women who should be at home with their children – if they have any'. She said they were 'just aping Englishwomen by shouting and screaming for the vote.' She always says that women can have a say in society by guiding and advising their men, which has always seemed a rather feeble way of having a say to me. I can't remember what Mother said to any of this. All I remember is that Aunt Josephine made being a suffragette sound like a silly, childish thing, a lot of foolish women having a big tantrum.

But the woman on the box wasn't silly at all. She was simply marvellous. Some men made rude remarks (at least I'm pretty sure they were rude, I couldn't understand some of them), but some seemed genuinely interested and asked lots of questions. After a while, I forgot all about Phyllis and just listened to the lady as she talked about how men and women have an equal stake in the world, and asked why women were being shut out of power (And the good bits of chicken, I thought). She talked about all the intelligent, brave women whose gifts were never used 'because they had no outlet'. She made me think about things I'd never thought of before.

Most of the time when I hear grown-up people talking about politics it's about Home Rule and independence, and it never seems to have much to do with real life. But what the woman said made me think that maybe politics *could* have something to do with real life. It even has something to do with us girls all giving the good bits of dinner to Harry and Father, and with us darning their socks, and with Phyllis having to fight to be allowed go to university when Harry took it for granted that he was going. Why should Mother not have a vote when Harry is going to have one in five years? And why didn't we ever talk about things like that? Maybe because we all took it for granted that boys deserved certain things and girls deserved other, less interesting things.

When the lady finished, quite a lot of the men clapped, though there were also a few boos. I clapped as hard as I could. And then I remembered Phyllis. She was standing near the chair, holding a stack of magazines. A man, better dressed than most of the others, went up to her and handed her a coin and she gave him a copy of the magazine. He walked past me as he left her and I could see that the name of the magazine was *Votes for Women*. I was just about to sneak away and get home as fast as I could when Phyllis saw me. She froze for a second and then she stormed over to me, her face furious. I don't think I've ever seen her so angry, even that time she came home and found Nora and me dressing up in her lace collars.

'What are you doing here?' she hissed. 'Did you follow me? Actually, don't bother answering that. You must have done, you horrid little sneak.'

I could feel myself blushing, because of course she was right.

'I knew you were hiding something,' I said, but even as I said the words I knew how feeble they sounded.

'It isn't any of your business,' said Phyllis. 'And you shouldn't be in a place like this. It isn't at all suitable.' She almost sounded like Aunt Josephine.

'Well, neither should you, if it comes to that,' I said.

'You're not going to tell Father and Mother, are you?' said Phyllis. 'You'd better not, you sneaking worm.'

'Of course I won't!' I cried. 'Oh Phyllis, I know I shouldn't have been following you, but I really don't want to get you into trouble. Honestly I don't.'

Phyllis's face softened, but not very much.

'I suppose I'd better take you home,' she said. She called over to another girl who was also holding a stack of magazines.

'Mabel,' said Phyllis, 'would you mind awfully selling my batch? My sister's turned up and I can't send her home on her own.'

'Of course,' said Mabel, who was a tall girl of about Phyllis's age with fair-ish hair and a nice, jolly face. Phyllis gave her the magazines as well as a small purse.

'I only sold one,' she said apologetically. 'And I bought one for myself.'

'People never buy much at the Wednesday meetings,'

said Mabel. 'Wasn't Mrs. Joyce wonderful?'

Mrs. Joyce must have been the woman who gave the speech. Phyllis agreed that she had been wonderful, said goodbye to Mabel and then, without saying anything to me, she grabbed my hand and we headed back down Eden Quay. She didn't say a word until we reached Sackville Street, and then she turned to me abruptly and said, 'Do you have any money?'

I shook my head.

'Wonderful,' said Phyllis. 'I'll have to pay for your tram fare, then.'

We got a tram straight away on Sackville Street and sat down next to each other in silence. Phyllis was holding the magazine she'd bought, and I looked at it curiously. I had never heard of a suffragette magazine before. Father sometimes gets *Blackwood's Magazine* or *The Strand*, and girls at school sometimes bring in ladies' magazines full of dramatic stories and things about clothes and what's going on in London. The nuns don't approve of them so the girls have to hide them and pass them around secretly. And then there are all the religious magazines, which are full of stories about saints and missionaries. I couldn't imagine that a suffragette magazine would be much like that. Or like the ladies' magazines either.

Neither of us said anything until we were halfway home. Phyllis looked too angry to speak and I felt too

The Making of Mollie 57

guilty. But eventually I said, 'Phyllis?'

For a moment, I thought she wasn't going to answer me but eventually she said, 'What?'

'How long have you been …' She was looking at me so fiercely I almost couldn't go on. 'Doing this,' I finished quickly.

'I'm surprised you don't know already,' said Phyllis, tossing her head back, 'seeing as though you appear to have been tracking my movements.'

One of her hairpins fell out. This has happened a lot since Phyllis started putting her hair up, because she has the usual Carberry unruly locks. I didn't dare point it out this time, though.

'Why were you going out the back way?' I said. 'I saw you sneak out a few weeks ago too.'

'Because the back lane is a short cut,' said Phyllis. 'And I was running late.'

I hadn't thought of that.

'But you climbed out the window the other week,' I said.

'That was because Mother knew Kathleen was sick and she and Aunt Josephine would have asked a lot of stupid questions if they thought I was going off on my own,' said Phyllis. 'And I couldn't go out of the front or the back door without passing one of them. How long have you been spying on me, anyway?'

'Oh, don't be like that, Phyllis,' I said. 'I honestly am

awfully sorry. And I really am interested too.'

Phyllis looked at me.

'Are you?' she said.

'Oh, I am,' I said. 'That woman's speech was very good.'

'I didn't think you were interested in this sort of thing,' said Phyllis.

'Neither did I,' I said. 'But I suppose I've never heard anything like it before.'

'I'm surprised you haven't,' said Phyllis. 'Some of the teachers in that school …'

'They've never said anything about it to me,' I said. 'Now do, please, tell me how you got started. Being a suffragette, I mean.'

'I don't particularly like that word,' said Phyllis. 'Lots of us use it, of course. But it's what the Antis call us. They invented it.'

I must admit that I rather liked the word and I still do.

'Well, how did you get started with votes for women, then?' I said. We were on Dorset Street now. Soon we'd be home, and who knew whether Phyllis would say anything then?

'Kathleen's aunt,' said Phyllis. 'Agnes.'

'The tall one with the curly hair?' I said. I'd met her at a Christmas party in Kathleen's house last year. She had lovely clothes.

'That's her,' said Phyllis. 'Kathleen and I went for tea with her a few months ago and I was talking about doing my degree and how strongly I felt about, you know, girls being able to do the same things as boys. And she lent me a book.'

'A book about being a suffragette?' I said. 'I mean ... about votes for women.'

'A novel,' said Phyllis. 'By a woman called Constance Maud. It's called *No Surrender*. It's about suffragettes in England but one of them is Irish. Well, she's awfully posh but she's Irish all right. Anyway, it made me ... I don't know. It made me see things differently. It made me notice things I'd never noticed before.'

Like me listening to Mrs. Joyce at the Custom House, I thought.

'And once I started noticing,' Phyllis went on, 'I couldn't stop noticing. So the next time I met Agnes at Kathleen's house I told her how much I liked the book and how interesting the whole suffrage question was. And she looked at me and said, "Do you want to do something about it?" And I did.'

Soon, Phyllis told me, she was reading more books and articles and pamphlets about suffragettes (I know she doesn't approve of the word but she still uses it quite a lot). She started buying *Votes for Women*, which is an English magazine. There's a newsagent on Great Britain

Street where you can buy it. And then she started going to these outdoor meetings. Apparently there is one almost every Wednesday and Saturday. The weekend ones are in the Phoenix Park. She even took part in a poster parade a few weeks ago when John Redmond (you must know him, the leader of the Irish Parliamentary Party) was having some sort of meeting. And sometimes she and Kathleen go into town and chalk suffragette slogans and notices about meetings in big letters on the pavement.

'But how does Maggie come into it?' I asked.

'She found my copy of *Votes for Women*,' said Phyllis. 'And when I asked her not to tell Mother about it, she said she wouldn't dream of it. And we sort of looked at each other for a minute, and then Maggie said that she was very interested in the cause herself but she never had time to do much about it. Her sister is a trade unionist, you know.'

'Jenny?' I said, surprised. 'I didn't.' Maggie's sister comes to visit her sometimes and we've all known her for years.

'Well, she is, and she supports the cause too,' said Phyllis. 'So I've been passing leaflets and things to Maggie and she's been passing some of them on to Jenny.'

And that was when we had to get off the tram. Once we were off, Phyllis seemed to remember that she was angry with me and barely said a word all the way home, even though I tried to ask her more questions.

Oh no, I can hear Mother coming up the stairs and I should have been asleep over an hour ago. And I haven't even said my prayers yet. I'll write more tomorrow.

Thursday

I don't know why I bothered turning the light off last night because I hardly slept a wink. I kept thinking about everything Phyllis had said. When I went down to breakfast I wanted to talk to Maggie about it all, but I didn't have a chance because she was so busy. I hadn't been able to say anything to her last night because Mother and Father were absolutely furious that I'd stayed away for so long.

'You know perfectly well that you're not allowed run off like that,' said Mother.

'I told you I was going to Nora's,' I said.

'I couldn't tell what you were yelling,' said Mother. 'And you shouldn't have stayed away for two hours anyway.'

I had to go to bed without any supper, even though I told them that Nora and I had been practising Latin verbs (which of course was a lie, but Mother didn't know that. If I had actually been practising Latin verbs, it would have been terribly unfair to punish me for it). But I know more punishments will be forthcoming.

Harry, of course, made his usual stupid remarks, this time all about how girls aren't able to tell the time. He is not nearly as funny as he thinks he is.

'We can tell the time perfectly well,' I said. 'We were just so engrossed in our Latin studies that we didn't notice it.' At this stage, I'd told the lie about me and Nora studying Latin so often I almost believed it myself, which is a bit worrying now I come to think about it. I reminded Harry that my school gets some of the best Intermediate Certificate results in the country, including maths. But he just laughed and said, 'Best results for a girls' school, which doesn't mean much', and strolled off.

Sometimes I really could kill him. And I thought again about what the lady at the meeting had said about men and women being treated differently.

Anyway. Even though I am still in disgrace today, I was very much looking forward to telling Nora that I had solved the mystery of Phyllis. Dreadful Harry walked us to school this morning so I couldn't say anything to her then, and as soon as he left us we bumped into our friend Stella. I didn't get a chance to reveal all until we were in our first class of the day, French, when I passed a note to Nora, saying 'PHYLLIS IS A SUFFRAGETTE!!!" As I said, passing notes is always risky in Professor Shields's

French class because of her supernatural hearing and hawk-like sight, but I really couldn't keep it in any longer. I scribbled the words on a scrap of paper and passed it to Nora, who was sitting at the next desk. She looked very surprised when she read it and as soon as Professor Shields turned back to the board again, she looked at me and mouthed 'How?'

But before I could write another note, Professor Shields whipped her head round like a cobra. It was clear that she'd noticed something. And she wasn't the only one. Grace Molyneaux was sitting behind Nora and she had definitely seen both the note passing and Nora's reaction to it.

'Is everything all right there, Miss Cantwell?' asked Professor Shields.

'Yes, Professor Shields,' said Nora. And I didn't dare look over at her for the rest of the class. It was very boring. We were practising verbs and learning how to say things like 'I have sold the pen of my aunt. I am selling the pen of my aunt. I will sell the pen of my aunt' in French. I don't know why, but we never seem to learn how to say any useful things in French class (or rather *en français*, as they say in France. I suppose I *have* learned something). If I ever tried to sell the pen of Aunt Josephine, she'd probably have me arrested for theft.

Finally, after half an hour of talking about the tables of

our uncles and the dresses of our mothers, French class was over and Professor Shields left the room, but Grace pounced on me before I chance to say anything to Nora.

'I hate to be a bore,' she said, untruthfully. 'But you know you shouldn't be passing notes in class.' She turned to Nora. 'Or receiving them. You do need to concentrate on your French.'

'I can concentrate perfectly well, thank you,' said Nora politely.

'I'm sure you can,' said Grace. 'But you know Aunt Catherine wouldn't like it. And besides, it's terribly distracting for everyone else. How am I going to win the Middle Grade Cup if you're throwing bits of paper around when Professor Shields is trying to teach us?'

Grace's Aunt Catherine is Nora's mother. Poor, poor Nora. Not only does she have to worry about Grace sneaking on her to teachers, but she also has to worry about her sneaking to Nora's parents as well.

'I could barely concentrate on my verbs,' said Gertie Hayden. She's not as bad as her great chum Grace, but she's still pretty bad. Whenever Grace does something annoying, Gertie backs her up, whether she agrees with her or not.

In this case, we knew Gertie didn't give a fig about concentrating on verbs. All she cares about is hockey and tennis. Sometimes I think that the only reason Grace is friends with Gertie is that Gertie poses no threat to Grace's ambition to win the cup.

Nora gave them both a haughty look. She is surprisingly good at looking like a grand old lady for a short red-haired girl from Drumcondra.

'Then why didn't you tell Professor Shields?' she asked.

Grace gave a sort of tinkling laugh.

'Don't be silly,' she said. 'I'm not a sneak.'

'Really?' said Nora. 'You do surprise me. Come on, Mollie.'

And she linked her arm through mine (which we are also not supposed to do, because the nuns don't really approve of close friendships between girls. They say they are 'unhealthy' though I really can't see why. It's not as though Nora or I have germs).

Grace smiled at us in a pitying sort of way, which was extremely irritating, and then she and Gertie went over to May Sullivan, who is a new-ish girl who sometimes goes about with Grace and Gertie (presumably because she hasn't seen through Grace's sugary sweet act, unlike me and Nora who've known her for years and years).

As Nora and I marched away to the science room for our next class, I said, 'You know, it's not that I think you were wrong, but maybe we shouldn't antagonise Grace.'

'Why not?' said Nora. 'She deserves it when she talks like that. Going on about Mother and telling us we shouldn't be passing notes!'

'True,' I said. 'But maybe we should try and avoid her wrath at the moment. Especially if …' I trailed off.

'Especially if what?' asked Nora.

I looked around to make sure Grace, or indeed anyone else, wasn't in earshot.

'Well, I rather think I'd like to find out more,' I said. 'About being a suffragette.' And as quickly as I could, I told her what had happened the previous evening, and what the lady, Mrs. Joyce, had said at the meeting.

'And you know, she's quite right,' I said. 'I mean, think of Harry. He gets away with doing all sorts of things that we could never do.'

'That's true,' said Nora.

'And he gets the best bits of chicken,' I said, warming to my theme.

'So does George, when he's at home,' said Nora. George is her brother, in case you've forgotten.

'I know, I've seen him,' I said. 'All brothers get treated better than we do. And it's been taken for granted since they were born that they're going to university, even though anyone can tell just looking at Harry that he's an absolute fool, and poor Phyllis who's so clever had to beg and beg and beg. And really, them getting the vote when they grow up is just the same thing as getting all the best bits of chicken.'

'Goodness me,' said Nora. But before she could say anything else Mother Antoninas suddenly loomed over us and said, 'What are you two girls dawdling for?' and we had to run into the classroom at top speed. It wasn't until break that we got a chance to talk properly while we drank our milk.

'So what exactly are you proposing?' asked Nora, after we'd found a suitably quiet corner of the refectory. 'Because I'm not actually sure I want to be a suffragette. I mean, it does sound quite exciting and I do see what you mean about all these things about brothers, but I haven't really thought about it much.'

'I'm not saying I want to be one either,' I said. 'I mean, I'm not even sure if you can be one at our age, but I'm not saying I definitely don't want to be one either.'

'That sounds like you do want to be one,' said Nora.

'I don't think it matters whether I do or not,' I said, taking a gloomy swig of milk. 'First of all because we're too young. But mostly because Mother and Father are never going to let me leave the house again after last night. And even if they did, they wouldn't let me go to meetings in town.'

'Oh, I'm sure we could think of ways around that,' said Nora. 'And around the being too young thing. There must be something we could do.'

'Does that mean you're interested too?' I said.

'Possibly,' said Nora. 'And possibly not. I'll have to consider it. Oh watch out, it's Stella.'

'Stella's all right,' I said, because she is. In fact, Stella Donovan is our friend. She's a boarder and she can be a bit wet and white-mouse-like, but I do like her a lot. Still, just because I like her doesn't mean I want her to know such secret information, so I immediately changed the subject and started talking about the pair of socks I'm knitting for Father's birthday (navy wool, very smart). I hoped Stella would be so bored by this not very exciting topic of conversation that she'd wander off and talk to someone else, but it turns out that she's become passionately interested in socks – knitting them, I mean, I don't think even Stella could be interested in socks in general. And she immediately started talking about cable patterns and different ways of turning the heel.

'If you start on a purl row, it looks so much neater,' she said, and she was so earnest and enthusiastic I didn't have the heart to stop the conversation, even though it was extremely dull. You simply can't be mean to Stella. It would be like kicking a puppy.

Anyway, Stella not only wanted to talk about her sock-knitting, she had taken it down from her dorm in a little bag and insisted on demonstrating her amazing sock skills for us. And so what with Stella's socks and Grace looking suspiciously at us all day, it wasn't until we were on our way home that Nora and I were able to continue our conversation.

'Thank goodness we're free of that prison,' she said as we turned the corner of Eccles Street. 'Poor Stella, being stuck there for weeks and weeks at a time.'

'It's not that bad,' I said. 'Some of the time, anyway.'

We walked along in silence for a moment. But it was a comfortable silence. It always is, with Nora.

'I've been thinking,' said Nora, 'about what we were talking about earlier. And we need to do some research. I'd like to find out more about it.'

I was very pleased to hear this.

'Really?' I said.

Nora nodded.

'After all, I wouldn't be able to be a doctor if women hadn't fought for the right to go to university,' she said.

I was so pleased to hear that she was interested in what Maggie had called 'the cause' that I didn't tell her I thought she would probably want to be something else in a few months. Or days.

'I agree about the research,' I said. 'Which means we'll have to talk to Phyllis.'

'How angry do you think she still is?' said Nora. 'About you following her, I mean.'

'By the time we got home yesterday she was quite friendly,' I said, 'but then this morning she grabbed me

when I was putting my coat on and told me I'd better
not sneak after her again. She might not want to tell me
anything in case I tell on her.'

'You'll just have to win her trust,' said Nora, which
was easy for her to say. She doesn't know what big sisters
are like. She only has George, her big brother, (and he's
away at boarding school most of the time) so I'm not
sure she appreciates quite how unreasonable an older
sister can be (or a younger one, come to think of it). It
does seem awfully unfair that I have to put up with not
only an older sister but an older brother AND a kid sister
too. You're so lucky, Frances, being an only child. I know
you think it can be a bit of a bore in the holidays but it
sounds awfully peaceful to me.

Saturday

I know I should have finished and posted this letter
already but more things keep happening and I want to
tell you all about them while they're fresh in my mind.
The letter is getting terribly long. I might have to ask
Father for an extra stamp to cover the weight. Anyway,
at the moment I feel jealous of you being away at school
as well as being an only child, not least because last
night my parents decided on my proper punishment

for running off on Wednesday. I wasn't allowed to go to Nellie Whelan's birthday tea after school today. Which is disappointing because Nellie's mother makes the most delicious lemon cake. I know this because she invited some of us to tea shortly after she joined our class and I had some of the cake then. When I mentioned this to Nora, she was not impressed.

'Is that the only reason you wanted to go to Nellie's party?' she said severely. 'It's not very nice to go to someone's birthday tea just because you like their mother's cakes.'

'Oh, don't be such a prig,' I said. 'You know I do like Nellie really. I was just looking forward to the lemon cake as an extra treat.'

'I suppose that's all right,' said Nora.

I must admit that I did feel awful when practically all the day girls and even a few of the boarders in our class, like Stella, went off to Nellie's after school today and I had to go home, even though Nellie very kindly promised to save me a slice of lemon cake and take it to school on Monday. To make matters (much) worse, because Nora was going to the party and I was in disgrace, I wasn't allowed to walk home alone and so I had to wait at the school's main entrance with Mother Antoninas looking at me very suspiciously until Harry turned up to collect me.

The only good thing about this arrangement was that when Harry arrived, he looked just as annoyed by the whole thing as I was. As usual, his chum Frank was by his side. Also as usual, Harry didn't bother saying hello or indeed anything even vaguely polite. Instead, he greeted me by saying 'I'm going to be late for the rugby match because of you.'

'It's not as if you're actually playing in it,' I snapped as we trudged along Eccles Street. 'You're just watching. No one cares if two of the spectators turn up late.'

Of course, that made him even more annoyed because he really, really wishes that he was playing. But it's ridiculous of him to expect to be in the first XV when there are boys in the school who are a whole year older than him.

Anyway, Frank tried to pour oil on troubled waters and politely asked me what I was planning to do when I left school. I don't know if I ever told you what Frank looks like. He's quite tall – even taller than Harry – and he has curly-ish golden hair that he keeps having to push out of his green-ish eyes.

'I don't know really,' I said, after considering his question. 'I suppose now Phyllis is going to the university, I'd like to go there too.'

'To study what?' asked Frank.

'English literature, I think,' I said. 'That's my favourite subject.'

'That's what I'd like to do too,' said Frank, but before

either of us could say anything else, Harry said, 'It's utterly ridiculous, girls going to college. What's the point? They'll just be looking after husbands and babies in a year or two. That is,' he added, giving me a pointed look, 'if any man will have them.'

'Oh shut up, Harry, don't be such an ass,' said Frank.

I don't know who was more surprised by Frank's words, Harry or me. I thought he'd reply with something typically obnoxious, but to my immense surprise he just muttered, 'I was only joking.' And then he started talking about some boy in their class who's supposedly an absolute wizard at rugby. It was all very dull but at least it took his mind off insulting me. They kept talking about boring boys' school things all the way home. I didn't particularly mind, though. Being ignored by Harry is vastly preferable to being talked to by him. Every so often Frank would politely ask me a question about my school: what sports do we play (none, in my case, at least not voluntarily) and whether the boarders are allowed out at the weekends. He doesn't know much about Dublin girls and their schools. He has a sister, but she's away at school in the country.

But mostly I was able to let the two of them have their conversation about rugby and how Father Jerome had made someone they kept calling 'poor old Sheridan' write out about twenty pages of the *Aeneid* as a punishment for falling asleep in class (even Mother Antoninas has never gone over five pages). And while they waffled on I was able to have a good think about the best way to approach Phyllis.

Somehow I'd barely seen her since the dramatic events of Wednesday night. On Thursday she and Kathleen went to some sort of art lecture with Kathleen's mother and then yesterday she was at a concert in town with Aunt Josephine. I must say that it would take more than Beethoven to induce me to spend a whole evening with Aunt Josephine, but I suppose she did also treat Phyllis to dinner beforehand. As for this afternoon, I knew she was going to Kathleen's house to help her trim a hat (I can only imagine what this one will look like) so I wouldn't be able to talk to her when I got home.

But of course, I realised, Phyllis wasn't the only person in the house who could tell me about suffragettes. There was also Maggie. And while I hadn't been able to talk to her on her own since I discovered Phyllis's secret, I knew that she wouldn't be too busy this afternoon because Father had to go to some sort of work luncheon, and what with most of the family being out of the house, she wouldn't be making a full dinner. Of course, I wasn't sure that she'd tell me anything. If Phyllis had told her about me following her on Wednesday – and she probably had – Maggie might not trust me. I was worrying about the best way to approach her when Harry shook my arm and said, 'Mollie? Are you listening to me? Get in there quickly so I can go to the match.' And I realised we were at our front door. It's quite surprising how much you don't notice when you're thinking hard about something interesting.

'Don't worry,' I said to Harry as I rang the bell. 'I don't want to spend any more time with you than I absolutely have to.'

Maggie answered the door.

'I've taken her home,' said Harry. 'Be a dear and tell Mother, won't you, Maggie? I'm late for the rugger match as it is.'

He smiled at Maggie and she smiled back. She actually *likes* Harry. I suppose I must grudgingly admit that he's generally quite nice to her. Possibly the only good thing about Harry is that he is always very polite to servants. Anyway, he and Frank went off and I followed Maggie into the hall.

'Wasn't it nice of your brother to walk you home?' she said.

'It certainly was not,' I said. 'He only did it because Mother and Father made him.'

'Ah, don't be too hard on him. He's a decent lad,' said Maggie. Which is clearly not true. But I didn't bother contradicting her because I had questions I wanted to ask once I'd poked my head into the drawing room and said hello to Mother. Mother was having tea with Mrs. Sheffield and Miss Harrington who live around the corner. They were talking about some sale of work the church is organising and they were all talking very passionately because some of the women who had been asked to take part refused because they think sales of work are 'Protestant things'.

I was able to escape to the kitchen quite quickly. As soon as I walked in Maggie produced the remains of a freshly baked lemon cake.

'I thought you might like a slice of this,' she said. 'Seeing as you're missing that party.'

'Oh Maggie, you're an absolute angel,' I said. And I gave her a hug.

'Get away with you,' said Maggie briskly. 'And don't tell your mother I gave you some. You're meant to be in disgrace, and besides, she thinks I made it for the sale of work committee. Which of course,' she added with a grin, 'I did.'

I couldn't reply because my mouth was full of lemon cake so I just nodded instead. The cake was very good – not quite as good as Mrs. Whelan's cakes, but of course I didn't tell Maggie that.

When I'd finished my cake and was drinking a cup of lukewarm, very strong tea from the kitchen teapot, I asked, 'Maggie, do you mind awfully if I ask you something?'

'Well,' said Maggie, looking amused, 'that depends what it is. Though I must say it's not like you to be so formal.'

'Well, it's about something ...' I hesitated, then took a deep breath and went on. 'It's about Phyllis.'

Maggie looked at me warily and didn't say anything.

'I know all,' I said. Even as I said the words I realised how melodramatic I sounded, like somebody in a cheap magazine serial (you must know the sort of thing, those stories where everyone is always turning out to be a duke's secret daughter or an earl in disguise and they all have masses of enemies who are trying to thwart them).

'And what exactly,' asked Maggie, with that same look in her eye, 'do you know?'

'I know about Phyllis being a suffragette,' I said. 'I think it's marvellous. And,' I said quickly, 'I'm not going to tell anyone. I know you know all about it, Maggie, and I swear your secret is safe with me.'

I was getting more magazine-serial-ish by the second but I couldn't help myself.

'I heard a lady called Mrs. Joyce talk in town on Wednesday,' I said. 'And she was so interesting and, well, I want to find out more about it, and I hoped you might help me.'

Maggie wiped her hands on her apron, took a cup and saucer from the dresser and poured out a cup of tea from the big kitchen teapot.

'I think that's probably cold,' I said, but she ignored me. She sat down on the opposite side of the table to me, took a sip of the tea, and said, 'You do know that if your mother and father thought I was telling you how to be a suffragette I'd lose my place before you could say "Votes for Women".'

'That would never happen!' I said. I almost laughed, because the idea of Maggie being dismissed was so silly. 'You're part of the family. Mother's always telling Aunt Josephine how lucky she is to have you. And besides, I won't breathe a word.'

'Words have a way,' said Maggie, 'of getting breathed. And I won't deny that your mother and father have been very good to me, and I may very well be part of the family, but it's a part that can be sent packing without a reference, and that's what they'd do if they thought I was getting you involved in anything they wouldn't approve of. It's bad enough that I've been talking about it with Phyllis.'

'But …' I began.

'No "buts",' said Maggie. 'I'm sorry, Mollie. But if you want to find out more, you'll have to talk to your sister.' She drained her teacup (the tea must have been practically cold) and stood up. 'And now I've got to finish the vegetables for later.' She went into the scullery.

I didn't dare follow her. I just sat there for a moment, thinking about how … shaky Maggie's life is here. I'd never really thought about it before. I do see her as part of the family, and it would never have struck me that my parents might ever send her away, no matter what she'd done. I still found it hard to imagine. But it was clear that Maggie knew better.

I put down my cup and went into the hall. Mother's church friends were just leaving so I had to say goodbye to them and promise to come to the sale of work. I wish I hadn't. Sales like that are always full of terrible stale buns and felt pen-wipers and a white elephant stall with lots of dreadful jumble that nobody wants (when I was smaller I thought a white elephant stall really was a stall selling white elephants. Obviously I knew they couldn't be regular-sized elephants, but I thought they might be special miniature ones. Or even toys. Imagine my disappointment when I discovered it was just a stall full of old fire screens and chipped tea cups).

I was just about to escape and slip up to my room when Mrs. Sheffield said, 'Now, Mollie, would you like to do something very helpful for me?'

If I were being perfectly honest, I'd have said, 'Not particularly,' but of course I couldn't say that. In fact, because Mother was glaring at me, I couldn't even make a polite excuse like telling her I had lots of schoolwork to do. Instead, I said, 'Of course!' as sincerely as I could, which was very sincerely indeed. I think I really might be quite a good actress. Maybe I will be one when I grow up, though I can't imagine Mother and Father would approve (and Aunt Josephine would probably disown me – which doesn't sound that bad, actually).

Anyway, Mrs. Sheffield was taken in by my acting and said, 'That's marvellous. I was hoping you'd be able to take Barnaby out for his walk in an hour or so. Thomas is away and I can't take him because Father O'Reilly is calling around to talk to me about this sale of work.'

I needed a lot of acting skills to do what I did next. I said, 'That sounds lovely' very enthusiastically. In fact, I might have gone a bit overboard on the enthusiasm because Mother gave me a very surprised look. She knows perfectly well that nobody in her right mind would describe taking Barnaby for a walk as 'lovely', not even Mrs. Sheffield.

Barnaby is not a person, in case you were wondering, but a very noisy and very fluffy little white dog who is also an absolute menace. Whenever anyone passes the Sheffields' house, he pops up in the bay window like a jack-in-the-box, barking his head off. And that's not the only annoying thing he does. They had to add an extra foot of fence to the wall of their back garden because Barnaby kept bouncing over the original one.

In fact, he is so bold and dreadful that Phyllis, Harry, Julia and I started calling him 'The Menace'. Even

Mother and Father sometimes call him The Menace by mistake. It's reached the point where I forget that his real name is actually Barnaby. And I couldn't think of a worse way of spending a Saturday afternoon when all my friends were at a party than taking him for a walk, but I couldn't get out of it. Mother doesn't usually like me wandering off on my own (as she puts it), but I suppose she thought nobody dangerous would go anywhere near me if I was with Barnaby. And so an hour later I was standing outside the Sheffields' front door, holding a lead with Barnaby at the end of it.

'Just about an hour or so should do it,' said Mrs. Sheffield, who looked delighted to have got rid of The Menace for a while (as well she might). 'Maybe you could take him to the Botanic Gardens, if they don't mind dogs.'

'All right,' I said, though I was quite sure you're not allowed take dogs into the Gardens and even if you were, I couldn't imagine they'd let The Menace in once they'd laid eyes on him. He just exudes badness. I looked down at him, and he stared boldly back at me with his bright button eyes. Then I said goodbye to Mrs. Sheffield and set off down the road.

The Menace always strains at his lead so much that the Sheffields became worried that a normal collar and lead would hurt his neck, so they had to have a sort of harness made for him which means the lead is attached to his back. I was worried that he'd break free from my clutches so I wrapped my end of the lead firmly around my wrist. As you can imagine, it wasn't a very relaxing walk, not least because when The Menace wasn't pulling on his lead (he is surprisingly strong for such a small fluffy dog), he was making sudden stops and barking so loudly that passers-by kept turning and staring at me in a disapproving manner, to see what I was doing to make him bark so much. I wished I was wearing a large rosette like the one the woman at the meeting was wearing, except instead of saying 'Votes for Women' it would say 'He's not my dog'.

I was so busy feeling sorry for myself as The Menace barked and strained his way along the road, I didn't notice that I wasn't grasping the lead quite as tightly as I should have. And just as we were passing a small green park, The Menace broke free and ran away from me as fast as his fluffy white legs could carry him.

For a split second I was frozen to the spot with horror, and then I raced after him. But he is surprisingly fast as well as surprisingly strong, and I couldn't catch him. He was soon far ahead of me.

'Oh, please, stop that dog!' I cried.

There weren't many people around, and none of them seemed eager to grab hold of Barnaby's lead, which swung out behind him as he ran. And which, I realised to my horror, was now swinging around a corner. Those streets are like a maze. If I lost sight of him in there, I was doomed. I'd never find him again. And while I didn't particularly care if I never saw Barnaby again as long as I lived, I didn't want him to be lost and alone on the streets. Besides, I'd get into terrible trouble once Mrs. Sheffield found out.

'Catch that dog!' I shrieked, or tried to. But by the time I staggered around the corner I could barely breathe, let alone shout, and I was starting to get a stitch. And then I saw a glorious sight.

If you'd told me last week that I'd ever be so happy to see either Barnaby the dog or Frank Nugent the boy, I'd have thought you were mad. But when I saw Frank walking towards me, holding the lead of a surprisingly docile Barnaby, who was trotting along beside him with a totally innocent look on his fluffy face, I was so overcome with joy I nearly burst into tears.

'I believe you must be looking for this little chap,' said Frank. 'I heard you calling after him.'

'Oh Frank!' I said. 'Thank you, thank you! How did you manage to grab him?'

'I've had plenty of practice tackling your brother at rugby,' said Frank, and smiled. He has a nice, friendly smile.

'Barnaby's almost as aggravating as Harry,' I said, as Frank carefully passed over the lead. 'I'd better take him home now before he does anything else dreadful.'

'Would you mind if I walked part of the way home with you?' said Frank. 'It's on my way.'

I told him I didn't mind at all, which was true, and asked him why he wasn't still at the rugby match.

'It's my father's birthday,' said Frank. 'We're having a special birthday tea. So I had to leave half way through.'

'Oh, I see,' I said. And I couldn't think of anything to say after that. I don't think I'd ever been on my own with Frank before. Or any boy, for that matter. He didn't seem to be able think of anything to say either, and we walked along in a slightly awkward silence until Frank said, 'Is he new?'

'I beg your pardon?' I said, confused.

'The dog,' said Frank. 'Harry didn't mention that you were getting a pet.'

'He's not ours!' I said, in tones of such outraged horror that Frank started to laugh, and then so did I, and I explained about Mrs. Sheffield and how awful The Menace was. After that things were much more comfortable between us. Even The Menace behaved himself and didn't pull on his lead, which was slightly irritating in one way because it made it look as though I had been too feeble to hold onto a normal dog earlier, rather than a monstrous fiend with superhuman – I mean supercanine – strength.

We had been walking along for about ten minutes when Frank mentioned that he was taking part in a debate at school about the future of the Home Rule bill.

'But I don't suppose you're interested in politics, are you?' he said. 'Most girls aren't.'

Well, I hadn't been particularly interested in politics, but I couldn't help resenting his assumption.

'Maybe I'd be more interested,' I said, a little stiffly, 'if I knew that I'd have a say in things when I grow up. I mean, if women had the vote.'

'Oh, well, yes,' said Frank. 'Maybe you would. I hadn't really thought of that.'

'What do you think?' I asked. 'About women's suffrage, I mean.' And for some reason, I don't know why, I really cared about what his answer would be.

'I don't know,' he said. 'I suppose I hadn't really thought about that much either.'

I was going to make a smart remark but then I remembered that I hadn't thought about it much until last week, so instead I said, 'Well, I think women should have the vote. Why shouldn't we? It's not fair that we shouldn't have a say in anything.' I remembered what Mrs. Joyce had said last week. 'We have to keep to the laws of the land, don't we? But we don't have a say in who makes them.'

I almost held my breath as I waited for Frank's answer. He ran a hand through his fair curls and then he said, 'I suppose you're right.'

I let out my breath.

'My mother did once say,' Frank went on, 'that she couldn't see why my uncle Stephen should have a vote when she didn't. And if you'd ever met my uncle Stephen, you'd see why.' He laughed. 'Oh, this is my turn.'

We paused at the corner.

'Thanks for grabbing The Menace,' I said.

'Don't mention it,' said Frank. He bent down to pat Barnaby's white fluffy head.

The Menace, as if aware that he'd soon have me all to himself again, started straining against his harness.

'Goodness, he's a strong little chap, isn't he?' said Frank, giving Barnaby's woolly curls a last rub. 'He doesn't look it. Well, goodbye. I'm sure I'll see you soon.'

'Goodbye,' I said.

He lifted his hand in a sort of salute, and headed off. I looked after him for a moment, but Barnaby was straining himself in the direction of home so I took him back to the Sheffields' house.

'Back so soon?' said Mrs. Sheffield, after her maid Agnes had fetched her. She looked slightly disappointed to be reunited with Barnaby so soon. 'Was he any trouble?'

'Not at all,' I said, which was my third convincing lie of the day. I'm starting to get a bit worried at how easily these lies spring to my lips, even if they do mean I'm a good actress.

Anyway, Mrs. Sheffield thanked me, and I was so immersed in my role as someone who had enjoyed taking Barnaby for a walk that I almost offered to do it again in the future, but luckily I restrained myself in time. And then I walked home and went into the dining room to write this letter. I am in a strangely good mood and I don't really know why. Maybe it's the exercise. I can't remember the last time I did so much running in one go. It must be good for me.

But I am finally going to finish this letter now. If I wait to write until after I've got something out of Phyllis, the letter will get so long it'll be more of a package and then it will definitely be too expensive. It's long enough as it is. I do hope you haven't been bored reading it. So I will bid you farewell.

Write soon!
Best love, and Votes for Women!
Mollie

13th May, 1912.

Dear Frances,

Thank you for the letter of the 10th. Your school has
always sounded very different to mine, what with
being in the middle of the countryside and not having
either nuns or day girls, but I was very surprised – and
impressed – to read about your Miss Bridges being so
keen on the cause. I can't imagine any of my teachers
taking suffragette magazines to the classroom. Since I last
wrote I have seen a few suffrage magazines. And books
– well, one. AND me and Nora have actually been to a
meeting, not that I got to hear much of it – oh, so much
has happened!

I'm afraid this will be another long letter. I hope you
don't mind. It will give you something to read while
all the others are playing hockey. What rotten bad luck,
spraining your ankle like that. I do hope it's a bit better
now, I know that a sprained ankle hurts like anything.

Do you remember the summer when you, me and
Nora all read *Treasure Island* and pretended the tree in

her garden was a pirate ship, and I tried to swing down from the 'mast' on a rope and landed badly? My left ankle was like a balloon for a week, and I couldn't get my boot on. I hope your ankle is less balloon-ish than mine was. And I'm sure it will be better by the time you start rehearsing your play. I'm very sorry that your plan to put on your own play was outvoted, but maybe it's for the best? Doing a play by someone else will be excellent practice and then you can perfect your own play for next year. And, after all, if you're going to be passed over for another playwright, it might as well be Shakespeare. I've read *Hamlet* now and it's awfully good.

So, as I said above, lots of things have happened since my last letter. Where exactly had I got to when it finished? Oh yes, I *still* hadn't talked to Phyllis about being a suffragette. Well, she finally showed up on the Saturday afternoon and after tea I followed her upstairs to her room, which in retrospect probably wasn't the best way to approach her. She didn't notice I was following her (I was wearing my indoor shoes and I am quite light on my feet. Maybe it's thanks to all the Drill and Dancing at school) until she turned to close the door of her room and saw me standing right behind her. She almost screamed.

'Mollie!' she said.

'I thought you knew I was behind you,' I said apologetically.

'Well I didn't,' said Phyllis. 'Anyway, you're sneaking around after me. Again.'

'Oh Phyllis, this time I really wasn't sneaking,' I said. 'Honestly, I thought you knew I was there. I just want to talk to you.'

Phyllis gave me a sceptical look but then she said, 'Come in, then.'

I went into her room and she closed the door. Then she folded her arms.

'Come on, then,' she said. 'What do you want to talk about?'

I took a deep breath. I had to do this properly and not annoy her.

'Ever since Wednesday, I've been thinking,' I began.

'That must make a nice change,' said Phyllis.

I ignored her jibe and kept going. 'I've been thinking about everything Mrs. Joyce said at the meeting,' I said. 'And, well, it all made sense to me. I mean, I could see how it fitted in with other things like … well, like Harry getting all the chicken.' I paused. 'I know that sounds silly.'

And to my relief and, I must admit, surprise, Phyllis shook her head.

'No,' she said. 'It makes sense.'

'Oh,' I said. 'Well, I told Nora about it and both of us would, well, we'd like to find out more. And get involved.'

As I said it, I realised that I really meant it. I wanted to stand up and actually do something to make the world fairer. But I wasn't quite sure Nora wanted to join in yet, so I added, 'At least I do. Nora wants to find out a bit more first.'

'Are you honestly serious about this?' asked Phyllis. 'You've never shown any interest in politics before now.'

I tried to explain how I felt. 'Politics never seemed connected to anything before now,' I said. 'Not to real life, I mean. At least my real life. But what she said about women not being able to do the same things as men, well, I can see that every day. And I suppose I never really thought about changing it. Until now, that is.'

'This isn't a silly game, you know,' said Phyllis. 'It's real. And sometimes it's dangerous.'

'I know,' I said. But Phyllis shook her head (which of course made a hairpin fall out).

'I don't think you do,' she said. 'You only saw one meeting, and it was a very civilised one. When we tried to do that poster parade down Dawson Street six weeks ago – Redmond and his lot were having a meeting in town – we were treated very roughly.'

'How roughly?' I said.

Phyllis sat down on the edge of her bed (which made another hairpin fall out).

'The stewards from the meeting tried to force us away,'

she said. 'Physically, I mean. And they wrenched our posters from us and tore them up. Mrs. Joyce fell over. And they didn't help her up or even apologise. They just laughed at her and ripped up her poster.'

I thought of the dignified woman I'd seen, and I imagined her lying on the ground while a crowd of men jeered at her. It made me feel a bit sick.

'Didn't the police do anything?' I said.

'They were jolly decent, actually,' said Phyllis. 'Not like in England. They stepped in and got us out of the crowd safely. But not before the crowd had, well, pushed us about a bit.' She looked down at her cuffs and started fiddling with a button. 'And thrown bits of horrid rubbish at us.'

I remembered the cabbage leaves on her hat.

'Was some of the rubbish rotten cabbage?' I said.

'Yes, as it happens.' Phyllis looked surprised. 'How did you know?'

'You had some leaves on your hat one evening,' I said. 'I did wonder.'

Phyllis sighed. 'Well, now you know,' she said.

'But who are they?' I asked. 'Were they Redmondites?

Phyllis laughed bitterly. People like Sherlock Holmes are always doing bitter laughs in books, but I don't think I'd ever heard someone actually do it in real life until now.

'They're members of the Ancient Order of Hibernians,' she said.

I had never heard of this Ancient Order before. It sounded terribly grand, but I didn't think grand organisations went around pushing women to the ground.

'Who are they?' I asked.

'Just a club of stupid old men that don't want anything to change,' said Phyllis. 'Some people call them the Ancient Order of Hooligans.'

'I didn't think anyone thought it was all right to go around shoving ladies,' I said.

Phyllis gave me a pitying look.

'My dear girl, you really don't know much about the struggle, do you?' she said, which was a bit unfair because I had already admitted I didn't. She got up from the bed and went to her bookshelf. Reaching behind the books on the top shelf, she pulled out a chunky volume and handed it to me. I opened it and looked at the title page. It was the book she'd mentioned on Wednesday: *No Surrender*.

'Read this,' she said. 'It's set in England so it's not quite the same as here. Their police are much, much rougher, for a start. But it'll give you an idea of the sort of minds we're up against. And some Irish women have been treated very badly by the police and authorities over there.'

And that was when I asked the question that I really

should have thought of asking on Wednesday evening.

'Who exactly are "we"?' I asked. 'I mean, are you all part of one organisation or society or something?'

Phyllis looked like she might give another bitter laugh.

'You don't even know?' she said.

Of course I don't, I thought, that's why I'd asked. But I didn't say anything.

'I'm part of an organisation. There are a lot of suffrage societies, but I'm a member of the Irish Women's Franchise League. That's who organised the meeting on Wednesday.'

'A league?' I said.

'Do you remember me talking about Mrs. Sheehy-Skeffington? She used to teach Kathleen's older sister in Eccles Street years ago, and I met her a few times,' said Phyllis.

I nodded. Phyllis had always been very impressed by what she knew of Mrs. Sheehy-Skeffington, whose father had been an Irish Party M.P. Phyllis said she seemed to be a teacher who encouraged girls to think for themselves.

'Well, she's one of the founders of the League,' said Phyllis. 'Not that her father approves of it. Her husband is a supporter too.'

But before I could ask any more questions I heard footsteps coming rapidly up the stairs. I shoved the book

inside my cardigan (under my armpit) just before the
door opened and Julia came in.

The thing about Julia is that she really does look
awfully saintly. Maybe that's why she's become so pious.
She's trying to live up to her virtuous looks. I'm quite
glad I'm stuck with very unsaintly features so there's
no danger of me becoming a little plaster saint. No one
looking at me would expect me to be particularly noble.
In fact, Maggie used to say that I just had 'a bold face'.
I don't think that's a compliment, but maybe it's better
than the alternative.

'Mother's looking for you,' said Julia. 'There's lots of
mending to do.'

When is there not? Honestly, I can't help thinking
Mother actually tears things up just to give us something
to do. How can so many things get torn or worn out in
one household? But there's no use arguing with Mother
about these things, so Phyllis and I followed Julia down
to the sitting room, where a basket of holey socks (not
holy in the Julia sense) and petticoats with sagging hems
awaited us.

Harry, of course, was nowhere to be seen while we
were put to work. He'd gone to some classmate's house
after that afternoon's rugby match. He really does
absolutely nothing around the house, while we girls have
to work like skivvies. I bet if women had the vote and

were making the laws boys wouldn't be allowed get away with this sort of thing.

It wasn't until all the mending was done and Mother was playing some rather strange but beautiful music by a French composer called Debussy that I finally got to start reading the book. I was a bit nervous in case anybody asked what I was reading. I could lie of course, and, as you know, I've recently found out that I'm surprisingly good at this, but still, all they had to do was glance at the spine and they'd find me out. So I found it quite hard to concentrate on it, and it wasn't until Julia and I were in bed and she was reading a book called *Little Lives of the Saints* (because that's the only sort of book Julia likes to read for fun) that I finally got to read it properly.

And once I started, I couldn't stop. After a couple of pages, I was totally engrossed in the story. There was a rather grand Irish girl (who seemed to live in England), and a girl who worked in a cotton mill in Lancashire, and they both became suffragettes. After a while, I heard Julia making her usual hideous grunts and realised she'd fallen asleep with her book in her hand. This was a very good thing (apart from the fact that I had to listen to her grunting away) because it meant that I didn't have to worry about putting out the light and could read for as long as I liked. Though just to make sure, I put a bolster against the bottom of the door so Mother or Father wouldn't see any light shining beneath it on their way to bed. It must have been at least one in the morning by the time my own eyes started to close and I reluctantly put the book under my pillow and turned out the light.

I had terrible dreams that night. I dreamed I'd been arrested and I was pounding on the door begging to be let out. And then I realised someone was actually pounding on my bedroom door and Harry was yelling, 'Get up, you lazy sluggards!'

Somehow, Julia and I had both managed to oversleep and now we were late for Mass. What with going to the church followed by the customary Sunday visit to Aunt Josephine – during which she spent the entire time talking about the 'dreadful behaviour of the young modern girl' – it was late afternoon by the time I was able to return to *No Surrender*.

I certainly needed something stirring to balance out all the nonsense I'd heard from Aunt Josephine all afternoon. Even Mother started to look like she was running out of patience after Aunt Josephine had given one of her speeches about how education was a waste of time for girls.

'I've seen the sort of girls Eccles Street turns out, Rose,' she said. 'Bluestockings. Office girls. That dreadful Mrs. Sheehy-Skeffington, or whatever she calls herself. It's a dangerous thing, filling girls' heads with rubbish they can never understand. Much better to send them somewhere nice where they can learn to be good young wives and mothers without all that bookish nonsense.'

'Robert and I believe that it's important for a girl to have a well-furnished mind,' said Mother, in the sort of voice she uses to her children when one of us has behaved badly in front of her friends and she doesn't want to lose her temper in front of them.

Aunt Josephine laughed, but it wasn't the sort of laugh that has any humour in it.

'Well, I suppose it depends on what you consider well-furnished,' she said. 'It's not as though they will have to earn their own living someday. And I believe most men would prefer to marry a girl whose mind is devoted to her children and family. And to God, of course,' she added.

Mother was making a great effort not to snap. I could tell.

'No man wants to marry an ignorant girl,' she said.

'You say that now, Rose,' said Aunt Josephine. 'But in a few years when Phyllis and Mollie are looking for husbands, you might regret it. And as for letting Phyllis go to that university …'

Mother hadn't been particularly happy when Phyllis first told her she was determined to go to college, but you'd never know that she had ever disapproved of it by the way she looked at Aunt Josephine now.

'Phyllis is going to study English literature,' she said haughtily. 'And I would rather she married a man who shared her love of books. Just as I have married a man who understands my love of music.'

This was a bit of an exaggeration, as Father isn't terribly passionate about music, but I suppose he does join in when we sing around the piano. And he does like listening to Mother play. Anyway, I couldn't blame her for wanting to exaggerate. Anything to wipe that superior expression from Aunt Josephine's face! But of course you can't wipe it away, not for long. She gave a tinkling little laugh and said, 'If you say so, Rose.'

Which I could see annoyed Mother even more, though she didn't respond. I don't think Mother actually likes Aunt Josephine very much. After all, she never visits Aunt Josephine herself apart from when we make these family visits with Father on Sundays, and I don't think she exactly invites Aunt Josephine to our house during the week. Aunt Josephine just sort of ... turns up. A bit like Dracula arriving at Lucy Westenra's house.

By the way, if you haven't read *Dracula*, DO NOT READ IT. I found Harry's copy of it a few months ago and devoured the whole thing in a couple of days before he noticed it was missing from his bookshelf. It was very, very exciting and I couldn't put it down, but then I had nightmares for a fortnight and couldn't go to sleep without putting my rosary beads under the pillow in case a vampire turned up.

Though, of course I've had nightmares about Aunt Josephine too, and rosary beads would be of no use against her. Nora told me that the man who wrote *Dracula* is actually from Dublin, and from a part of the city that's not too far away from here. I do wonder if he ever met Aunt Josephine.

Anyway, even Father seemed tired of Aunt Josephine that day, and he doesn't have to put up with her during the week too because he's always at work when she makes her afternoon calls, so he doesn't see her at her absolute worst. Father developed a headache when we got home (possibly as a result of having to listen to Aunt Josephine) and went for a lie down, and was too exhausted that evening to read us any more of Peter Fitzgerald's adventures. But I didn't mind missing out on P. F. because it meant I could read *No Surrender* in peace.

It was an usually quiet evening. Father was snoring away upstairs, Mother was playing something soothing by Bach on the piano, Julia was reading her saints book, and Phyllis was embroidering what is going to be a sash for Kathleen's birthday. Even Harry was quiet for once. He was reading a story about Harry Wharton and Co. in the latest issue of the *Magnet*. He pretends he's far too old for 'stupid kids' school stories' but I know he sometimes still buys the *Magnet* and the *Gem*. I made a note to swipe the magazine later because even though I may be too old for school stories myself I love reading about Harry Wharton and Bob Cherry and Billy Bunter. But right now I was more interested in reading about Mary O'Neill and Jenny the mill girl and the other brave suffragettes.

Oh Frances, you must get a copy of it. It made me cry with sorrow and with rage at the awful things that are done to women and girls just because they want to stand up for what's fair and right. I don't know how anyone could read it and not agree with the justice of those brave women's cause.

By the time I arrived at school the next day I felt like smashing some windows and chaining myself to some railings. I told Nora this as we waited in the cloakroom for the second bell to ring.

'I'm not sure smashing anything is a good idea right now,' she said, after I'd handed her the book and told her to read it quickly so I could give it back to Phyllis. 'And you definitely couldn't do the other thing. For one, we don't have any chains.'

'I could use a skipping rope,' I said.

'That's not quite as dramatic,' said Nora. 'Though I dare say it would create a sensation.'

'Imagine if I roped myself to the gates of Dublin

Castle,' I said. I pictured the dramatic scene. Me crying 'No surrender!' as a policeman tried to untie the ropes. 'What a stir it would cause.'

'Especially if your father saw you,' said Nora.

I hadn't thought of that. Because he's a civil servant, he does have to go in there a lot. But anyway, I'd think about that later, when I was actually chained (or tied) to the railings. And I supposed there were other places I could chain myself to. Even a post office might count as a government office.

'Hello there, what are you two whispering about?' said a familiar, sugary voice. It belonged to Grace, who is always sneaking about trying to catch people doing or saying something they shouldn't so she can pretend to be sorry for our lack of discipline and/or tell a teacher. All of a sudden, I felt the urge to really give her something to talk about.

'If you must know,' I said, 'we were talking about suffragettes.'

Grace looked horrified.

'Surely,' she said, 'you're not interested in those dreadful women.'

Nora rolled her eyes.

'We might have known that you wouldn't approve of them,' she said. 'You never like anything interesting.'

Grace smiled pityingly.

'If you call making a show of yourself in public interesting …' she said.

'I certainly do,' said Nora. 'In fact, I admire them for it.'

I should have known that the way to make Nora really warm to my new cause was to show her that Grace was against it. I should almost be grateful to Grace, really.

'Nora, you're clearly not in your right mind,' said Grace. 'I really think I ought to tell your mother about all this.'

But now she had gone too far. Nora glared at her so ferociously that Grace actually took a step backwards.

'Go on, then,' growled Nora. 'Tell her.'

Grace pulled herself together and tossed her annoyingly perfect curls. Then she smiled at us in her awful way.

'You poor thing,' she said. 'I won't deign to respond to that. I'm going to find May and Gertie.' And she swept out of the cloakroom. At least, she tried to sweep out, but Mary McCarthy's coat had fallen off its hook and Grace tripped over it. I must admit that she managed to regain her footing with more dignity than I would have managed in the circumstances.

When she'd gone I looked at Nora.

'Did you really mean that?' I asked. 'About admiring the suffragettes?'

'Well yes,' said Nora. 'I suppose so. Though I was partly saying it to annoy Grace.'

'Oh,' I said.

'But honestly,' said Nora. 'I have been thinking about everything you said – about brothers and votes and all that. And I do think it's right. I mean, why shouldn't we have a say in the country when we grow up? Especially when you look at some of the ridiculous boys who might be running the place.'

'That's exactly it!' I said. I was awfully glad. Discovering this suffragette movement was so thrilling for me that I really wanted Nora to share my excitement. It's always more fun when your friends share your interests. Of course, Nora and I don't always like the same things. She absolutely hates knitting, for example, while I actually find working the stitches quite soothing (AND you get a cardigan or a scarf or a pair of socks when you've finished the soothing part).

She also loves learning French. A while ago she started talking about wanting to go to Paris after she finishes school (this was before the doctor business. And her desire to be a lady mayor). I did point out to her that the things we learn at school won't be much use to her in Paris.

'You won't want to talk about your aunt's pens,' I said. 'You'll want to ask how to get to the train station and how much that loaf of bread is.'

But Nora said she'd learn that sort of thing when she got there.

Anyway, back to the cloakroom.

'What shall we do first?' asked Nora. 'If we want to be actively involved, I mean.'

'Well, there are meetings,' I said. 'Like the one I followed Phyllis to.'

Nora looked sceptical.

'I don't think we'll be able to go to many of those,' she said. 'Not if they're on Wednesday evenings outside the Custom House.'

She was right. It's so unfair, Harry is always popping off to Frank's house (and vice versa) and rugby matches and heaven knows what else whenever he feels like it, but if I want to go anywhere but Nora's house Mother is always finding some reason why I shouldn't go. And then she often finds reasons to stop me going to Nora's house too.

'They have other meetings too,' I said. 'Less, well, rough ones. They have them at the Phoenix Park at the weekends. So we might actually be able to go to one.'

Nora looked as though she was considering all this, but before she could say anything else, a fair-haired head suddenly popped through the coats and gave us such a fright that we both shrieked (though not very loudly. Despite what Harry says, I hardly ever shriek).

'Stella!' I said, when my heart stopped pounding.

'Sorry,' said Stella. 'I heard your voices and it was

quicker to look through the coats than walk all the way around to you. What are you talking about?'

Nora and I glanced at each other and I knew we were thinking the same thing. How much should we tell Stella? On the one hand, she's our friend and it seemed awfully mean to keep something so big and important a secret from her, especially if we were going to get involved and start chaining ourselves to things. On the other hand, I wasn't sure if Stella would approve of our new interest. She may be our friend, but she can be a little bit … well, whenever Nora and I sympathise with her about being stuck in school all the time and having to share a dorm with Gertie Hayden, she always says that she doesn't mind at all and that she LIKES being at school and that they have quite a lot of fun in the dorm and that the sodality (that's a sort of religious club, I don't think you have them in England) is lovely, and that Gertie isn't half as bad when Grace isn't around, and that the nuns are all very kind to them. And I'm sure all this is true, but anyone who won't even say a bad word against Gertie is … well, I suppose what I'm trying to say is that Stella has never been very rebellious. She never really breaks the rules. In fact, I think she quite likes rules in general. So what would she think when we told her we wanted to break quite a lot of them?

All of these thoughts seemed to flash through my brain

in just a few seconds, but at the end of those seconds I knew what I wanted to do. Our friendship with Stella was important, and you have to trust your friends. Besides, it wasn't as if we were asking her to join in. And even if she didn't approve of the whole thing, I knew that she wouldn't tell anyone about it who would get us into trouble. So I gave Nora a tiny nod, and she nodded back, and then I turned to Stella and said, 'We want to be suffragettes.'

Stella looked more baffled than shocked.

'Suffragettes?' she said. 'Like those women who wear posters? And the ones in London who get carried off by policemen, kicking and screaming?'

'Well, yes, sort of,' I said. 'At least, I hope we don't get carried off by policemen. And we do have suffragettes in Ireland too, you know.'

'Oh, I know,' said Stella. She was fiddling with the end of her thick fair plait, which she always does when she is thinking hard. 'They just don't seem to be as dramatic as the English ones. They don't seem to break windows and things.'

'So far,' said Nora.

I was pleasantly surprised by Nora's attitude. Now she'd decided she wanted to get involved, she seemed to be becoming more enthusiastic by the second.

'But aren't they stopping Home Rule?' asked Stella.

'The suffragettes, I mean. One of the older boarders was reading a paper the other week and she said that if the suffragettes didn't stop making a big fuss about women getting the vote, we wouldn't get Home Rule at all.'

I had to admit that I didn't know much about this. I suppose I've just been thinking of how important it is that women should be treated fairly. I hadn't really bothered finding out much else. Nora didn't know either. Then I remembered something.

'When I went to a suffrage meeting at the Custom House, it seemed like the lady who spoke was all for Home Rule,' I said. 'And I know Phyllis has always been in favour of it. Besides, one of the suffragette leaders is the daughter of an M.P.'

As soon as I'd said all this, I realised that it sounded as though I had made the bold and daring decision to go to the suffrage meeting all by myself, rather than sneaking after Phyllis and going to a meeting by accident. But I didn't feel like telling Stella the full story right then. I also didn't feel like telling her what Phyllis had said about Mr. Sheehy not approving of his daughter's activities.

'Is it a secret?' asked Stella, still fiddling with her plait. 'You wanting to be suffragettes, I mean.'

'Not exactly,' I said. 'After all, Grace just found out. And besides, there's not very much to know. We're still just finding out about it all, really. Nora's only just decided to be one.'

'Mollie,' said Nora, 'is surprisingly convincing.'

I felt rather pleased to hear this. Who knew I had such effective powers of persuasion? I've never been particularly good at getting people to follow my lead before now. If I had been, I'd have used my powers to persuade Harry and Grace to be less awful. I wondered if this was a sign that I was destined to go into politics myself one day and I was just thinking that 'Mollie Carberry, M.P.' sounded very fine when I realised that Nora was waving her hand in front of my face.

'Are you listening, Mollie?' she asked.

'I was just wondering if I could be an M.P.,' I said.

Nora looked alarmed.

'Now, steady on,' she said. 'I've only just decided to get involved in all of this. I didn't mean I was going to help you run for parliament. Anyway, you're far too young.'

'I know that, you goose,' I said. 'I meant some day in the distant future.' I turned to Stella. 'Anyway, I suppose we should probably make sure the nuns and teachers don't find out. I don't think Grace or Gertie would dare sneak, though.'

'It wouldn't be the end of the world if the staff did find out,' said Nora. 'They can't expel us for having opinions. They're always encouraging us to think for ourselves.' I wasn't sure about that, but she was probably right. And then the bell rang and we had to go back to class. We didn't get a chance to talk about it much for the rest of the day, but Nora took home *No Surrender* that night and the next day she looked exhausted.

'I was up all night reading,' she said dramatically. 'Well, almost. I used practically all the oil in the lamp, I stayed up so late.' I think she was exaggerating but I didn't say anything about that.

'Isn't it awfully sad?' I said. 'And horrible, too. The way they treat all those poor women!'

'It's the awful unfairness of it,' said Nora, passionately. 'Jenny's sister! And the government doing all those terrible things to them just because they want the same rights as men! I don't think I realised quite how unfair it was until now.'

'That's exactly it,' I said. I was very pleased that we felt the same way.

'When did you say the next meeting was?' said Nora.

'Tomorrow,' I said. 'But that's just outside the Custom House. We could go to the Saturday one, though. I mean, I bet we could make an excuse to go to the park. Phyllis might even take us.'

'Then you'd better start buttering her up,' said Nora.

'I'll start tonight,' I said. And I did, though the results were mixed. Harry was off playing some match or other and Father was at some sort of work-related dinner, so it was just Phyllis, Mother, Julia and me. Mother, as usual, was playing the piano (something very loud by Beethoven), Julia was concentrating very hard on making an elaborate house of cards on a small and dangerously wobbly table, and me and Phyllis were reading. I have started reading *Jane Eyre* – which is very good. There was a waiting list for it at the school library so I hadn't read it until now. Have you read it? It is all about a poor downtrodden orphan that has horrible cousins (a bit like Harry only even worse), and then she goes to an even more horrible school where she has to eat burned porridge and makes friends with a very saintly girl. I'm not making it sound very good but it is, especially when she goes off to be a governess for a rich and rude yet interesting man called Mr. Rochester. Jane is small and ordinary, and nobody thinks she can do anything important, but she is full of fire and rage. I know how she feels.

Anyway, even though Jane Eyre is very good I wasn't really concentrating on it because I was trying to think of ways to butter up Phyllis, who was totally engrossed in reading a book called *A Room With a View*. I knew there was no use in just asking her nicely if she would take us. I had a feeling she was already regretting lending me the Constance Maud book. So I said, 'Your hair looks awfully nice, Phyl.'

And instead of being flattered and saying, 'Oh, thank

you very much, Mollie,' she looked at me suspiciously and said, 'What do you want?'

'Nothing!' I said. 'I was just hoping that when I put my hair up it looks as nice as yours.' Even as I spoke I realised I couldn't blame Phyllis for suspecting my motives. Her hair was already coming out of its pins and a thick curl kept falling into her face. She tucked it back up and said, 'Are you being sarcastic? It sounds as though you are.' The curl came untucked and fell back over her eyes.

'No!' I said. 'I was trying to be nice. But,' I added peevishly, 'apparently my niceness is wasted on you.' And strangely enough, that seemed to have a positive effect because Phyllis said, 'Then I'm sorry I didn't believe you.'

And I said, 'It's all right' and I knew that the first part of my mission to butter up Phyllis had been a success.

I made my next move the next day. It was Wednesday, so we still had plenty of time, and I thought it was best to move slowly. Softly, softly, catchee monkey, as Father likes to say. If you've never heard the expression before, it has nothing to do with actual monkeys (sadly), it just means that the best way to get what you want is to go slow and steady. I knew that Phyllis would probably be going to the meeting in town that evening, so when I passed her on the landing on my way down to breakfast I said, 'Good luck.'

Phyllis gave me another one of her most suspicious looks. It's starting to feel as though she can't look at me any other way.

'Good luck for what?' she said.

I was starting to wish I hadn't said anything.

'The Custom House meeting,' I said. 'I presume you're going?'

'Shut up!' hissed Phyllis. 'Someone might hear you.'

'No they won't,' I whispered back. 'They're all downstairs already. Listen, Phyl, I promised I wouldn't let anyone know about all your ... activities, and I meant it. You can trust me, honestly you can.'

And before Phyllis could reply, I skipped down the stairs. I didn't want to push her too far. As I said to Nora at school that day, softly, softly is the best approach. But she wasn't convinced.

'You can't be too soft,' she said. 'Saturday isn't all that far away. And anyway, it's all right for you. Even if it doesn't work, you've already been to a meeting. But I haven't.'

'Stop fussing,' I said. 'I'll persuade her. And if the worst comes to the worst, I bet we can think of an excuse to get away on Saturday.'

'Aren't you still sort of in trouble for sneaking off last week?' said Nora.

'Not really,' I said, but Nora had raised an important

point. As a rule in my family, once a punishment has been carried out (like me missing Nellie's party), my parents say no more about the bad behaviour that led to it. But even so, I wasn't sure they would be happy about me heading off with just Nora quite so soon. For a moment I thought about asking if Maggie could take us for a walk, but then I realised it wouldn't be fair to Maggie. And even if I could bring myself to do such a low thing, she'd probably see through the ruse and refuse to take us to the Park anyway. Phyllis was our only hope.

She didn't come home that evening until it was quite late, and I didn't get a chance to talk to her on her own (I could have barged into her room but I didn't think that would be very helpful). It wasn't until Thursday evening that I finally managed to bring up the subject. For once, the two of us were on her own. Mother was talking to Maggie about tomorrow's meals, Harry was off with Frank, Father had one of his headaches and had gone for a lie-down, and Julia was in the dining room doing her home exercises.

'Phyllis?' I said.

'Um?' she said absently. She was still reading *A Room with a View*, which was clearly more interesting than a younger sister.

'You know the League meetings you were telling me about?' I said.

That got her attention. She looked sharply at me.

'What about them?' she said.

'Nora and I would really like to go to Saturday's one,' I said. 'Just to see what they're like.'

'You must be joking,' said Phyllis.

'Oh, come on, Phyl,' I said. 'It's the Phoenix Park! Lots of people go there on Saturdays. And it's the afternoon! It's not as though we're hanging around town at night.'

Phyllis was clearly considering it. I think there is a part of her that is genuinely pleased that her sister has been recruited to the cause. But there is another part of her that doesn't want an annoying little sister hanging around. Not that I am annoying. But I think most people think their younger siblings are a bit irritating. I certainly do. Anyway, I could tell that she was on the cusp of agreeing so I didn't say anything else in case it tipped her over into the 'no annoying sisters' camp. I just gazed at her imploringly instead. And it worked!

'You and Nora can come,' she said. 'But only if you stay where I can see you and keep out of trouble.' She stood up and looked down at me in a very stern sort of way. 'And this is a once-off, just to stop you going on about it. I'm not going to take you to any more meetings. All right?'

We'll see about that, I thought. But I didn't say it. I just said, 'Thanks awfully, Phyl. We'll be good as gold.' And then I went out of the room before she could change her mind. I was so pleased I bounced up the stairs and as I bounced I found myself singing 'The Kerry Dance', but instead of the normal words I sang 'Oh we're going to get votes for women! Oh we're going to a meeting too.' But I sang it very quietly so nobody would hear.

I told Nora the good news as soon as we met the next day.

'I told you I could persuade her,' I said.

'All right, there's no need to be so smug,' said Nora. 'But well done.'

'I've been thinking,' I said. 'I know we can't go out with posters and things. Or smash windows like they do in England. But maybe we could do something else to feel like we're part of the cause. Something fun.'

'Like what?' said Nora.

'We could write a song,' I said. And I told her about my new version of the 'Kerry Dance' song.

'That doesn't sound very good to me,' said Nora dubiously. 'Sing it.'

I did.

'It is quite memorable,' Nora admitted.

'Well,' I said. 'It's a memorable tune. Not that I wrote it.'

'I suppose we could write more words,' said Nora. Her face brightened. 'It might even become an anthem! For all the Irish suffrage campaigners.'

'That's the spirit!' I said. And then we were at the school and had to go in to English literature where we are reading dreadful Walter Scott, who everyone hates. I wish we could read *Jane Eyre* instead, it's much better. But even Walter Scott can't last forever (although it certainly feels like it), and at break, after we'd had our lunch, we found a quiet corner of the garden (the weather was so nice we could sit outside). Nora took out a notebook and a pencil.

'It's a very jaunty song,' she said. 'So we need quite dramatic lyrics.' She hummed the tune. 'What about – and I'm just thinking aloud – something like, "Irish girls and Irish women, hear the cry of the suffragettes"?'

'That's not bad,' I said.

Nora sang the line. 'Not bad at all.' She wrote it down in the notebook. 'What rhymes with suffragette?'

We both thought for a bit, but it was surprisingly hard. Finally, I thought of something.

'Clarinet?' I said.

'I suppose it's better than nothing,' said Nora.

'Well, that's what you've come up with – nothing,' I said crossly. 'What about … we will make a joyful noise with drums and bells and clarinets?'

'But we don't have drums and bells,' said Nora. 'Or clarinets for that matter.'

'Nora!' I said. 'It's just a song. It's a ... what do they call it? A metaphor.'

'For what?' said Nora.

I didn't really know myself.

'For making a noise!' I said. 'You know. To get attention for the cause.'

'I see,' said Nora.

'And I think we should have something about our brothers not thinking we should have the vote,' I said.

'You haven't actually talked about it with Harry, have you?' said Nora. 'Maybe he wouldn't mind you having the vote. And I don't know what my brother thinks.'

Nora was being a bit too literal. It was most unlike her.

'I mean brothers in general,' I said. 'And fathers. I mean, clearly lots of people's brothers and fathers don't think we should have the vote or we'd have it by now.'

'Fair enough,' said Nora. 'What rhymes with vote?'

A few minutes later we had come up with this: one verse and a chorus.

Irish girls and Irish women,
Hear the cry of the suffragettes!
We will make a joyful noise
With drums and bells and clarinets

Though our fathers and our brothers
Don't think we should have the vote
We will fight and we will win it
And then we will gladly gloat.

'Heavens,' said Nora. 'That's actually rather good.'

'Maybe it really will catch on,' I said. 'And become the suffrage anthem.'

We sang it through again.

'I'm not sure about the gloating bit,' said Nora. 'It's a bit ungracious.'

'Well, if women get the vote I will gloat,' I said firmly. 'We've got to be honest.'

Nora wasn't convinced, but she agreed that it would do until we came up with a better phrase that ended in a word rhyming with vote.

'We can try it out on Saturday,' said Nora. 'If all goes well. I hope nothing happens to stop us getting to that meeting.'

I hoped so too. We had both asked our parents if Phyllis could take us to the park and they had given us permission to go but that didn't mean they couldn't suddenly change their minds. So what with my nervousness and I my excitement I felt quite giddy the next morning. In fact, after breakfast Phyllis dragged me out into the hall and told me to calm down.

'As far as Mother and Father are concerned, this is just a walk in the park,' she said. 'And if you're giving me all those meaningful looks and dreadful winks they'll know something's up.'

'I am not giving you dreadful winks!' I said. 'I was giving you encouraging smiles.'

'Well, it looked awful and very suspicious,' said Phyllis. 'Calm down or I won't take you anywhere.'

So I did. I read an improving annual called *Aunt Judy's Yearly Book*, though I'm not sure who Aunt Judy is. Anyway, her book isn't very interesting – you would have been very bored by it – but it is also not the sort of thing a daring suffragette would read so I hoped it would throw Mother and Father off the scent and stop them suspecting my true plans for the day. And I suppose it did help me to calm down as I waited for Phyllis's summons. Which finally arrived at about three o'clock.

'Come on then,' she said. 'And don't look too excited. We're only going for a walk. And we're getting the tram there, so I hope you have some money.'

I wish Phyllis wouldn't always act as if I was trying to cadge things off her. Anyway, I wasn't. I am quite good at saving (mostly because I don't have anything exciting to buy with whatever money I ever get) so I had more than enough for my tram fare. Mother and Father came into the hall as we were putting on our coats, and for a moment I thought they were going to suggest we take Harry or Julia with us, but they didn't and soon we were out of the house and trotting down the road. Well, Phyllis was striding down the road and I was trotting after her, trying to keep up.

'Come on' she said. 'I've got to be there to sell *Votes for Women*.'

'But you don't have any magazines,' I said.

Phyllis shook her head, as if she couldn't believe what an idiotic sister she had.

'I'll collect them there,' she said. 'Ah, there's Nora.'

To save time, we'd agreed to meet Nora at the corner rather than calling to her house. 'Thanks awfully for taking us, Phyllis,' she said when we approached.

'I hope you don't make me regret it,' said Phyllis. 'Look, there's a tram coming.'

We had to run to catch the tram, but when we were finally on it I asked, 'What exactly will the meeting be like? Will it be like the one I saw?'

'A bit, I suppose,' said Phyllis. 'There's usually three or four speakers. Sometimes there's a lorry and the speakers stand on the back.'

I thought it sounded very dramatic, and I told Phyllis so.

'Well, it can be,' said Phyllis. 'And not always in a good way. So if there's the slightest hint of trouble, you're to go straight to the park tearooms and I'll find you there afterwards. If I haven't been arrested, that is.'

I hadn't bargained for this.

'Are you likely to be arrested?' I asked, nervously.

'Well, probably not, but anything could happen,' said Phyllis. 'And there's another thing.' She looked at me sternly. 'You have to promise that if we see anyone you know – anyone who might tell Mother and Father – you're to run to the tearooms immediately.'

'But what about you?' I said.

'I'm prepared to take the risk of being caught,' said Phyllis. 'But whatever trouble I might get into for doing this, I'd be in much, much more if they thought I was encouraging you pair to get involved.'

She had a point.

'All right,' I said. 'I promise.'

'So do I,' said Nora.

And that was when we'd reached our tram stop. We had to get out and then get another tram. While we were waiting for it I said, 'You know, Phyl, me and Nora have written a suffrage song.'

'Have you really?' said Phyllis. 'Good heavens.'

'Well, we wrote the words,' said Nora. 'The tune is "The Kerry Dance".'

'This I must hear,' said Phyllis. 'Go on, then. Before the tram arrives.'

'All right,' I said. 'But quietly. We don't want everyone to hear until it's been perfected.'

And so we sang the song, as quietly as we could. Phyllis had a very peculiar expression on her face by the time we'd finished. She made a sort of coughing sound and said, 'Sorry, there's something in my throat. That is ... well, I'm not sure about the line about gloating.'

'I told her that was too much!' said Nora, triumphantly.

'It doesn't seem to be in the right spirit,' said Phyllis. 'But, well, it's a good effort.'

'I suppose we can change those gloating lines,' I said, as the tram turned up. I would just have to think about something else that rhymed with vote (I haven't found anything suitable yet, so, Frances, all suggestions would be gratefully received).

Eventually we were at the park. There seemed to be hundreds of people milling about the place as we walked through the gates. I could hear lions roaring in the zoo.

'Where do they have the meetings?' I asked.

'It's quite a walk,' said Phyllis, leading the way through the throng. And it was. But eventually I saw a lorry with a few men and lot of women, some of whom were carrying poster boards, standing around it. I recognised Mabel from the Custom House, who was now helping to unfurl a large banner that read IRISH WOMEN'S FRANCHISE LEAGUE. There was a pole attached to each end of it so it could be held up to the crowd.

'Right,' said Phyllis. 'You two, stay here. And remember what I said.' She went to join her comrades.

'This is very exciting,' said Nora. 'Look, Phyllis is holding the banner.'

I must admit that Phyllis looked very impressive as she held up one of the poles. Her hair was starting to come out of its pins but now it only added to the dramatic effect. She looked a bit like Joan of Arc. Only without the armour. And without the short hair. So not all that much like Joan of Arc, really. Anyway, she looked very good and some passersby were starting to stop and look at the suffragist group with interest.

A moment later, a bespectacled woman got on the platform and cried, 'Ladies and gentlemen!' She had a loud and ringing voice and it certainly got the attention of people walking past. 'I am going to talk to you today about why women should and will get the vote.'

Some of the gathering crowd booed, some groaned, but others cheered. Some women paused in their walking and drew closer to the makeshift stage.

'As you know,' the woman continued, 'since last winter Irish women have been allowed vote for local and county councils. But that is not enough!'

The audience were listening attentively.

'We know that Ireland will soon have Home Rule,'

said the woman. Several people in the audience cheered. 'But what use is an Irish parliament to Irish women if we can't vote for its members?' the woman went on, her voice becoming more passionate. 'How can Ireland gain its freedom if half of the population are not free? If we are treated like children and lunatics? If we aren't given a chance?'

Nora squeezed my hand. 'She's marvellous,' she said.

I turned to her and was about to tell her I agreed when, over my shoulder, I saw a terrible sight in the distance. I'd know those fluffy ears anywhere, especially when they were accompanied by the imposing height of Mrs. Sheffield, out on a Sunday stroll with her terrible dog.

'Oh no,' I said. 'The Menace!'

'The what?' said Nora.

'He's a dog who lives near me,' I said. 'And he's coming this way.'

'Is that all?' said Nora, annoyed. 'Who cares about a stupid dog? I want to listen to the speeches.' She turned back towards the platform.

'You don't understand,' I said, grabbing her shoulder. 'He's with his owner. She's a friend of Mother.'

'Why didn't you say so?' said Nora. She looked around. 'Is it that very fluffy one? I don't think his owner has seen us. They're still quite far away.'

'Well, she'd better not see me,' I said. Another thought struck me. 'Or Phyllis.'

'Phyllis said to go to the tearooms if we saw someone you knew,' said Nora.

'But we can't let her get into trouble on her own,' I said. I knew Mrs. Sheffield would run straight to Mother if she saw Phyllis holding a suffrage banner in public. 'It wouldn't be fair.'

But how, I wondered, could we save Phyllis? She couldn't just run away – she was holding the banner, after all. I pulled my hat down over my face and glanced at Mrs. Sheffield and The Menace. Luckily she walks slowly (I could see The Menace straining against his sturdy harness, eager as ever to race ahead) so they were still a good few yards away.

'Come on,' I said, and pulled Nora around the side of the crowd.

'Where are you going?' said Nora. 'The tearooms are that way.'

'But Phyllis isn't,' I said. We were quickly circling the edge of the crowd, making our way towards the back of the lorry. Mrs. Sheffield wouldn't be able to see us now, but Phyllis and her banner were still in a very prominent position. If Mrs. Sheffield glanced at the speakers as she passed them, she couldn't miss Phyllis. 'If we go round this way, we can approach her from behind.'

'But your mother's friend will see us then,' said Nora. We were near the front of the crowd now. The woman's speech was over and now a man with a moustache had taken to the stage.

'Not if we crawl,' I said. 'Come on.' I got down on my hands and knees and started to creep behind the platform as fast as I could. Luckily the man with the moustache was a very good speaker, and I don't think many of the crowd noticed us as we made our way behind the lorry, which blocked us from the audience's view, as did the skirts, bags and posterboards of the other suffragettes. Now we were just a few feet from Phyllis.

'Phyllis!' I hissed, in as loud a whisper as I dared. She didn't look down. I tried again, slightly louder this time. 'Phyllis!'

This time she heard. She glanced towards us, and the confused look on her face turned to horror as she saw us practically lying on the grass.

'What on earth …?' she began, in a ferocious whisper, but I interrupted her.

'It's Mrs. Sheffield,' I hissed. 'She's here. In the park. Hide your face!'

Phyllis looked out at the audience and she must have seen something because she immediately moved her end of the banner in front of her face, shielding it from the crowd.

'Go to the tearooms,' she said. 'Now!'

'But we've barely heard any of the meeting,' I whispered back. Phyllis turned towards me, still hiding her features from the audience.

'Do you want me to hit you with this pole?' she snarled. She didn't look much like Joan of Arc now. She just looked like an angry big sister.

'No,' I said. 'But I think you're being extremely unfair. Come on, Nora.'

And we crawled off. We kept crawling until Nora said, 'Why aren't we walking? Your mother's friend will have gone past now.' And when we stood up we saw that the front of our skirts were covered in grass stains. Our mothers would be very annoyed when they saw that.

'We could actually run back to the far side of the crowd and hear some more speechifying,' I said. 'We need to do something to make these grass stains worth it.' So we did. The moustachioed man had finished his speech to great applause, but another woman was talking now. She was saying that without women having a say, the concerns of women and of children were ignored.

'There are children starving and uneducated in this city,' she said. 'And with the vote, we women could change all that.'

I thought of the ragged children I'd seen when I followed Phyllis just a few weeks ago. Quite a lot of people clapped, though there were a few laughing jeers. But there was something about the conviction in her voice, and in the voices of the other speakers, that made you feel sort of hopeful, that made you believe that though things were unfair, they had to change and get better for everyone. We clapped very hard when she finished, but when it was announced that the next woman, a Mrs. Cousins, would be the last speaker, we knew we had to leave now to make sure Phyllis didn't see us hanging about.

So we finally went to the tearooms. It was quite a walk, but Nora had a shilling besides her tram fare so we bought tea and a reviving bun each.

'I'm very glad we went,' said Nora, through a mouthful of bun. 'Even though we didn't get to hear everything.'

'They were awfully good,' I agreed. 'And quite a lot of the crowd seemed to agree with them.'

'We're proper suffragists now,' said Nora. 'Or is it suffragette? What's the difference?'

'Phyllis doesn't like suffragette,' I said. 'Though I rather like it. As a word. Anyway, the suffragists are the ones who believe in just, I don't know, writing letters to M.P.s and all that. The suffragettes are the ones who believe in militant action. You know, breaking windows and chaining and that sort of thing. '

'Maybe the next time we go to a meeting we should

wear a disguise,' said Nora, pouring out the tea. 'Just in case someone we know comes along again. Though I'm not sure what sort of disguise.'

'We could ask Kathleen to trim some hats for us,' I said. 'No one would recognise us if we had giant pineapples or cabbages or what-have-you on our heads. They'd be too busy looking at the felt vegetables.'

'Sssh!' said Nora, gesturing towards the door. I turned and saw Kathleen herself come in, closely followed by Phyllis.

'Oh, you're here,' said Phyllis.

'You told us to come here!' I said indignantly.

'I wasn't sure you could be trusted to do it,' said Phyllis.

'Well, I must say that's a fine way to talk to someone who just saved your life,' I said.

'Saved your life?' said Kathleen, and laughed in a very annoying fashion. I don't think she ever takes me seriously.

I explained to her about Mrs. Sheffield and Barnaby. Phyllis had the good grace to look a bit sheepish.

'Sorry,' she said. 'You're right. Thank you, both of you, for warning me. I'd rather not have to row with Mother and Father unless it's absolutely necessary.'

She handed over a copy of *Votes for Women*.

'Read this,' she said. 'While we go to the lavatory.'

Nora and I flicked through the pages as they made their way to the small wash room. It was very interesting, with lots of stories about dramatic events in London.

'It's like *No Surrender*,' said Nora. 'Only real.'

Phyllis and Kathleen returned and Phyllis put the *Votes for Women* back in her bag.

'Right, girls,' said Phyllis. 'We're going home.'

'Aren't you going to have tea?' I asked.

'We don't have time,' said Phyllis. 'Mother and Father will start asking questions if we get back too late.'

I actually didn't mind going home because I was quite exhausted. Being an active suffragette – well, we did crawl around on the ground to save Phyllis, which is pretty active if you ask me – is very tiring. In fact, I was so tired by the time we got home that I could barely defend myself when Mother noticed the grass stains on my knees. Luckily Phyllis did the decent thing and stood up for me.

'It's my fault, Mother,' she said. 'We were walking over the grass and I distracted her by pointing out the Lord Lieutenant and she tripped over a root. And it wasn't even the Lord Lieutenant at all,' she added. 'Just a man in a top hat.'

'Oh,' said Mother. 'Well, I hope you'll both be more careful in future. Now, go and get changed and you can have some tea.'

As Phyllis and I made our way upstairs I said, 'Thanks for that, Phyl.'

'Well, you deserved it,' she said. 'But,' she added, her voice, stern, 'I'm not taking you to any more meetings.'

'Oh, Phyllis!' I said.

'I think it's wonderful that you've embraced the cause,' said Phyllis. 'But I can't be responsible for you doing anything else Mother and Father wouldn't approve of. You'll just have to support the cause from a distance until you're my age. Though of course I hope we'll have the vote by then.'

'Just one more meeting,' I said.

But Phyllis ignored me and went into her room. Still, I bet I can change her mind. Nora did say I was persuasive.

But I haven't had much time to think about how I will persuade Phyllis because the next day, after Mass, we had to go for our weekly visit to Aunt Josephine.

'It looked like rain this morning.' said Mother, as we walked down the long road that led to Aunt Josephine's house. 'Aren't we lucky it held off?'

I didn't feel very lucky as I sat in Aunt Josephine's stuffy drawing room and listened to her complain about her servants. She has two of them, even though she's the only person in the house. Her son is in the army and her husband, Uncle Gerard, died a few years ago. He was nicer than Aunt Josephine, though quite boring. Anyway,

Aunt Josephine is looked after by one cook-general, one house-parlourmaid, and a charwoman who comes in twice a week to do the rough jobs. Which is more than twice as many servants as we have and there are six of us. Aunt Josephine doesn't even have a dog or a cat.

'I don't know why I pay that girl,' she said crossly. 'I went down to the kitchen the other day and she was fast asleep with her head on the kitchen table when she should have been polishing the silver.'

'That girl,' by the way, is as old as Mother and if she was asleep it was because Aunt Josephine makes her servants get up at half past five to set all the fires 'so they have time to heat the house properly'. She has a fire in practically every room all year round because she says she 'feels the cold'. And then the servants aren't allowed go to bed until after she's asleep, and she has trouble sleeping so they're forced to stay up very late and make her hot milky drinks. She is a dreadful tyrant.

Mother said, 'Well, you do work her rather hard,' which Aunt Josephine didn't like at all.

'Just because I don't let them do what they like, doesn't mean I work them too hard,' she said, in frosty tones. 'You're far too lenient on that girl of yours.'

'Maggie is an excellent worker,' said Mother, firmly.

'She leads you a merry dance,' said Aunt Josephine, with an unpleasant laugh. 'I don't know what you're thinking of, letting her have visitors in your kitchen. It'll be gentleman callers next, you mark my words.'

'Maggie is perfectly well behaved,' said Mother, standing up. 'And now, Josephine, I think we should leave you in peace. She looked at Father, who had been dozing over the paper while all this was going on. 'Come on, Robert.'

Once we'd left the house and set off for home, Mother seemed almost giddy to be free of Aunt Josephine.

'Why don't we have pirate tea later?' she said.

And even though Harry and I are far too old for games, we all cheered. Pirate Tea is an excellent game that we used to play quite a bit when I was younger. Instead of having a proper meal at the table, we dress in old clothes with scarves around our heads and make a sort of cave out of a clothes horse, and then we all sit on the floor outside it and have a feast and make lots of hot buttered toast (when I was very, very small I wasn't allowed use the toasting fork in case I burned myself but that was a long time ago.).

Anyway, it is the best possible antidote to an afternoon of Aunt Josephine and I was very pleased Mother had suggested it. It was so much fun that even Harry forgot to be rude and annoying and told a quite funny story about some boys in his class. By the time we were all lolling on cushions, delightfully full and greasy thanks to the toast, I felt perfectly happy and content. In fact, I still feel rather happy as I write this letter. And I am quite sure that I'll be able to persuade Phyllis to let us carry on supporting the cause.

Best love, and votes for women!
Mollie

Monday, 27th May, 1912.

Dear Frances,

Thank you so much for your letter. It is a great relief to know you really don't mind me going on for pages and pages. I am sure that once this campaigning is all over and we've won the vote (that can't possibly take too long, can it?) and my life goes back to its boring old self, then my letters will return to normal length.

I am very glad that your leg is on the mend and that rehearsals for the play have begun. How exciting that you are playing Polonius! That bit where he gets stabbed behind a curtain is awfully dramatic, you must tell me how you perform it. Will you have a false beard and everything?

I haven't even bothered putting anything in my own letters about school recently because then the letters would be even longer. But you can take it for granted that while all this has been going on, we have been going to maths and Latin and stupid Drill and Dancing and all the usual boring school things. Oh, and the nuns have told Grace that if she keeps up her work and good behaviour then she has a very good chance of winning the stupid cup she's so obsessed with.

'I know they were just being kind,' she told Gertie and May at the top of her voice, so that everyone in the refectory could hear her. 'But it's awfully encouraging to hear them say so. I just hope everyone else is concentrating on their work too and not getting distracted by nonsense.' And she looked over at Nora and gave her one of her fake smiles.

But of course my most important news is all about the movement. There is going to be a big meeting soon, on the first of June. Lots and lots of suffrage campaigners from all over Ireland – unionists AND nationalists, according to Phyllis – are going to turn up. And the I.W.F.L. (the Irish Women's Franchise League) – you know, Phyllis's group – have launched a new magazine, which is terribly exciting. It's called *The Irish Citizen* and we found out about it the other day thanks to Phyllis's friend Mabel. We were all sitting around the drawing room reading and listening to Mother play the piano, when there was a ring at the door and a moment later, Maggie showed in Mabel, who was carrying a large bundle and looking very excited. Phyllis was very taken aback.

'Mabel!' she said. 'I wasn't expecting you. Mother, this

is my friend Mabel Purcell.'

'How do you do?' said Mabel, still looking rather red in the face.

'Very well, thank you, Mabel,' said Mother. 'Won't you sit down?'

Because Mabel was still standing in the doorway clutching her parcel.

'Actually,' said Phyllis, 'I think we'll go to our room. Mabel is getting married soon and she's ...' I could see Phyllis thinking fast. 'She wants to show me her, um, trousseau.'

I could tell that Mother thought it was a bit odd of Mabel to carry over her new clothes in a parcel rather than inviting Phyllis over to see them hanging in her own wardrobe. And the bundle Mabel was carrying didn't much look like clothes to me. But Mother didn't seem to suspect anything untoward as she said, 'How nice. Well, do come down for some tea afterwards.'

'Thank you, Mrs. Carberry,' said Mabel, and then Phyllis practically shoved her out of the room and closed the door behind them.

I was dying to know what was going on. I knew it had to have something to do with the I. W. F. L. But of course I had to just sit there and pretend to read my book as Julia asked Mother to play '*Salve Regina*', which is a Latin prayer/hymn that we sing a lot at school. That's

Julia's idea of a jolly song. Mother wasn't very keen and said it was really designed to be sung on its own, not played on the piano, so I asked her to play 'Daisy, Daisy'. But Mother doesn't much like music hall songs either and played some more Mozart instead. Not that I was listening to her, I was just waiting for Phyllis and Mabel to come downstairs so I could find out what was going on. Eventually they appeared, and now Phyllis looked quite excited too, though she was trying to hide it as they sat down on the sofa.

'So Mabel, tell us when you're getting married,' said Mother. 'I presume you're not going to university like Phyllis?'

'Oh, I am,' said Mabel, and then Phyllis glared at her and she said, 'Um, my fiancé is a student there already. We shall study side by side after we get married. Which will be in, um, September.'

'Yes,' said Phyllis. 'Just a few weeks before we start lectures.'

'How very modern,' said Mother, looking faintly astonished.

'He's an awfully nice boy, Mother,' said Phyllis. 'His father is a barrister.'

Mother looked very impressed by this and before she could ask any more questions about Mabel's imaginary fiancé and his family, Phyllis distracted her by asking how the church sale of work was going. I had to wait until Mabel had had a cup of tea and two of the best biscuits before I could get Phyllis alone and find out what was going on.

'What did Mabel want?' I said. 'And don't tell me she wanted to show you her wedding clothes because I know perfectly well you were making all that up.'

'Do you think Mother guessed?' said Phyllis.

I shook my head.

'Does Mabel even have a fiancé?' I asked. 'I bet she doesn't.'

'No,' said Phyllis. 'It was the first thing I could think of.'

'I knew it,' I said. 'So what did she want?' Phyllis hesitated. 'Go on, Phyl, you have to tell me.'

'All right,' she said. 'Come up here.' We went up to her bedroom and she took down a pile of magazines from the top shelf of her wardrobe.

'Behold!' she said, handing me one. 'I'm going to be out selling this tomorrow.'

'Heavens!' I said. The magazine was called *The Irish Citizen*, and in big letters on the front it said, 'FOR MEN AND WOMEN EQUALLY, THE RIGHTS OF CITIZENSHIP. FROM MEN AND WOMEN EQUALLY, THE DUTIES OF CITIZENSHIP.' Which is quite a long-winded way of saying that men and women need equal rights and then they can serve their country equally. Unlike now, when women have to obey laws and pay taxes to a government they can't choose.

'Mr. Sheehy-Skeffington is the editor,' she said. 'Well, one of them. Mrs. Cousins's husband is the other one.' Mrs. Cousins is another of the I.W.F.L. leaders.

'Oh Phyl,' I said. 'I can't believe you didn't tell me that this was coming out. You must have known.'

'Well, yes, I did,' said Phyllis. 'But you and Nora already know far too much about all this League business. I need to put my foot down somewhere.'

'Can I at least read it?' I asked.

But Phyllis didn't look enthusiastic about this prospect.

'How do I know you won't leave it lying on your bed or something?' she said. 'Or read it in front of the drawing room fire?'

'Don't be silly,' I said. 'I'll only read it in my room when Julia's not there, and I'll hide it under my mattress. The only person who's likely to look under there is Maggie when she's changing the sheets, and she's hardly going to say anything.'

'Oh, all right,' said Phyllis, as I knew she would. 'But you have to pay for it.'

I thought this was a bit much, but I didn't want to push her too far so I got a penny out of my money box and gave it to her. She handed me a copy of the magazine.

'I shouldn't really even sell it to you,' she said. 'It's not officially on sale for a few days.'

'Are you going to sell it at meetings and things?' I asked.

Phyllis nodded. 'And me and Mabel are going to sell it in town on Saturday,' she said. And that was when I had a good idea which I will tell you about later in this letter. Then Phyllis said, 'Now we'd better go back downstairs before Julia or Harry starts sniffing after us.'

So we did, but not before I ran into my room and slid the magazine under the mattress. It wasn't until after supper, when Julia had finally persuaded Mother to sing Latin hymns with her, that I was able to sneak up and read it (it wasn't a Peter Fitzgerald night so it didn't matter that I wasn't with the rest of the family). The magazine was awfully interesting. There was information about various suffrage groups. It said there were about 3,000 active suffragists in Ireland, which seems like a lot, and I bet that isn't even counting girls like Nora and me who have just discovered the cause and haven't been able to actually do much about it yet.

When I said this to Nora and Stella the next day, Nora strongly agreed with me.

'And,' she said, 'I bet there are even more who would call themselves suffragettes if they really knew about it, and not just the nonsense they hear grown-ups saying when they read the papers.'

'I think I might be one too,' said Stella.

We both stared at her in surprise.

'Well, maybe not a proper suffragette,' Stella added. 'I don't think I approve of breaking things and chaining yourself to things and going around wearing a big poster. I would never want to do anything like that.'

'Fair enough,' I said.

'But I do think women should have the vote,' said Stella. 'I mean, it just makes sense, doesn't it? When you look at people like Professor Shields or Mother Antoninas, they're terribly clever. I mean, if anyone should have their say, they should.'

'Quite right too,' cried Nora. 'Bravo, Stella.'

'But I really, really mean it about not breaking things,' said Stella nervously. She looked a bit as though she expected us to immediately drag her out to Dublin Castle and put a brick in her hand.

'That's quite all right,' I said. 'I mean, we haven't any plans to break anything either.' Yet, I thought, but I didn't say it out loud. Not that I really want to break any windows, but I do want to do something, and I told Nora and Stella what it was.

'Phyllis is going to sell the magazine in town on Saturday,' I said. 'Somewhere around Sackville Street, she said. Why don't we go in after school and see if we can help?'

'Are you sure she'll let us?' Nora asked.

'Well, not if we ask in advance,' I said. 'But if we just turn up I'm quite sure she wouldn't turn down the help. After all, we did save her at the last meeting.'

'I won't be able to leave the school,' said Stella, with obvious relief.

'Don't worry, Stella, I didn't expect you to,' I said.

'I suppose we could both get away,' said Nora. 'All right, let's do it!'

Anyway, both Mother and Mrs. Cantwell were quite happy to do without us for a few hours on Saturday afternoon, especially when we each told our mothers we were going to the other's house. Which was why we were able to walk into town as soon as lessons finished.

'Where do you think she'll be?' said Nora as we approached Rutland Square.

'Well, it must be somewhere fairly prominent,' I said. 'She wouldn't bother going down some side street. She could even be on the Square.'

We walked the whole way around Rutland Square and Phyllis was nowhere to be seen, although there was a boy selling newspapers, a man selling matches and another playing a barrel organ. But luckily we didn't have to hunt too long, because just after we reached Sackville Street we saw her. She was on her own, standing outside the Gresham Hotel, holding up a copy of *The Irish Citizen*.

She had a bag slung across her front with a strap, and I could see more copies of the magazine sticking out of the top of it.

'Support votes for Irish women!' Phyllis cried. 'Buy *The Irish Citizen*!' Then she glanced in our direction, and when I saw the expression on her face I started to wonder if my good idea had really been so good after all.

'What on earth are you doing here?' she said in a voice that was more like a hiss. 'Sneaking after me yet again?'

I didn't think this was very fair, especially after last week.

'You told me you were selling magazines in town today!' I said. 'We're hardly sneaking if we happen to find you. And besides, we want to help.'

'Oh, for goodness' sake,' said Phyllis.

'Come on, Phyl,' I said. 'You must know by now that we really do want to help the League. And we stopped Mrs. Sheffield finding you last week. Can we, I don't know, hold your bag or something?'

The bag really did look very heavy, which is probably why Phyllis started to look slightly less fierce.

'What if someone we know sees you?' she said. 'Another friend of Mother and Father? Or even Aunt Josephine?'

'You know Aunt Josephine never comes into town on Saturdays, she hates crowds,' I said. 'And besides, the same goes for you. You don't want Mother and Father to know that you're doing this, but you're out here anyway.'

'Well, I've told you, that's a risk I'm prepared to take for myself,' said Phyllis. 'And it's not that I don't appreciate you helping me last week. But it was too close a call, and I'm not having you around if it happens again.'

'Oh please, Phyllis,' said Nora.

'If anyone asks, we'll say we forced you to give us the bag,' I said. 'Or that we stole it.'

Phyllis sighed. And then she took off her bag and put it at my feet.

'Right,' she said. 'You can look after that while I go to the lav. But I wouldn't be doing this if I didn't really, really need to go.' And she took a much-folded piece of paper out of her coat pocket and glanced at it for a moment.

'What's that?' I said.

'My lavatory list,' said Phyllis. 'Now, stay there and mind the bag. Do. Not. Sell. Anything. I'll be back in about ten minutes.'

And before I could ask her what the lavatory list was, she was trotting down Sackville Street in the direction of the bridge. Nora and I stared at each other.

'Now what?' asked Nora.

'I suppose we really do have to do what she said,' I said, a little sadly. It did seem a bit of a shame that we were out with a bag full of suffrage magazines and couldn't do anything. Though when I thought of actually holding out the magazine to strangers and asking them to buy it, I felt my stomach churn with nerves, so maybe it was all for the best.

'Do you think you could actually bring yourself to sell it?' said Nora, who was clearly thinking the same thing.

'Well, if Phyllis can do it ...' I said. But I had to be honest with Nora. 'Not really. Not yet. Maybe I could build myself up to it by handing out something free first. Like leaflets.'

We wondered if there were any leaflets in the bag, so we could have a go, but when we looked inside there weren't any.

'It's probably a good thing there aren't,' I said. 'Phyllis would be furious. Even though she didn't specifically tell us not to give out leaflets.'

Nora glanced down at the bag at our feet.

'Maybe we should hold on to the strap,' she said. 'In case someone tries to steal it.'

I didn't think that was very likely but I haven't really spent any time just hanging around the streets before, so for all I know there are bag-stealers everywhere who wouldn't be put off by the fact that a bag was clearly full of magazines. Just to be on the safe side, I bent down and took hold of the bag's sturdy leather strap, and I was just standing up again when a voice said, 'Aren't you Phyllis Carberry's sister?'

It was Mabel, she of the pretend-fiancé. And she was looking at the bag of *The Irish Citizens* with a slightly concerned look on her face.

'Um, yes,' I said. 'Phyllis left them with us.' I wasn't sure whether I should mention Phyllis going off to the lav to Mabel. 'She'll be back in a minute.

'We didn't steal them or anything, in case you were worried,' said Nora. I kicked her to shut her up, though actually I had wondered if Mabel had been trying to work out how we'd got hold of them. I suppose it must have looked a bit odd, two fourteen-year-old non-League members lurking about the streets with a bag full of I.W.F. L. magazines.

'Of course I wasn't worried,' said Mabel. 'But she was meant to be selling them with Kathleen.'

I noticed that she was carrying a similar bag herself. 'Have you been out selling them too?' I asked.

Mabel nodded.

'At the end of Westmoreland Street, near Trinity,' she said. 'Quite a few people bought them.'

'Did you get any bother?' said Nora. 'From people who don't, you know, support the cause?'

But Mabel hadn't.

'I got a few funny looks, but that was all,' she said. 'Oh,

and one man who said we were setting back the cause of Home Rule, but his friend told him not to talk like that to a young lady.'

Really, I think Mabel and Phyllis are awfully brave. If I was selling magazines I'd spend the entire time worrying about strange men saying rude things to me. Even the funny looks didn't sound very nice.

'We do support the cause, you know,' I told Mabel, just to make sure she knew that Phyllis hadn't left her bag of *Citizens* with any old sister. 'We just wish we could do more for it.'

'I'm sure there are lots of things you can do,' said Mabel.

'Like what?' asked Nora.

But Mabel wasn't exactly sure.

'Maybe you could make rosettes or something?' she suggested.

I thought of Nora's hatred of knitting and all things craft-related.

'I don't think that's our, um, natural sphere,' I said.

'Well, I must say it's good to see girls your age interested in the movement,' said Mabel. 'And I'm sure you'll be able to think of something active to do. It will be the making of you both!'

Just then, Phyllis returned.

'Sorry, Mabel,' she said. 'I left my post for a bit. These

two weren't causing any trouble, were they?'

'Of course not,' said Mabel. I beamed at her. She was much nicer than some of Phyllis's friends. Kathleen always seems to find me and Nora rather irritating. 'Where's Kathleen?'

'She had to help her mother buy a hat in Switzers',' said Phyllis. 'I only hope her mother didn't see me from the tram on their way home. It goes right past here.'

'Oh, don't worry about that,' said Mabel. 'Kathleen knows your patch and I'm sure she could keep her mother distracted while the tram goes by. Besides, they'd have been on the other side of the road. When are you finished for the day?'

Phyllis sighed. 'I might as well finish now,' she said. 'I sold quite a few at first but it's sort of tailed off. And besides, I'm boiling hot AND starving.'

'Tell you what,' said Mabel. 'Why don't we go to the Farm Produce? It's only around the corner.' She looked at me and Nora. 'We could invite these young recruits.'

I didn't dare beg Phyllis to let us go in case it annoyed her and she told us to go home, but I couldn't help staring at her pleadingly. Nora was gazing at her in much the same way. She rolled her eyes and said, 'Oh, why not. It'll be an adventure for them. And I suppose they deserve a treat after helping me out in the Park.'

Nora and I thanked her as enthusiastically as possible

and then we followed them down Sackville Street. I wondered what the Farm Produce might be. There certainly wasn't any farm around Sackville Street, unless they meant one of those awful little city dairies that keep cows in a tiny shed behind a house. But the Farm Produce wasn't an actual farm. It was a shop about a hundred yards down Henry Street called the Irish Farm Produce Company, with a restaurant in it where Phyllis and Mabel were greeted with warmth and recognition by some of the staff.

'We go here quite a bit,' said Phyllis by way of explanation, when we'd taken a table. 'They're very suffrage-friendly. They've got an advertisement in *The Irish Citizen*.'

'And they're on the lav list,' said Mabel.

'What is this list?' asked Nora.

Phyllis and Mabel smiled at each other.

'It's what Phyllis and Kathleen and I call our list of all the places in town that let you use their lavatory when you're out leafleting or chalking or what have you,' said Mabel. 'Shops and cafés and things.'

'There are quite a lot of them,' said Phyllis. 'You'd be surprised.'

'And you'd also be surprised,' said Mabel, 'at how often you need to go when you're out for the whole day. Even if you've barely drunk a drop.'

A waitress arrived at our table, and Phyllis ordered tea and cakes for everyone. I was pleasantly surprised when she got me and Nora a little cake each. Not just because I wanted a cake to myself (though I did), but because on the rare occasions that Mother takes me and Julia into town to buy new hats or underwear or winter coats, she always takes us to Bewley's for tea and then buys one tiny cake for both of us and cuts it into bits for us to share. I'm sure that everyone is staring at her and marvelling at her miserly ways, but she says that this is nonsense and that everyone else is concerned with their own cakes. But I bet they're not.

Anyway, maybe it was because Phyllis too has experienced Mother's stingy approach to cakes over the years, but it was very generous of her to buy us some (not least because Nora and I only had enough money for our tram fare home so we wouldn't have been able to buy even a stale bun on our own).

'So, are you girls coming to the big meeting on the first?' Mabel asked, when we were all drinking our tea and eating our (delicious) cake.

'They certainly are not,' said Phyllis.

'You can't stop us,' I said indignantly. 'We can buy tickets like any member of the public.'

'I can refuse to take you,' said Phyllis. 'Which I will. And good luck coming up with an excuse for going out alone on a Saturday evening.'

I didn't want to have a fight with Phyllis in front of Mabel, especially as they'd both been quite decent with us so far, so I said, 'Maybe we can discuss this later,' in a very grown-up voice that Phyllis and Mabel seemed to find very amusing.

'Well, I'm sure Phyllis will tell you all about the meeting,' said Mabel. 'It should be very impressive.'

'If we fill the hall,' said Phyllis. 'Kathleen and I are going to try and do some chalking tomorrow. Just to make sure people know.'

'We'd better fill it,' said Mabel. 'Lots of very important people are sending messages of support. And there'll be some excellent speeches.'

'And maybe trouble,' said Phyllis. 'If those Ancient Hibernians show up.' She looked at us sternly. 'Which is why I'm not taking you pair.'

It was a very nice afternoon, even though Phyllis was determined not to take us to the meeting. She and Mabel talked about the League and a lot of important people involved with the movement, some of whom we'd heard when we went to the Meeting in the Phoenix Park. And Mabel asked us both lots of questions and was very impressed by Nora's plan to become a lady doctor (oh yes, Nora has gone back to the doctor plan after a few weeks of wanting to be a veterinarian, I can't remember if I told you. Trying to keep up with her plans can be very confusing). I did remind her that she nearly fainted last week when Agnes O'Hara cut herself on a broken glass during break, but she kicked me under the table and told Mabel and Phyllis that she was training herself to overcome her fear of blood, which they also seemed to find quite funny. I don't understand girls their age sometimes.

Eventually Phyllis realised that we'd finished our cakes and tea nearly an hour ago and that even a suffrage-friendly place like this one probably didn't want people taking up tables for hours on end without buying anything else, so she and Mabel paid, and we all left. As we walked up Henry Street towards Sackville Street, I said, 'Thanks, both of you, for taking us to tea. It was lovely.'

'Well, I'm not going to make a habit of it,' said Phyllis, drily. 'And *you'd* better not make a habit of sneaking after me. This is the second time.'

'Oh Phyllis, I only sneaked once, and that was ages ago,' I protested.

'That's as may be,' said Phyllis. 'But next time, I won't buy you tea.'

Which was fair enough. We bid Mabel a friendly farewell on Sackville Street – she had to get her tram home to Clontarf – and then we jumped on a tram ourselves. I wanted to go upstairs but Phyllis said the wind on the top deck always does terrible things to her hats (this is unsurprising, given all the ridiculous trimmings Kathleen puts on them) so we sat in the boring downstairs bit.

Actually Phyllis was in quite a good mood, and when we'd got off the tram and reached the turn for Nora's road she said, 'My pleasure,' when Nora thanked her for the tea and cake. But she probably shouldn't have worried about the top deck damaging her hat because, thanks to the hot weather and the dust and the general mugginess, the trimmings were all started to droop anyway by the time we reached home. We were both quite hot and red and dusty when Phyllis let us in the front door with her latch key (she is the only one of us who has her own key). We trooped into the drawing room, where we could hear Mother playing the piano, and Phyllis was just saying, 'Look who I found on my way home,' when I realised that we had a visitor.

Frank was standing by the piano, where he'd obviously been turning the pages of Mother's music, while Harry was lolling (as usual) in the most comfortable arm chair. And suddenly I was very conscious of just how red and hot and dusty I was, and how my stockings had gone baggy around the shins so my legs looked like an elephant's knees, and how the muggy weather had made my hair fluff up even more than usual, and not in a good way like the pretty actresses you sometimes see on postcards. The fact that Harry sniggered horribly when he saw us and said, 'Look at the state of you! Have you been running?' certainly didn't help. Nor did Mother saying, 'Mollie! What have you been up to? Go and wash your face', as if I were five years old. And I knew that if I started to argue with her I would end up looking even more childish, so I had to go upstairs and wash my face and hands. Luckily, the cold water made me less red, but I still looked rather shiny and even after I'd pulled a comb through my hair it still looked absolutely dreadful. But there was nothing I could do about that in this humid weather. I decided to change my stockings, so at least I didn't look quite so baggy and scruffy. But it all took so long that by the time I got back to the drawing room, looking at least slightly presentable, Frank was putting on his jacket.

'The music was lovely, Mrs. Carberry,' he was saying politely. 'And thank you for tea.'

'You're always welcome, Frank,' said Mother, fondly. 'Thank you for turning my music for me.' She was probably wishing her own horrible son were half as polite and friendly as Frank always is. I bet she asked Harry to turn the music first and he refused.

'Come on, Nugent,' said Harry. 'I'll see you out.'

He strolled out to the hall, with Frank following him. But as Frank passed me by, he paused.

'Sorry I have to go just as you arrive,' he said. And he smiled in a very nice way before he went out to Harry. But it didn't stop me feeling hot and embarrassed. Then Mother started asking me about tea in Nora's house and I had to make something up so I didn't have time to think about Frank and my red face after that.

Anyway, that was a few days ago and ever since, Nora and I have been thinking about what we can really do to help the movement, but we're not quite sure yet. After all, we can't go out and sell magazines like Phyllis and Mabel or wear posters or speak at meetings because we're too young, but surely there must be something. Actually, I have been thinking a lot about the whole business of tying oneself to some railings. I know a rope is no use but was wondering how exactly the women in England did it. Did they use the sort of chains that people put over gates? And what bit of themselves did they put chains around? So I asked Phyllis.

'Some women get leather belts with chains attached,' she said. 'They get them made specially.'

Well, there's no way we can do that. Unfortunately. But there must be something we can do on our own. We just have to think of something.

Wednesday

Nora and I have taken to the streets at last! Yes, we finally took action and went chalking. As the English suffragettes say, 'Deeds not Words'. And we really needed to do some deeds after talking about it for so long (do you 'do' deeds? Or commit them? I suppose that's not very important right now). We had a very good reason to go chalking because, as I said before, there is going to be a huge meeting this Saturday and we knew from what Phyllis and Mabel said that they wanted as many members of the public as possible to come along to it. It's not free – entrance is one shilling and sixpence – so they need to do lots of advertising because unlike the outdoor meetings they can't rely on passersby. Which all meant that it was the perfect opportunity for me and Nora to stand up for the cause (or rather kneel down).

We made the decision at school yesterday. And actually, Stella helped us make it, when we were telling her about this meeting.

'Are you going to go?' she asked.

'If we can,' I said. 'I've got just enough money.'

'Me too,' said Nora. 'It's definitely worth one and six to see all those speakers and really feel like we're, you know, part of the movement.'

Stella didn't look convinced but she was too polite to say anything.

'The only problem is,' I said, 'that we'll have to persuade Phyllis to take us. And you know what she's like. Mercurial moods. Especially after we turned up on Saturday.'

'Imagine if we could go on stage and speak at it,' said Nora dreamily. 'The young politicians of the future.'

'I can't imagine anything worse,' said Stella, alarmed. 'The thought of standing up there in front of all those people.'

'Well, they're going to have lots of important speakers,' said Nora. 'I do hope enough people turn up. It'll be a terrible waste if the hall is half empty.'

'How do they spread the word about these meetings?' asked Stella. 'I mean, do they have advertisements and things?'

'Yes,' I said. 'But they do other things too, like the posters. You know, women going around with poster-boards hung over their shoulders. And then other girls go out chalking the details on the pavement.'

As soon as I said those words, the idea struck me. I could see that Nora was thinking the same thing.

'Could we?' she said, her eyes wide.

For a split second I hesitated. I know we'd been dreaming of chaining ourselves to things and speaking on platforms, but this wasn't just a dream. Did I really want to do something so public as kneel down in the street and chalk slogans? What would people say? Would they stop us? Then I chided myself for my own cowardice. It was time to stop imagining things and actually do them. The English suffragettes are definitely right about 'deeds not words'. Well, maybe not right about setting fire to postboxes (imagine if one of your letters to me got burned up) but right about lots of other things.

'I don't see why not,' I said, trying to sound casual. 'I mean, all we need is chalk.'

And that was that. As there was no time to waste, we decided to go out the next day after school.

Finding chalk wasn't very difficult. There was some in the bureau drawers in the dining room, along with scraps of string and spare pen nibs and a forgotten half empty bottle of ink that looked as if it had turned into tar. This morning I slipped in there before breakfast and wrapped a few sticks of chalk in my handkerchief and put them in my pocket. There was no point in getting totally covered in chalk dust before we went on our mission, though I was slightly nervous that I might sit on them at the breakfast table and end up with a pocketful of chalk crumbs.

'You haven't forgotten I'm going to tea at Nora's house after school today, have you?' I said. Nora and I had decided that this would be our cover – she would tell her mother that she was coming here. It's quite usual for one of us to invite the other to visit at short notice, so our parents shouldn't get suspicious.

'No,' said Mother. And then, just as I was starting to feel a bit worried at how easy it had been recently to get our mothers to agree to let us go to tea in each other's houses (it's almost as though they WANT to get rid of us for a while), she said something that made my blood run cold. 'But I do feel we've been imposing on Mrs. Cantwell by letting you go over there so much. Maybe I should send her a note and tell her that Nora is always more than welcome in our house too.'

My stomach lurched. The last thing Nora and I want is our parents realising that sometimes when we say we are going to the other one's house, we are actually roaming the streets getting up to goodness knows what. We've always been grateful that our mothers don't really know each other very well. And I certainly didn't want that to change.

'Oh, you don't need to do that,' I said. 'She always says the house is very quiet with George away at school. She likes having me around the place.'

'I find that very hard to believe,' said Harry, who was sitting next to me.

'Stop that, Harry,' said Father.

'I bet the last thing the Cantwells want is another girl in the house squealing and shrieking,' said Harry, but he said it to me in a sort of mutter so our parents couldn't hear exactly what he'd said. Which of course allowed them to pretend he hadn't said anything. He always gets away with things like that.

Anyway, Mother and Father didn't say anything else about writing to the Cantwells, and I managed to get myself and the chalk to school without incident. I showed the chalk to Nora and Stella at lunchtime. We were in the music corridor, and for once, hardly anyone was around.

'Excellent,' said Nora, taking a piece of chalk.

'I got three sticks, so we have one each and then a spare in case one of us loses one,' I said.

'I do wish I could go with you,' said Stella. 'Not to do actual chalking. Just to keep sketch in case anyone came along who might want to stop you.'

Poor Stella, it is hard lines on her being a boarder, no matter how many plays they put on and how much dressing up they do (though all of that does, as I've said before, look like jolly good fun).

'Couldn't you say you were going out to tea with one of us?' said Nora.

But Stella shook her head. 'I'd need to give more notice,' she said. 'You know the nuns don't just let us go off like that without checking exactly where we're going. They are responsible for us, after all.'

'I wish you could come,' I said, and meant it. Though a part of me thought that Stella might funk it at the last minute. She can still be a bit white-mouse-ish at times. Maybe it was for the best that she was staying at home with her knitting.

'What exactly are you making?' asked Nora, peering into the embroidered bag full of wool and needles that Stella often carries around so she can knit a few rows between classes. I could see some rather nice soft moss green yarn and a bundle of something knitted in garter stitch.

'Oh, just a scarf,' said Stella. 'Well, two scarves, actually. They're going to be presents.'

'Scarves?' I was surprised to hear this. 'I thought you'd be doing something more complicated.'

Stella looked slightly affronted.

'You know perfectly well that scarves can be complicated too,' she said. 'It just depends what stitches you use. And these ones are especially fancy.'

I supposed we'd have to take her word for it. It didn't sound very interesting for an expert knitter like Stella, though.

'Well, have fun,' said Nora.

'I'd tell you to have fun too but it doesn't sound right when you're doing something so serious,' said Stella. 'You don't think you'll get arrested, do you?'

'We can't get arrested,' I said. 'Chalk washes away, so it's not like paint. It's not illegal.' I glanced at Nora nervously. 'Is it?'

'I'm quite sure it's not,' said Nora, confidently. 'We have nothing to fear.' But when Grace, Gertie, and poor May Sullivan, who still hasn't escaped their clutches, walked by, she quickly shoved the chalk into her pocket. Not before Grace noticed, of course.

'What are you messing about with over there?' said Grace. 'There's something white coming out of your pocket.'

Nora had somehow crushed part of the chalk and released a lot of chalk dust.

'None of your business,' said Nora, brushing her skirt clean.

'There's no need to be so rude, Nora,' said Grace, sounding hurt. 'I didn't want you to get your skirt all dusty.'

'Well, it's not,' said Nora. 'But thank you.'

The trio walked on, and I turned to Nora.

'You really must stop antagonising Grace,' I said. 'She'll be looking out for an excuse to tell on you.'

'I'm just hoping I'll trick her into showing her true colours in front of May,' said Nora sheepishly.

'Well don't,' I said. 'It's not worth it, especially if she

tells your mother about this and you're not allowed to leave the house for months.'

By the time lessons finished for the day, we were all feeling a little nervous. Especially Stella, even though she wasn't going.

'Are you sure it's safe?' she asked, as she walked us out to the school entrance.

'Was it safe when Mrs. Pankhurst was clapped in irons?' said Nora grandly. But I could tell she was being dramatic to cover up her fear. Besides, neither of us actually wanted to be clapped in irons.

'Right-ho,' I said, as briskly as I could. 'Let's go and do it, then.'

We said goodbye to Stella, who trotted back into the school with her knitting, and set off towards town. It was only then that we realised that we hadn't chosen the exact location of our first chalked message. Nora suggested Sackville Street, but I said there were too many flower sellers and other people hanging around and it would be hard to find a clear space to chalk. I thought Stephen's Green would be better, but Nora said that was too far to go because we didn't have any tram fare to get home and it would all take too long (I still think she was being ridiculous. It wasn't that far and I'm sure we could have been home by six. Anyway, there was no reasoning with her).

In the end, we decided we'd start a place in between those two locations: a corner of Westmoreland Street, near College Green. It was just across from the place where Mabel told us she always sold suffrage magazines, though when we eventually got there after a rather hot and dusty walk, there was no sign of her. Which was probably for the best. I wasn't sure I was going to tell Phyllis about this.

'This will do,' I said when we reached the corner. The street was busy enough. Some clerks and bank workers were already making their way home, and the road was full of lorries, delivery vans, bicycles and quite a few motor cars.

'All right,' said Nora. 'Who'll go first?'

I took a piece of chalk out of my pocket and unwrapped it from the now very dusty handkerchief.

'Me,' I said.

We both knelt down on the ground and I wrote in large letters:

VOTES FOR WOMEN!
GRAND MEETING AT ANTIENT CONCERT ROOMS
1ST JUNE, 8PM
ADMISSION 1/6

We looked at it for a minute and then scrambled to

our feet. Passersby were already looking at us, curious to see what we were writing.

'Come on,' said Nora. 'Let's go and do the next one before anyone says anything to us.'

And we scampered across the road to the front of Trinity College, dodging a laundry van as we went. We stopped before we reached Trinity's gates. The pavement was more narrow than the one where we'd chalked the last message, but there weren't too many people as we knelt down, facing the railings. Nora took out her chalk. As she wrote the same message that I'd chalked a few minutes earlier, I could hear a pedestrian pause behind us.

'Look at those admirable young girls,' he said in a very respectable voice. 'Praying in the street! For the souls of those Trinity College heathens, I have no doubt.'

That was when Nora and I got to our feet, dusted off our knees and turned to move on.

'I must say how nice it is,' began the man, who was an elderly gentleman in a very neat suit, accompanied by a well-dressed lady of similar age whom I presume was his wife, 'to see such devout…'

But he didn't finish his sentence because now he had seen exactly what we'd been doing down on our knees.

'Lord bless us and save us!' he cried. 'Those shameless hussies have got children out now, have they? You should be ashamed of yourselves!'

'I'm afraid we're not,' said Nora. 'Come on, Mollie.'

'You seemed like such good little girls,' said the woman. She almost looked like she was about to cry, she was so horrified.

'We're not very little, but we *are* good,' I said. 'So are the women speaking at the meeting. You should come along and see.'

The man and his wife were lost for words.

'Let's go, Mollie!' said Nora, and we walked as fast as we could past Trinity's front gate. As we went off, the woman regained the power of speech and cried, 'I never thought I'd see this day! Irish girls behaving like little hooligans!'

As soon as we were out of sight, we both started to laugh.

'Praying!' said Nora.

'Well in a way we are,' I said, daringly. 'Praying that people will turn up at this meeting.'

'I'm not sure anyone at school would see it like that,' said Nora. 'Or our parents, come to think of it. They're more likely to agree with those two.'

'Will we do one more?' I said, glancing up Grafton Street, which was full of people and horses and vehicles both motor- and horse-powered. The pavements were far too narrow and it looked far too crowded to attempt a chalking, unless we did it on the wall of one of the shops, and I was quite sure that would get us into trouble.

'Let's just do a general Votes for Women one,' said Nora. 'It's quicker.'

So we did. I knelt down on the pavement and wrote VOTES FOR IRISH WOMEN in big letters. And when I'd dusted down my frock (avoiding the curious and, I must admit, amused glances of the passersby), even I had to admit that the time really was getting on, so we set off for home.

Mother and Father would be very angry if they knew I was roaming around town like this, but it's quite safe really. They always say the city is dangerous, but I'm not sure what they think might happen to us. Nobody would bother robbing us because we never have any money. I said this to Nora and she said, 'What about Florence Dombey in *Dombey and Son*? She gets lured away to a side street by a horrible old lady who steals all her good clothes to sell them.'

I had read the book but I couldn't think this was very likely to happen to us.

'Florence was only about six,' I said. 'I'm sure Dickens didn't think fourteen-year-olds would be lured away by thieving old ladies.'

Nobody tried to lure us anywhere, but some rather frightening-looking men did call things at us that we couldn't understand but which they clearly thought were very amusing. After we turned on to Dorset Street, some ragged children started to follow us asking for pennies.

'Go on, missus,' said one girl with flaming hair the colour of Nora's. 'Give us a ha'penny.'

'We don't even have a farthing,' said Nora.

'Sorry,' I said, as politely as I could. But I still felt bad.

They were very thin and dirty. I remembered Maggie's sister once telling me that there are tenements near that part of town where dozens of people live in houses not much bigger than ours, with only one lavatory shared between hundreds of people. I wished I had some pennies to give them, even though a few pennies wouldn't really make much of a difference. But I didn't know how to say that I wished I could give them something without sounding like I was taunting them, or looking down on them. And, although I was ashamed of feeling like this, I was also a little bit afraid of them because they were so loud and dirty. Which I know was very snobbish and foolish of me. I would be dirty, and probably loud too, if I was cramped into a tiny space with lots of other people.

It didn't take long before they realised we really didn't have any money. The red-haired girl said, 'We should do a collection ourselves and give you a few bob if you're that hard up.' And with a laugh, they turned and went back towards the streets where they lived. Maybe if women had the vote, things would get better for children like that, I thought. But then I thought of Aunt Josephine, who was fond of saying that poor people were just lazy and that she couldn't understand why they didn't make more of an effort to wash their clothes. She would never vote to improve things for them.

I wondered how Aunt Josephine would manage washing her clothes if she lived in a cramped house with no indoor water and no money. Of course, she's never washed an item of clothing in her life; she sends everything to the same laundry we use. And she gets her housemaid to wash all her lace by hand. So it's a bit rich of her to criticise anyone for their own washing skills.

'You're very quiet,' said Nora, as we approached the turn for her road.

'I was just thinking of Aunt Josephine,' I said absently.

'Well, don't,' said Nora. 'Think of how we're going to get away to the big meeting.'

'I already have,' I said. 'I'm going to get Phyllis to take us.'

Nora didn't seem very impressed by my excellent scheme.

'What makes you think she will?" she said. 'She's already said no. And I know she thinks we're getting too interested. It's obvious she thinks that if we get involved your parents will find out. So why should she take us?'

'Blackmail,' I said smugly.

Yes, it's an ugly word, but it works.

That evening, after Father had read us the latest extremely exciting installment of Peter Fitzgerald's adventures (he has escaped the gang by climbing up a chimney and hiding there, but now the housemaid, unaware of Peter's hiding place, is starting to lay a fire beneath him), I cornered Phyllis in the hall.

'I need to talk to you,' I said.

'Do you really?' said Phyllis wearily.

'Yes,' I said. 'I want you to take me and Nora to the meeting on Saturday.'

'No,' said Phyllis. 'How many times do I need to tell you this? I am not taking either of you anywhere again. It's too risky.'

'But why?' I said indignantly. 'We're supporters of the cause.'

'You're fourteen,' said Phyllis.

'So?' I said. 'We're still supporters. And after all, if we win, we'll be able to vote in seven years.'

'What a hideous thought,' said Phyllis. 'The prospect of you voting is enough to turn me off the cause altogether. Anyway, you may well be right ...'

'I am,' I said.

'But I don't want the responsibility of looking after the

pair of you,' said Phyllis. 'There might be trouble at the meeting. Those awful Hibernians might turn up.'

I hadn't really thought of that. But even if they did, I still wanted to be there.

'You won't have to look after us,' I said. 'We're quite capable of looking after ourselves.'

'I'll be the one our parents will blame if you get taken off to hospital in an ambulance,' said Phyllis, who was surely exaggerating. No suffragette had ever needed an ambulance after the protests (as far as I knew). 'It's bad enough that I took you to that park meeting, and to the Farm Produce restaurant,' Phyllis went on, 'but if they find out about all this, they might even stop me going to College in October.'

I had had a feeling she would say something like this. So I took a deep breath and drew myself up to my full height (which is still three inches shorter than Phyllis).

'Then you leave me no choice,' I said dramatically. 'If you don't take me and Nora, I will tell our aged parents everything.'

Phyllis looked horrified.

'You wouldn't,' she said.

'I definitely would,' I said. Even though actually, I wouldn't. It would be far too low and sneakish and cruel. I just had to hope Phyllis would believe my threat and wouldn't call my bluff. 'Oh go on, Phyllis. We won't get you into trouble. Honour bright, we won't.'

'You're an absolute monster,' said Phyllis.

'Please, Phyllis,' I said. 'It's just one meeting. And if there's even a hint of trouble, we'll sneak out and run home. You know those awful old Hibernians wouldn't hit a girl my age, anyway.' At least, I hoped that was true.

'I'll think about it,' said Phyllis. 'You sneaky little beasts.'

But I am pretty sure she will take us. I'm going to bed now and I do feel a bit bad about this blackmailing business, but surely it is worth it for such a good cause? I will ask God about it when I say my prayers.

Later

I woke up at four o'clock in the morning (I know because I could see the clock on the mantelpiece in the light shining in from the street), and I couldn't get back to sleep again because I felt so guilty about blackmailing Phyllis. I know 'thou shalt not blackmail' is not one of the ten commandments, and I don't think I've ever seen anything about it in the Catechism, but maybe that's because it's so bad God didn't think He had to tell you not to do it (although I suppose you could say the same about killing people, which is definitely worse than blackmail). Anyway, whether it's in the Bible and the Catechism or not (and it might be in the Bible somewhere. I haven't read all of it), I do know God wouldn't approve of what I said to Phyllis last night. I know in my heart of hearts that it is a terrible sin.

I wouldn't feel right going to such a good and important meeting through such nefarious means, so at breakfast this morning, around the time everyone had finished their toast and Mother was reminding us that she was going to Mrs. Sheffield's this afternoon to talk about church fundraising things, I made my best Significant Face at Phyllis to indicate that I wanted to talk to her. So she waited for me in the hall when everyone was leaving the breakfast table.

'What do you want?' she said. 'More blackmail?'

I took a deep breath. No one likes admitting that they're wrong, even when you know that it is absolutely the right thing to do.

'The opposite,' I said. 'I feel awful about saying that I'd tell on you. You must know I wouldn't ever really do that.'

Phyllis raised an eyebrow. Just one. I don't know how she does it. I've tried it myself because it does look so wonderfully supercilious, and I'd love to be able to do it at Grace, but every time I make an attempt both my eyebrows go up and I just look surprised. Though Phyllis definitely couldn't do it a year ago, so maybe by the time I'm her age I'll be able to do it too.

'Really?' said Phyllis.

'Honestly, Phyl, I really wouldn't,' I said. 'I just said it because we really, really want to go to the meeting. But I'd rather not get there under false pretences. Or,' I added, 'blackmailing pretences.'

Phyllis looked unmoved.

'So why should I help you then?' she asked. 'You're certainly not behaving in a way worthy of the cause.'

I knew she was right.

'I can't think of a reason,' I said honestly. 'Only that we really do believe in the cause, and we really would like to go. And in fifty years I want to be able to tell my descendants that I was at the most important suffrage meeting Ireland had ever seen.'

'Your descendants,' said Phyllis. 'What a horrible thought.'

'I do understand why you wouldn't want to take me,' I said. 'But surely it's important to encourage the new generation of fighters for the cause! That's me and Nora,' I added, lest Phyllis be confused. 'And we've both got money for the tickets.'

'You're not going to give me any rest about this, are you?' said Phyllis.

I shook my head.

Phyllis sighed. 'Fine,' she said. 'I can't believe I'm giving in to your nonsense, but I'll tell Mabel to keep tickets for both of you. But only because I believe hearing all the speakers will be good for you. It might build your character, which is clearly sorely in need of building. And you'll have to pay me for the tickets in advance, because you've proven that you can't be trusted.'

'Thank you,' I said humbly. 'I really am sorry about, you know, the blackmailing.'

'You'd make a terrible criminal,' said Phyllis. 'You confess all far too easily. And right now, you'd better go to school.'

And so that was how Phyllis agreed to take me and Nora to the meeting. I knew she'd give in eventually – she always does. That afternoon, after I'd handed over money for my ticket (she said Nora could pay on the day), she got Mabel to reserve tickets for all four of us. Afterwards, she told Mother and Father she was taking us to a recital on Westland Row. Luckily, she'd made sure that Mother was otherwise engaged – she and Father were going to visit Father's old school friend Mr. Campion in Clontarf – so there was no chance of Mother inviting herself along to the show. I still feel guilty about even mentioning blackmail, though. Sometimes I wonder if politics is good for one's soul. It does seem to have made me terribly ruthless. Though

I comfort myself with the knowledge that I would never have told on Phyllis, really. I hope you know that, Frances, because I can't imagine you'd approve of blackmail, even for a good cause.

To make up for my wickedness, I decided to do some more chalking. After all, there are still a few days until the meeting, and Mother wasn't going to be at home that afternoon. But when I suggested doing it to Nora and Stella they both thought we might be pushing our luck.

'I know that man on College Green was quite amusing,' said Nora, 'but imagine if he'd dragged us off to the police or written to our parents or something. Maybe we should wait a while before we try it again.'

'Are you a girl or a mouse?' I said. 'Besides, the meeting's on Saturday. We won't get another chance to chalk about it.'

'I am most definitely not a mouse,' said Nora. 'As I think you know. But I can't tell my mother I've gone to your house for two days in a row.'

She had a point. I would only have to make excuses to Julia and Harry. And while both of them would probably tell Mother and Father if they actually knew I was out doing suffragette things, they wouldn't bother telling Mother and Father if I was a little bit late home. Mostly because they knew I could tell on them for doing the same thing. Even Julia dawdles with Christina some days.

'Well, I'll do it by myself,' I said. I felt I owed it to the cause. 'And I don't need to go as far across town this time. I can just do it in Rutland Square.'

So that's where I went. I still had some chalk in my coat pocket from the day before. I did feel a bit nervous walking into town on my own. I tried not to think about the dreadful old lady stealing all Florence Dombey's expensive clothes, and comforted myself with the thought that none of my clothes looked particularly expensive. Not expensive enough to tempt a mad thief, anyway.

It didn't take long to reach Rutland Square, which was fairly quiet, to my great relief.

I got out my chalk and found a nice prominent spot outside Charlemont House. I was kneeling on the ground writing VOTES FOR WOMEN! COME TO THE MEETING IN ANTIENT CONCERT ROOMS 1ST JUNE, 8PM. ADMISSION 1/6 in nice large letters when a voice somewhere behind me called, 'Mollie?'

I scrambled to my feet and whirled around to see a boy walking towards me.

It was Frank. He was carrying a paper parcel and staring at me in a baffled sort of way.

'What are you doing on the ground? Did you fall?'

'I'm fine,' I said, as Frank's glance fell on the chalked letters. His greeny-blue eyes widened. They are rather a nice colour. I mean, you notice it, unlike the colour of my own eyes, which are a sort of nondescript grey (as you have probably forgotten – that's how unexciting they are).

'Did you write this?' he said.

'Of course,' I said. I tried to sound defiant, but all I could think of was what would happen if Frank told Harry about this. Harry would definitely not keep it to himself. And I could only imagine what Mother and Father would say if they knew I was crawling around on the ground chalking suffragette messages for all the world to see. I felt sick at the thought.

'What are you doing in town?' I said, in a rather accusatory fashion. I hoped my haughty tone would distract him from thinking about what I'd just written.

'My school's around the corner, you know,' said Frank. He held up his parcel. 'And my rugger boots were being repaired in a place down the road. I just collected them.'

'Oh,' I said.

'Look here,' said Frank. 'If you think I'm going to tell, well, anyone about all this, then you needn't worry. I promise I won't say a word.'

I felt a flood of gratitude as I gazed up at him (he really is a lot taller than I am), but then I had to remind myself that no matter how nice he may seem, Frank is a friend of Harry. So I tried to sound very stern as I said,

'Good. Because this is terribly important and if anyone found out about it, I'd get into awful trouble.'

'I know it's important,' said Frank. 'I do think women should have a say, remember?'

I thought of that conversation when he helped me catch Barnaby The Menace. He had been awfully nice that day. And I know he hadn't told Harry about me losing The Menace, because if Harry knew about that he would have had plenty of rude things to say about me being a feeble girl who couldn't even hold onto a small fluffy dog (even though Harry knows perfectly well that the dreadful Menace has the strength of a dog three times his size).

'I remember,' I said.

Frank looked down at the chalk.

'I didn't realise you were really, you know, an active suffragette,' he said. 'Aren't you awfully young?'

'I'm only a year younger than you,' I said indignantly.

'I didn't mean it like that,' said Frank. 'I just meant, well, I knew you agreed with their ideas. But I thought all the women who went to meetings and wore posters and all that were grown-ups.'

'Well, they are,' I said. 'Nora and I have just been doing this chalking on our own. I mean, we haven't got any official connections with any of the suffrage societies and leagues.'

I didn't tell him that Phyllis did. I might not mind Frank knowing about my activities (such as they are), but I knew Phyllis wouldn't want me to tell anybody about her own involvement without her permission.

To my surprise, Frank looked impressed by my revelation. It was rather nice to see him look at me with something a bit like admiration. He's the only boy who ever does, after all. Not that I really see any boys besides Harry. I might as well be in a boarding school like you for all the contact I have with the opposite sex.

'Have you done lots of this chalk business?' he asked then.

For a wild moment, I considered telling him that yes, we went out five times a week and gave speeches on Saturdays too. I bet he'd have been impressed by that. But I couldn't bring myself to lie.

'Well, this is only the second time,' I admitted. 'We were out yesterday.' And I told him about the man that thought we were praying.

He laughed. He has an awfully nice laugh, the sort that makes you want to laugh too.

'I wish I'd seen that,' he said, smiling.

'His face was a picture,' I said, smiling back at him.

'What do they think about all this at your school?' asked Frank.

'Well, our teachers don't know about it,' I said. 'As

far as I know. But I don't think all of them would be against it. I mean,' I added, 'I don't think they'd be against women getting the vote, but they probably wouldn't want any of us girls going around, well, doing things like this.'

'Especially in that hat,' said Frank.

We don't have a uniform in our school (though there is talk of bringing one in next year) but I did have a brooch with the school crest pinned to my hat ribbon. It's been rather a craze in the Middle Grade this year.

'I hadn't thought of that,' I said. 'Oh dear, do you think someone might tell them? The school, I mean?' I had a horrible thought of that man turning up at the school and telling Mother Antoninas all.

'Oh, I doubt it,' said Frank. 'It sounds like he was too shocked by your daring deeds to notice things like hats.'

'Oh, good,' I said. 'I mean, it's not like I don't want to, you know, stand up for my beliefs. But I'm not keen on getting into trouble if I don't have to.'

'That sounds like a very sensible attitude to me,' said Frank. He looked down at the chalked slogan again. 'Are you going to do any more chalking? I can keep sketch for you if you like.'

I stared at him.

'Would you really?' I said. A rather low suspicion came into my head that Frank was somehow being put up to all this niceness by Harry as some sort of trick. They are friends, after all. And Harry is definitely the sort of boy who would pretend to keep sketch and then run away just when a policeman walked by – at least if he was meant to be keeping watch for *me*. He probably wouldn't do it to his actual friends.

But Frank seemed to be genuinely sincere.

'Well, yes,' said Frank. 'I think what you're doing is marvellous. None of the boys at school are brave enough to do something like this.'

Well, I hadn't intended to chalk any more, but really, Frances, how could I just go home after he'd said something like that?

'All right,' I said. 'Let's go round the corner, the Frederick Street side. It's on the way home.'

We walked around the corner in companionable silence. He is very easy to be around, for some reason. When we were at the side of the church, I said, 'All right, I'll do it here. Watch out for policemen.' Of course, I still had no idea whether policemen would mind chalking or not, but it made it all sound much more dangerous and exciting. I got down and used the last of my chalk to write VOTES FOR WOMEN MEETING! ANTIENT CONCERT ROOMS SATURDAY 8PM. TICKETS 1/6 as quickly as I could.

'Right,' I said. 'That'll do.' I sounded very brisk and

businesslike, even though I felt all wobbly and excited inside. I know I keep saying this, but I really think I must be a good actor. I should try taking part in the next school production if they ever actually let us day girls do something again.

'We'd better go before we get arrested, for defacing public property' said Frank, but not in a serious way. He looked as if he was enjoying himself tremendously as we walked quickly towards Dorset Street.

'To be honest,' I said,' as we crossed the road, 'I'm not entirely sure you really need to watch out for policemen. I think chalking is all right. It's just paint that they object to. Legally, I mean.'

But this didn't seem to bother Frank.

'Oh well,' he said cheerfully, 'it still felt like we were breaking the law. Quite thrilling, really. I only wish I could tell the boys at school about it.'

I looked at him anxiously.

'You won't, though, will you?' I said. 'You promised.'

Frank looked affronted.

'Of course I won't,' he said. 'My word is my bond. Or something like that. You needn't worry.'

I was glad to hear it.

'You know what Harry's like,' I said. 'If he found about this he'd go straight to my parents. And then I wouldn't be allowed out of the house for months.'

'You know, Harry's not that bad really,' said Frank. 'I bet he wouldn't tell on you.'

'You don't know what he's like at home,' I said. 'No, actually, you do. You've seen him throw socks at me.'

'I'll admit he can be a bit ... boorish,' said Frank.

'A bit?' I said.

'All right, then, very,' said Frank. 'But well, he's a lot nicer about all of you when you're not there.'

'I find that very hard to believe,' I said.

'The other day Murphy — he's a chap in our class — said something about it being hard lines on Carberry having a house full of girls,' said Frank. 'He knows Harry has three sisters.'

'Well, I can only imagine that Harry agreed with him,' I said. 'He tells us how awful it is for him often enough.'

'To tell you the truth,' said Frank, 'he defended you. And your sisters. He said that you were all "decent sorts".'

I couldn't believe my ears.

'You're making that up,' I said.

'I'm honestly not,' said Frank. 'He really did. He said he'd rather have sisters than a brother who was always going to be better at rugby than you. Murphy's brother,' he added, 'is on the first XV and Murphy isn't even in the junior team with me and Harry.'

I honestly couldn't think of anything to say. I was so surprised.

'I know he can be very annoying,' said Frank. 'And I won't pretend he isn't a rude beast to you. But you know, he might grow out of it.'

And for the first time, I actually wondered if that could be true.

After that, we didn't talk about Harry. We mostly talked about books (we both love *Three Men in a Boat* and the Sherlock Holmes stories. I told him that my favourite book when I was younger was *Five Children and It*, and he said his was *The Story of the Treasure Seekers*).

'I do like that one,' I said. 'But I rather like books where magic things happen. They make you feel as though everything could change all of a sudden, and be more interesting than it used to be.'

'But I suppose things can change,' said Frank. 'I mean, a few months ago I bet you never thought you'd be chalking political slogans on pavements.'

'I suppose you're right,' I said. It was rather a nice thought. Although not as magical as actually finding an ancient Psammead creature that granted wishes, like in *Five Children and It*.

We had turned onto Dorset Street now, which is not a very magical place (though I remembered the bit in *The Story of the Amulet* when the children find the magical Psammead in a dingy pet shop on a street rather like it).

'Do the boys at school ever say anything about

suffragettes?' I said. I was curious to know what boys around my age thought of it, and I couldn't ask Harry without rousing his suspicions. Frank looked a little awkward.

'I don't think I should really tell you,' he said.

'It'll be nothing I haven't heard from Aunt Josephine and Grace Molyneaux,' I said. 'She's an awful girl in my class.'

'I'm pretty sure they say worse things than even Grace Molyneaux,' said Frank. 'However bad she might be.'

'Oh, go on,' I said. 'I might as well know.'

'If you insist,' said Frank with a sigh. 'All right. They say that suffragettes are just frustrated spinsters who want a vote because they can't get husbands.'

'Well, that's not true,' I said. 'Lots of the leaders are married. And by the way, that's exactly the sort of thing Grace would say.'

'And,' Frank went on, 'they say that London will never give us Home Rule if suffragettes keep demanding the vote. That they'll use it as an excuse not to pass a Home Rule bill in parliament.'

'I don't see what the point of Home Rule would be if only men had a say in it,' I said crossly as we crossed Dorset Street.

'I see what you mean,' said Frank. 'But I don't think the fellows at school would agree. Hey, watch out.'

I was so cross I hadn't noticed a large coal van coming

towards us. Frank grabbed my arm and pulled me out of its path.

'You can't fight the good fight if you're run over by a coal van,' he said, smiling. He does have an awfully nice smile. Did I tell you that already? I realised he was still holding my arm. It was rather a nice feeling, but then he let go and we scampered across to the opposite pavement.

After that, we went back to talking about books. It was so much fun that when we reached the corner where we had to go our separate ways I felt quite disappointed.

'Thanks for keeping watch for me,' I said.

'Don't mention it,' said Frank. 'I hope the meeting goes well. You are going, I presume?'

'Of course,' I said proudly.

'Well, I hope it goes marvellously,' said Frank. 'And don't worry, I won't tell a soul.'

I watched him head down the road and then sighed and walked the rest of the way home. Maggie let me in when I got there.

'Where have you been?' she said. 'Your mother didn't tell me you were going out.'

'Oh, I just called in to Nora's house,' I said. This was yet another of my worryingly easy lies. 'You don't have to mention that to Mother, do you? I didn't tell her I was going there.'

'I suppose I won't have cause to mention it,' said

Maggie with a smile. She glanced down at my skirt and her smile disappeared.

'What on earth is that?' she said. 'That skirt only came back from the laundry last week.'

I glanced down and saw that there were white chalk marks where I'd been kneeling. I hadn't brushed myself off when I chalked the second message.

'It's nothing,' I said. 'Just some chalk. We were, um, playing hopscotch.'

'Aren't you a little old for hopscotch?' said Maggie.

And there was something about the way she said it that made me think she knew that I was lying. And that it was something to do with the movement. But she wasn't going to ask too many questions.

'It's awfully good exercise,' I said. Father's clothes brush was sitting on the hall stand and I grabbed it. 'I'll just go out in the back garden and brush this off. I don't want chalk dust flying everywhere.'

And before Maggie could say anything else, I trotted down to the kitchen and out the back door. The chalk brushed off my skirt easily enough, but I realised I had to be more careful in future. I know Maggie is on my side really – or at least the side of the cause – but I can't forget what she said about how my parents would react if they knew that she knew about my activities. And I probably won't go out chalking on my own again.

I feel utterly exhausted from all the worrying about being caught. It is very hard being a secret suffragette sometimes. Still, I'm glad I did it. And I'm glad I met Frank. I can't believe Harry has said nice things about us in school. Life really is full of surprises.

I will finish this letter now. Good luck with your play's first night. I'm sure you'll be marvellous. I hope someone takes photographs of you all in your costumes, then you can show them to me when you're over here in the holidays. I can't imagine what you'll look like in your false beard. I wish we were doing some acting this year but the only middle-school girls who have been allowed put on a play are the boarders. Nora and I agree that this is extremely unfair. Some of the older day girls were in a production of *Twelfth Night* before Christmas, though, and Phyllis was surprisingly good as Juliet in her last year, so maybe we will get our chance to shine. Anyway, I hope you all shine this week - do write and tell me all. And the next time I write, I'll have been to the big meeting. Let's hope all our chalking has paid off and the hall is packed to the rafters!

Best love and VOTES FOR WOMEN!
Mollie

Sunday, 2nd June, 1912.

Dear Frances,

I don't even feel like writing because I feel so annoyed
and disappointed, but I might as well tell you all my woes
when they're still fresh. Last night was a disaster. Not the
meeting itself – that went quite well. At least, I presume
it did, because Phyllis says so. But Nora and I didn't get
to see any of it AND we had a fight, and it's all stupid
Mabel's fault. Oh, all right, she's not stupid – she's been
very nice to us in the past. And the fight with Nora
wasn't her fault. But I really am very annoyed with her at
the moment.

Yesterday seems like years ago now. I was looking
forward so much to going to a proper meeting and being
a real part of the movement at last that I was counting
the minutes until it was time to go. Unfortunately Aunt
Josephine came over for tea in the afternoon, and there
was a terrible moment when Mother mentioned that
Phyllis was taking me to a concert that night.

'I don't think Phyllis is old enough to look after

Mollie at a public concert,' Aunt Josephine sniffed.

I held my breath, terrified that Mother would say, 'Actually, Josephine, you're right, I shan't let her go after all,' but she just said, 'Oh, don't worry, Josephine, I trust my girls.' Which was a relief but did make me feel a bit guilty because, after all, we had told Mother a lot of lies. But the bad feeling had vanished by the time I got ready to go out. I wore my best frock and my new summer coat, and Mother said I looked very smart though she didn't know what on earth I do to my hat ribbons because they looked as if someone had been chewing them.

'You'll do, though,' she said, and she was smiling so I knew she didn't mind that much about the hat ribbons. They weren't so terribly bad really, just a little bit frayed at the ends. And so Phyllis and I stepped out into the sunny evening.

'We've done it!' I said, as soon as the door had closed behind us.

But Phyllis hissed at me to shut up and practically dragged me down the front steps.

'The window was open,' she said, when we had made our way a few yards down the road. 'Mother might have heard every word. You've got to be more careful.'

'Sorry, Phyllis,' I said soberly, but I couldn't stay sombre for long. I almost felt like skipping as we walked along, but of course I'm far too grown-up to do anything like that. I did find myself walking very fast though, to the extent that Phyllis had to tell me to slow down.

'We haven't even got to Nora's house yet,' she said. 'If you keep racing along at this rate, we'll all be bright red and absolutely sodden with sweat by the time we get to the meeting.'

'Phyllis!' I said, shocked.

'Perspiration, then,' said Phyllis. 'Anyway, slow down.'

I suppose I really didn't want to turn up scarlet and smelly, so I did slow down a bit. But it was hard to walk along in a decorous and civilised fashion, especially when we collected Nora and she was practically bouncing with excitement too. Phyllis was not pleased.

'Calm down, you girls,' she said. 'I said I'd take you to this meeting because I thought you could behave in a civilised fashion. Please don't make me regret it.'

So we had to stop bouncing along. But it was difficult, especially when Phyllis started talking about all the speakers who were going to be there.

'Countess Markevicz will be there – she's terribly impressive, everyone says so,' she said. 'I heard that she turned up at a suffrage protest in England driving a coach and four. With white horses.'

I couldn't help hoping she would do something like that this evening, though Phyllis said it was unlikely.

'Do you really think there'll be protests?' said Nora, after we'd got on the tram and were speeding up Dorset Street. 'Against the meeting, I mean.'

Phyllis shrugged her shoulders.

'I don't know if they'd dare,' she said. 'They tend to be there when we protest other things – like the Irish Party in the Mansion House. But this time, they'll definitely be outnumbered. And remember, if there's a single sign of trouble you're to leave straight away.'

We got off the tram in College Green and made our way along the high wall of Trinity College towards Great Brunswick Street. The clock at the front of the college had showed us we were actually a bit late, so we probably should have hurried earlier, though I didn't dare say anything about that to Phyllis in case she refused to give us our tickets when we arrived (I wouldn't have put it past her). She was already looking a little harassed.

As we went along, I noticed a couple of women wearing suffrage badges on their coats, also making their way to the meeting. One even had a rosette in green, orange and white, the I. W. F. L. colours, attached to her coat with the words VOTES FOR WOMEN emblazoned across the middle. I wished I had one myself, though I knew I'd never have the nerve to wear it anywhere any of my family could see it. Not for the first time, I wondered if I'm being awfully cowardly being a secret suffragette (at home, anyway). But I reminded myself that if Mother and Father knew, then I'd never be allowed leave the house at all, which would rather defeat the purpose of being open about my views. Nora was clearly thinking along similar lines because she said, 'I wish we could wear those rosettes' in a rather wistful voice.

'Here we are,' said Phyllis. She glanced at her very pretty watch that was a present for her eighteenth birthday. 'And just in time, it's practically eight o'clock.'

We had arrived at the Concert Rooms. And that was when everything went wrong.

The green-coated woman I'd seen giving Phyllis the pamphlets (it seems like so long ago now) was waiting for us at the entrance, but she looked rather surprised to see us.

'Hello, Phyllis,' she said. 'And ... I don't think we've met.'

'This is my sister Mollie,' said Phyllis. 'And her friend Nora. Girls, this is Mrs. Duffy.'

'They do know what's on tonight, don't they?' said Mrs. Duffy. 'It's not a concert, girls.'

'Of course we know,' I said, indignantly. 'We're here to support the movement.'

Nora looked as if she were going to say something

very rude, but luckily Mabel emerged from the vestibule of the Concert Rooms. Mrs. Duffy told her and Phyllis that she'd see them inside and headed into the building.

'Have you got our tickets?' Phyllis asked Mabel.

'Do you mean tickets for the girls too?' said Mabel.

'Of course I do,' said Phyllis. 'I gave you the money.'

And that's when everything started to go wrong. I realised Mabel was looking distinctly guilty.

'I'm terribly sorry,' she said. 'But I didn't realise the tickets were for them. I thought they were for Kathleen and Margaret.'

'Well, I'm sure those two can get their own tickets,' said Phyllis.

'No, you don't understand,' said Mabel. 'I've already given *them* the two tickets you asked me to get. And they're already inside. I suppose I made them think that you'd told me to hold tickets for them.'

'Really, Mabel, it's not like you to be so scatty,' said Phyllis crossly. 'Your imaginary fiancé is clearly a bad influence. Well, I suppose we'd better get two more tickets, then.'

But when she went to get us some tickets, she was told that there were none left!

'There's not a spare seat to be had,' she said when she returned. 'And there are already people standing at the back.' And I must admit that she looked genuinely sorry to be the bearer of bad tidings, especially when you consider that she hadn't wanted to take us at all and that I had almost blackmailed her about it. Maybe she was wishing she'd followed my lead and walked faster.

'So what can we do?' asked Nora.

I think we were both expecting a seat to be produced from somewhere.

'Well, you can't go home on your own,' said Phyllis. 'I'm not having you roaming the streets at this time of the evening.' A thought struck her. 'I know, maybe you can wait in the vestibule. You might be able to hear the speeches there.'

We went into the vestibule, and through the open door that led into the hall I could see that the big concert space was decorated in wonderful banners and posters. Just then, there was an announcement that the meeting was about to begin and that everyone should take their seats.

'I'm so sorry,' said Phyllis, 'but I'll have to go in. Excuse me, sir!' An attendant hurried over to her. 'Is it all right if my sister and her friend sit here while the meeting is going on?'

The man didn't look pleased.

'We're not a public waiting room,' he said.

'Oh please, sir,' said Phyllis, gazing at him with wide eyes. 'They'll be as good as gold.'

'They'd better be,' grunted the man, and left us.

'There you go,' said Phyllis. 'I really am sorry.'

And off she went, closing the door behind us. There was nothing for us to do but sit in the boring old vestibule while the attendants looked at us suspiciously. I suppose we should have grateful there were chairs and we didn't have to sit on the floor. A moment later, we could hear the rumbling of applause and a muffled sound that meant someone was speaking to the crowd, but we couldn't make out what they were saying.

'This is even worse than the last time,' I said. 'At least we got to hear *some* of the meeting when we were crawling around on the ground.'

'And the park is slightly more interesting than this place,' said Nora.

We did, of course, consider opening the door and sneaking in, or just leaving and strolling around town.

'But knowing our luck,' said Nora gloomily, 'we'd get thrown out if we sneaked in, or get run over by a tram if we went out. And no matter what, our mothers and fathers would find out.'

She was probably right, unfortunately.

'And after all we did for this meeting too!' I said. 'Maybe we shouldn't have bothered chalking. I bet some of the people who saw those chalkings are sitting in there right now instead of us.'

'Maybe the man who lectured us is there,' said Nora. 'Maybe we converted him.'

It was a nice idea, but I was fairly sure we hadn't. I felt terribly bitter.

'I bet there are people in there who haven't done half as much for the cause as we have,' I said. 'I bet there are people who haven't done a thing.'

It was quite satisfying to grumble for a while, but the satisfaction didn't last long. It felt like we were sitting in the vestibule for about five hours (even though it wasn't nearly that long). Of course we couldn't hear anything that the speakers were saying, but every so often we would hear an enormous cheer or a round of applause, which just served to taunt us. It was so unfair.

Normally Nora and I can talk to each other for hours and hours, but somehow the feeling of being shut out depressed both of us and after a while we didn't really have much to say. And then eventually – I don't know why – I said, 'Do you like Frank?'

Nora stared at me in confusion. 'Frank who?' she said.

'Frank Nugent,' I said. 'You know, Harry's friend.'

'Oh yes, him,' said Nora. 'I barely know him, though. I haven't seen him for ages. I thought you barely knew him too.'

And I realised that even though I have been thinking about Frank quite a lot in recent weeks, I haven't really said anything about him to Nora. Maybe it's because I do rather – yes, I will admit it at last – like him, and I know that we're not meant to think about boys like that yet. I know I've written to you about him, but it's different telling someone face to face. It makes it all more real, somehow. And that's why I hadn't said anything to Nora. But I couldn't go back now.

'I've actually bumped into him a few times recently,' I said cautiously. 'And he really is awfully nice.'

'You're going bright red,' said Nora. She stared at me. 'Mollie! Are you in love with Frank Nugent?'

I could feel myself going even redder. It can't be normal to blush like this, can it? Maybe I have a terrible disease. Like consumption. Does that make you blush or make you all pale? I can't remember. I must ask Maggie tomorrow, I bet she'd know.

'Of course not,' I said. 'I'm only fourteen.'

'Juliet was only fourteen when she met Romeo,' said Nora. 'Why didn't you tell me you were in love with him?'

'I'm not!' I said crossly. 'I just like him, that's all. He's much nicer than you'd think any friend of Harry would be. AND he supports the cause.'

'Really?' said Nora, surprised.

'Yes!' I said. And I told her about meeting him when I was out with Barnaby, and about bumping into him on my second chalking outing. Nora looked rather hurt.

'I can't believe you didn't tell me any of this,' she said. 'We're meant to be friends and you've been having a ... a secret love affair.'

'Nora!' I said, horrified. 'Don't be so vile. You sound like one of those awful cheap romance serials. And I have NOT been having a secret anything.'

I was so angry with her for implying such a thing that I couldn't even look at her. We sat next to each other in silence for a few moments. But gradually my rage started to calm down and I couldn't help thinking that if Nora had been having all these meetings and conversations with a boy and hadn't told me about it, I would have been quite hurt too. So even though I was still annoyed about her saying that nonsense about me being in love, I muttered, 'Sorry for not telling you about meeting Frank.'

And Nora said, 'Sorry I said you were in love with him.'

And then neither of us said anything for a bit.

'I don't know why I didn't tell you,' I said eventually. 'I suppose I didn't want you to think I was getting soppy over him. Or something. Because I don't think I am.'

'Are you sure?' said Nora.

I sighed. 'I do like him more than I've liked any other boy I met,' I said. 'But first of all, I've barely met any boys, and second of all, I know we're far too young to think of boys at all. That's what everyone says. And don't go on about Juliet again because that was hundreds of years ago. You know things are different in the twentieth century.' And I wondered what it would be like if everyone thought it was all right for a fourteen-year-old girl to be in love with someone, but I couldn't really imagine what we'd do if they did.

There was another pause and Nora asked, 'So, what was he like when he found you chalking?'

'He kept watch for me,' I said. 'He really does support the cause.'

'Hmm,' said Nora. 'Then I suppose I must approve of him.' And she said it in such a funny, dramatic voice that I couldn't help laughing.

Suddenly we could hear very loud cheering and applause coming from the hall, and what sounded like people stamping their feet. And then the doors opened and the crowd began to stream out of the hall. It was mostly women but there were quite a few men too, and most of them were talking enthusiastically to each other. They looked as if they'd enjoyed the meeting very much. Which was, of course, a good thing for the cause, though it did make me even more jealous. Finally, Phyllis appeared with Kathleen, Mabel and another girl who turned out to be Margaret. Their eyes were positively sparkling with excitement.

'Oh, there you are!' said Phyllis, who had clearly forgotten all about me while the meeting was going on. She pointed towards a bearded man who was talking earnestly to a woman in an excellent hat. 'That's Mr. Sheehy-Skeffington. You know, the editor of the *Citizen*.'

'How was it?' I asked flatly.

'It was marvellous,' said Mabel. She had the good grace to look guilty. 'Sorry about giving away your seats,' she said.

'It's all right,' said Nora, nobly, even though it clearly wasn't. I knew I would find it very hard to forgive Mabel for her foolishness.

'Some of us are going to Margaret's house for tea,' said Mabel. She looked at me and Nora. 'Why don't you all come? It won't make up for missing the meeting, of course, but it could be rather fun. Kathleen's aunt has made the most magnificent cake and she's taking it along.'

Imagine, us going to a late-night suffragette party! Maybe I could forgive Mabel after all. But of course I should have known that Phyllis would have to do her responsible-big-sister act.

'Sorry, Mabel, but Mother and Father would kill me if I kept these girls out late,' she said. 'I'd better get them home.'

So we missed the party too. And the worst thing was that when we came home, Mother and Father of course asked me how the concert was, and I had to smile and say it was wonderful.

'It was very good of Phyllis to take you,' said Mother.

'Josephine certainly wouldn't have taken me anywhere when I was your age,' said Father, with a grin. And I had to grin back and say, 'I suppose I'm lucky to have Phyllis.' Which in a way is very true, because if it weren't for her we'd never have found out about the movement at all, and she did take us to the meeting despite my almost-blackmail, but at the same time, I was still feeling terribly disappointed so it was very difficult to hide my gloomy mood. But I had to, until I got into bed (Julia was fast asleep) and then I must admit I cried. But only for a minute.

So there you have it. I went to the biggest, most important suffrage meeting of the year and I didn't hear or see anyone. And me and Nora almost had a serious falling-out (though I suppose I am glad that my Frank meetings are out in the open). I can't believe we didn't get to see that glamorous countess (she didn't come on a white horse – which at least we might have been able to see, seeing as we were right at the entrance – but Phyllis said she gave a good speech). I almost wish we hadn't bothered chalking about the meeting now. Oh, all right,

I don't wish that, but it does seem rotten bad luck after all our work. And I feel terribly flat. Last night was such a grand affair that there might be no other big meetings or suffrage events for ages. I'm trying to tell myself that the most important thing is that the meeting was a big success and lots of people came AND the awful Ancient Hibernians didn't show up and ruin it all by throwing eggs and lettuces and things, but I still feel very glum. Oh well. I will write more tomorrow, if I'm not too depressed.

Monday

Something rather dramatic happened today, though I'm not sure whether it will turn out to be good or not. Grace told our classmates that me and Nora are suffragettes. As you know, we hadn't really planned to tell anyone else at school. I suppose the whole time we have been torn between wanting to stand up for our beliefs (new though they might be) in public and not wanting to get into trouble. But anyway, everyone in our class knows now.

It happened, like most vaguely interesting things at school, at break. We were in the refectory, and Nora, Stella and I were talking to Daisy Redmond and Johanna

Doyle about what we might do when we leave school. Nora, Daisy and I want to go to university, but Stella and Johanna don't.

'So what will you do?' asked Nora. 'You'll have to do something. You know what the staff always say. We can't expect to just live at home doing nothing until we get married. If we get married,' she added.

'That's just what I'm going to do,' said Johanna, but she didn't sound very happy about it. 'Father doesn't believe in women working. He doesn't really think girls should be educated at all, to be honest. There were awful rows at home about me coming here.'

Of course, one knows that plenty of people don't believe in educating girls. Look at Aunt Josephine. But our school has always been rather progressive in that regard, so it's quite rare to find anyone here whose parents think that way.

'I was thinking I might be a nurse,' said Stella.

I wasn't sure I could imagine Stella dealing with all the blood and such like. But if Nora thinks she can be a doctor, I suppose Stella can be a nurse.

'You'd have to go to England,' said Daisy. 'That's where the only Catholic training place is. Sister Augustine said so.'

But Stella didn't like the sound of going that far.

'Maybe I could be an instructress in poultry keeping,' she said.

We all stared at her.

'A what?' I said.

'You know, someone who teaches people how to look after chickens,' said Stella.

'But why on earth would you do that?' said Nora. 'You're not interested in chickens, are you?'

'There was a talk about jobs a few months ago for us boarders – remember, Daisy?' said Stella. 'And it was one of the things they mentioned. Like joining the civil service or the bank. Or teaching in a school. But I don't think I'd be much good at those other ones.'

I wasn't sure I could imagine Stella being much good teaching people about chickens either, but I wasn't rude enough to tell her that. Besides, I had been struck by another thought.

'It's so unfair,' I said.

'What is?' said Stella. 'Do you mean unfair to the chickens?'

'No, to girls,' I said. 'The idea that there are only about five jobs we can do. I mean, if we were boys, we wouldn't just have teaching and nursing the bank and the civil service and, and … chickens. We could try being anything we liked and nobody would say we couldn't.'

'I suppose you're right,' said Daisy.

'I am right,' I said. 'And you know, if women had the vote, then maybe that would change. Eventually, at least.'

Grace, who was sitting at the next table with Gertie, stood up and went over to us.

'Can you please keep the noise down over there?' she said. 'Some of us need peace and quiet in our lunchbreak.'

'We weren't being that loud,' said Daisy.

'You weren't, Daisy,' said Grace. 'But I'm afraid Mollie was being very noisy. I'm sorry Mollie, but you were.'

'It's break,' said Nora. 'Not French class. We're allowed to talk.'

'You're not allowed to scream and shout,' said Grace primly. 'Though I suppose I shouldn't be surprised at you pair.'

'What's that supposed to mean?' I said sharply. 'I wish you'd stop making these snide remarks. If you've got something to say, just say it properly, instead of pretending to be nice.'

Grace was so offended that she forgot to put on her nice voice.

'Well, isn't making a racket what you suffragettes do?' she snapped.

'You what?' said Johanna.

'They're not suffragettes, you goose,' said Daisy. She looked at me and Nora. 'You're not, are you?'

I caught Nora's eye. What should we do? Should we deny it? But surely that's wrong, if we really believe in the cause. And we do, we really do. So I said, 'Yes, we are.'

Daisy and Johanna looked astonished.

'Are you really?' said Johanna. 'What do you do?'

'We'll tell you,' said Nora, 'when certain sneaky tell-tales aren't listening.' And she gave Grace a very meaningful look.

The funny thing was, Grace didn't look particularly pleased by her revelation. In fact, as soon as she said it, she looked as though she wished she hadn't. I suppose she liked having something secret to hold over us. Anyway, she didn't stick around. She tossed back her curls and said, 'I'm sorry you think I'd do anything so low as tell tales. I thought you'd told your chums about your ... activities. I didn't realise you were ashamed of them.' And before we could think of a reply to that, she had returned to her seat.

'We're not ashamed of them,' I said.

'Do tell us all about your suffragette business,' begged Daisy.

'Not here,' said Nora. 'Let's go to the library.'

We didn't have too much time before break finished so we scurried down the corridor to the library and found a quiet corner where no one could overhear us.

'Go on then,' said Daisy, when we were all settled at the round table.

'We go to meetings,' said Nora. 'Suffrage meetings.'

She didn't say that we'd only been to two. And that we hadn't actually got into the last one.

'And we helped sell a suffrage magazine in Sackville Street,' I said, which was almost a lie but not quite. After all, we had looked after the bag, so we were helping Phyllis.

'Goodness!' said Daisy.

'And you mustn't tell a soul about this,' said Nora, impressively, 'but we chalked suffrage things on the pavement in town. Telling people about the meeting.'

Johanna and Daisy looked so astonished we might as well have told them that we'd set fire to a postbox.

'Is that against the law?' said Johanna.

'No,' said Nora, very confidently. 'It just washes away.'

It did strike me again that we had been taking it for granted that it was all right to chalk.

I wasn't sure whether Daisy or Johanna approved of all this or not. They just looked a bit stunned. And then the bell rang for class, and we didn't really have a chance to talk to them for the rest of the day.

'You don't think Daisy or Johanna will side with Grace about all this, do you?' I asked, when me and Nora were walking home.

'I don't think so,' said Nora. She kicked a stone along the pavement. 'But how unfair it all is, that we have to live in fear of Grace getting us into trouble just because we want to fight for our rights!'

'Including,' I said, 'the right to do more jobs than just teach people about chickens.'

I was still thinking about the unfairness of the world when I arrived home from school. Maggie let me in and told me she'd made another lemon cake.

'And Jenny is here,' she said. 'If you'd like to come down and say hello.'

'Of course I would!' I said. Jenny is Maggie's sister – her name is Jane really. She and Maggie are orphans, which I think is very sad, though Maggie says she is used to it now as their parents died a long time ago when they were quite young. That's when Maggie first went into service and came to live with us, and Jenny went to work in a biscuit factory. Jenny comes and visits Maggie regularly, and sometimes Maggie goes to visit her on her afternoon off. I've always liked Jenny, and not just because sometimes she gives me a broken or misshapen biscuit (they get them at the factory and sometimes they taste even nicer than the perfect biscuits). So I was very pleased to see her when I followed Maggie down the steps and into the kitchen.

'Hello Jenny!' I said.

'Hello there, young Mollie,' said Jenny, smiling back at me and holding out a plate. 'Have some cake.'

Maggie poured me some tea, and soon I was sitting at the table with the two Murphy sisters. Their surname is Murphy, did I ever tell you that? I suppose I never think about it because we always call them by their Christian names. It's funny that I call some grown-ups, like Mother's friends and Nora's mother, Mr. and Mrs. whatever their surname is. But Jenny and Maggie and servants in general are always just called by their first names. It seems a bit rude to them, now that I think of it. Imagine if I suddenly called Mrs. Sheffield 'Maria'. She'd never let me take out The Menace again. Actually, maybe I should try it the next time she's here …

But I'm getting distracted (again). We were at the kitchen table, and I was drinking tea and eating the extremely delicious lemon cake, which was possibly as good as Nellie's mother's cake. I asked Jenny about the biscuit factory and she said that she and the other women who work there weren't happy at the moment.

'Because we've found out that we're going to be expected to cover the men's lunch breaks,' she said. 'But we won't be paid for it.'

I remembered what Phyllis had said about Jenny the other week.

'Aren't you a trade unionist?' I said.

'I certainly am,' said Jenny happily.

Maggie shot her a warning look. 'We'll have none of that talk in this kitchen,' she said.

'Oh come on, Maggie,' said Jenny. 'We were talking

about it here just before Mollie came in.'

'That,' said Maggie, 'was when we were among ourselves.' She looked at me. 'And, Mollie, before you say anything about not minding, we've been through this before. I'm not going to be responsible for you hearing all sorts of radical talk.'

'That's what happens when you have your feet under another man's table,' said Jenny. 'You think it's a good thing, bed and board and all that, but once you're there you can't call your soul your own. No offence meant to your mother and father, Mollie.'

'That's all right,' I said.

'I might have to slave away in that factory,' said Jenny. 'But as soon as I walk out through those gates, I can do what I like and say what I like.'

'Well, isn't that nice for you?' said Maggie. 'Not everyone can have a wonderful job in a factory. In case you hadn't noticed, there aren't that many jobs for girls like us.'

'Well, if you had a union job, at least you'd be able to fight for your rights,' said Jenny. 'And at least you'd actually have rights. The things you hear about some generals! They're made to do the work of ten maids all on their own.'

And even though we don't make our general-servant – Maggie, of course – do all that work, I knew Jenny was right. Just think of how Aunt Josephine treats her servants!

'Jenny!' said Maggie, with a pointed look at me.

'Actually,' I said, hoping it would calm things down a bit, 'my friends and I were just talking today about how boys can work at anything but there are only a few jobs that girls can do. I mean, the only jobs they say we can do are teaching, being a nurse, the bank, and the civil service. Or telling people how to keep chickens, of all things. Only five jobs!'

'Only five jobs for girls like you,' said Jenny. 'Girls like us don't have a chance of working in a bank. Just service or the factory, or farms if you're in the country and, well, you don't want to know about some of the other jobs.'

I felt myself go red AGAIN. I hadn't even thought about that until now. Of course, girls from families like Maggie and Jenny had other jobs they could do. But they were generally much nastier, and always much worse paid, than the jobs the nuns encouraged us to try.

'Sorry,' I said. 'I didn't mean to be rude.'

Jenny looked as though she were regretting her sharp tone. She put her arm around me.

'And neither did I,' she said. 'It's not your fault things aren't fair.'

'I do want to change things,' I said. 'My friend Nora and I ...' And then I remembered what Maggie had said about not wanting to know about our activities. It wasn't fair of me to say anything in front of her. So I just said, 'We support the suffrage cause.'

'Good for you,' said Jenny. 'Maybe I'll make a trade unionist out of you too.'

'Jenny!' said Maggie again. 'I think it's time you went home.'

'I'm only codding you,' said Jenny. She stood up and reached for her coat, which was hanging on the back of a chair. I realised with a start that it was an old one of Mother's. I remember the distinctive cuffs. Mother always gives her old coats to Maggie, and Maggie must have passed this one on to Jenny. Jenny must have noticed me staring because she said, 'Nice coat, isn't it? I'm not too proud to accept anyone's hand-me-downs, especially when it's such a fine garment as this.' She gave Maggie a kiss on the cheek.

'Bye now, Maggie,' she said. 'I'll be in better humour the next time I see you.'

'Bye,' said Maggie, a little stiffly, but then she hugged her sister firmly. 'What would I do,' she said into Jenny's shoulder, 'without you to keep me on my toes?'

'Ah, you'd be all right,' said Jenny. 'You'd rise up on your own eventually.'

She released herself gently from Maggie's embrace and patted me on the shoulder.

'Goodbye, young Mollie,' she said. 'Keep fighting the

good fight.' And then she let herself out of the back door and went out the back gate.

'That girl,' said Maggie, with feeling, 'will get me sacked one of these days.'

'Not if I have anything to do with it,' I said. Even though I knew that if Mother and Father really did decide to let Maggie go, I wouldn't have much say in the matter.

Maggie knew this too, of course, but she smiled.

'Off you go, now,' she said. She gestured towards a soft bundle wrapped in brown paper that was sitting on the kitchen cabinet. 'I've got to run around to the laundry with this in a minute. Your mother forgot to send some of your father's shirts.'

So I went upstairs to write this letter. Which I will finally finish writing now. I do hope you are well and that you aren't studying too hard. After all, even if you do go to Oxford, you've got a few years to prepare for it. I should probably be studying a bit harder myself, but sometimes it's very difficult when so many exciting and dramatic things are happening ....

Best love,
Mollie

P.S.

Tuesday

I meant to send this letter this morning on my way to school, but I forgot, so I am opening up the envelope (I will have to gum it down afterwards with glue) because I need to tell you that Nora and I have made a big decision. We are going to take militant action! We're not going to set off a bomb or chain ourselves to the railings of Dublin Castle, or anything like that. But we are going to do something that is almost certainly breaking the law. And we're going to do it soon.

We made the decision this afternoon at the end of break. Nora, Stella and I were sitting out in the garden, as were most of the school because the weather was so nice. But we had found a quiet corner where we could talk about secret suffragette things in peace. We needed to do this because of course Johanna and Daisy told other people about our suffrage leanings ('Well, you did say you weren't ashamed of it,' said Johanna, which was fair enough), and now everyone knows. At the first break today we were besieged by classmates asking questions. First of all, they all asked if we did things like the suffragettes in England.

'Did you set fire to anything?' asked Nellie Whelan, hopefully.

'No,' said Nora. 'We keep telling you, we haven't done anything like that.'

'But you might,' said Mary Cummins.

'Probably not,' I said.

'I don't really see why it's all so important,' said Maisie Murray. 'I mean, our mothers don't seem to need the vote. Mine doesn't, anyway.'

I sighed. I didn't want to get into a fight with Maisie, who's quite a nice girl really, and I certainly didn't want to insult her mother, but really, I had to say something.

'It's about fairness,' I said. 'Women have to stick to the laws, but they don't have a say in making them. It's not fair. Same as it's not fair that our brothers are allowed to do whatever they like – well, practically – and we're not.'

'I don't have any brothers,' said Maisie.

'Well, boys in general, then,' I said. 'You know what I mean.'

'Not really,' said Maisie.

'I do,' said Mary. 'Why shouldn't our mothers have their say? And our aunts.' Mary's parents died a few years ago, and she and her sister live with their Aunt Margaret. I've met her and she's much nicer than Aunt Josephine.

'It seems a bit silly to me,' said Maisie. 'I don't mean to offend you.'

'Well, it's not silly at all,' said Nora, who did look quite offended. That was when the bell rang, which was probably a good thing because Nora looked as if she were going to start yelling at Maisie. But for the rest of the morning more people kept coming up and asking questions, and when the big break came along we were so tired of saying the same things over and over again that we hid in the most secluded bit of the garden we could find.

'Well,' I said. 'Even if I didn't think it was necessary to promote the cause before today, I certainly do now. When I was coming out of the lav, Cissie Casey asked me if it was true that I wanted women to rule the world!'

'You don't, do you?' said Stella.

'Of course not,' I said.

'We just want fairness,' said Nora. 'And the chalking is all very well. But I can't help feeling we should do something else. Something bigger.'

I knew exactly what she meant.

'The thing about chalk,' I said, 'is that people just walk over it and smudge it, or it gets washed away the next time it rains. Which is usually about five minutes after you've chalked something.'

'Exactly,' said Nora. 'And I don't think people take it seriously. I mean, they think it's silly, or funny.'

'Well, some of them take it seriously,' I said, remembering the man who had thought we were praying. 'But you're probably right.'

'So why don't we do it properly?' said Nora. 'Why don't we use paint?'

If you had asked me to think about it logically, I could have given plenty of reasons why we shouldn't use paint. For one, I *knew* that painting on something without permission was illegal. But then, so was breaking government windows, and the women in London were doing that all the time.

'We could,' I said cautiously. 'That would definitely cause a stir.'

'Oh, I'm really not sure this is a good idea,' said Stella, nervously.

'But where should we do it?' said Nora.

'Well, I suppose it should really be government property,' I said. 'I mean, that's meant to be the point.'

'If only your father's office was closer to our houses,' said Nora.

I was quite glad it wasn't. I was fully prepared to paint something on a government building, but not the one Father worked in. Then I thought of something.

'What about a postbox?' I said. 'Like the one on Eccles Street, at the Nelson Street corner. Lots of people walk past that one.'

'A postbox?' said Stella.

'It's government property,' I said.

'That,' said Nora, 'is an excellent idea.'

'I don't think it is,' said Stella.

'And all we need,' I continued, ignoring Stella's foolish objections, 'is some paint and a brush. We can find them easily.'

'I know for a fact,' said Nora, 'that there's some in our shed.'

Apparently Mr. O' Shaughnessy, who does their garden every week, had recently painted their back gate.

'Oh please don't,' said Stella unhappily.

'But when will we do it?' I said. 'We can't just pop into town after school and start painting like we did with the chalk. I mean, we don't actually want to be caught.'

'Well, it would make quite a statement if we were arrested,' said Nora. 'I bet it would make all the papers.'

'Oh Nora, no!' cried Stella.

And I had to agree with Stella. I know I was the one who got Nora involved in all this, but when she's involved in something, she does sometimes go a little too far. Still, maybe her attitude is what I need to keep myself going.

'We are absolutely NOT getting arrested,' I said. 'At least I hope not. Why don't we get up really, really early? At four or five in the morning? Hardly anyone will be around then, not even policemen.'

'But how would we do that?' said Nora. 'I don't have my own alarm clock. And neither do you.'

'No,' I said. 'But Harry does.' He got one for his

birthday last year and it is awfully impressive. It even has numbers that glow in the dark. 'And I bet I could muffle it up so it didn't wake the entire house.' Luckily, Julia is quite a sound sleeper so I should be able to muffle it from her too.

Nora nodded.

'Then that's what we'll do,' she said.

'The only thing is,' I said, 'that it won't be easy to get the clock from Harry. I mean, he'll definitely notice if it disappears. He's frightfully proud of it. He doesn't even need it because Father knocks on our doors to wake us up, but he sets it to go off anyway.'

'I don't suppose he's going away on holiday any time soon,' said Nora, hopefully.

'He's going away for a rugby match next week,' I said. 'But only for the day.'

'We'll just have to watch out for an opportunity,' said Nora. 'I mean, all sorts of things might happen.'

'One of us might be given an alarm clock as a present,' I said. (Well, it is possible.)

'Exactly,' said Nora. 'We'll just have to wait and see. I'm sure something will turn up.'

So that's what we are hoping. I will write very soon and let you know if something does. Though knowing our luck recently, it could take months and months.

Friday, 14th June 1912

Dear Frances,

Before I write anything else, I want you to swear by
everything you hold dear that you will not let another
living soul see this letter. You must burn it, if necessary.
Because besides me and Nora, you should be the
only person who knows what happened on Thursday
morning.

Have you sworn? Then I will continue. I'm sorry
about all this cloak-and-dagger stuff, but it really is
necessary. Because we finally did it. We took militant
action. We are proper suffragettes at last! And, as it turned
out, we weren't the only ones out on the streets that
morning. But I will tell you more about that later.

Anyway. Here's how it all happened. I suppose it all
began with Harry and his illness. On Monday he left the
house early because he was going to Dundalk on the
train with the rest of the Junior Team to play a rugby
match with some school up there. Our uncle Piers,
Mother's brother, who is a solicitor in Dundalk, was

going to go to the match to cheer them on and take Harry and Frank out for lunch afterwards. But Harry nearly didn't go at all because when he was having breakfast he barely touched his toast, which is very unusual for Harry, who normally gorges half a loaf of bread every morning.

When Mother noticed how little he was eating, she said, 'You do look pale, darling. I'm not sure you should go.'

Harry looked horrified.

'I'm perfectly well,' he said. 'I'm just nervous about the match.' And he crammed some more toast into his mouth and bolted it down. After he swallowed it, he looked even queasier.

But maybe Mother didn't feel like having an argument with him. She said, 'All right. But if you're not feeling well, you mustn't play.'

And if you want proof of just how spoiled Harry is, there you have it. If I'd been sick, I'd have been packed off to bed, no matter how much I protested! But she believes everything he says. And she regretted it later, because that evening we were just sitting down to some Peter Fitzgerald when a telegram arrived from Dundalk. I was looking forward to Peter because school had been rather awful that day. I had made an utter mess of my Latin translation and Professor Brennan was absolutely

horrible to me and nearly made me cry. And then I
was daydreaming in maths – not even thinking about
important political things, just about Mr. Rochester in
Jane Eyre, which I have nearly finished – and Professor
Corcoran surprised me with a complicated maths
question which of course I couldn't answer. And then
she asked Nora, who had also been daydreaming, and she
couldn't answer it either. So we both have to do some
extra maths exercises tonight.

On a more positive note, our classmates have stopped
badgering us about being suffragettes. But in another way
that's rather depressing because none of them seem to
care about the cause very much. Or at all.

So, all in all, I was feeling glum when the telegram boy
came. Mother looked very pale when Maggie handed
the envelope to her, and I must say I felt pretty awful
myself when she opened it and said, 'Oh my Lord, Harry.'
I knew something bad had happened, and I know he's
very annoying, but I don't actually want him to DIE.
What if there had been a train crash? They do happen
sometimes and people do die in them.

'Is he all right?' I asked, and I was surprised at how
wobbly my voice was.

Julia started to cry. Father put his arm around her and
said, 'It's all right, you little mouse', but his face looked
very worried. And that made me feel very worried too.

My stomach felt most peculiar.

'He got sick at the match and couldn't travel home,' Mother said. 'Piers has taken him back to his house.'

'Is it serious?' said Father.

There was barely a second before Mother answered but somehow my mind managed to think of all sorts of terrible things: Harry with a terrible fever. Harry screaming in pain. Harry coughing up blood and dying of consumption like Daisy Redmond's mother.

'Piers thinks it's just bilious influenza,' said Mother. And she showed Father the telegram.

'Is that serious?' I asked. Somehow my voice didn't sound entirely steady. And Father said, 'Not at all, just not very pleasant.' He kissed the top of Julia's head. 'Now, why don't the two of you make yourselves comfortable and I'll tell you what Peter Fitzgerald has been up to.'

But Julia didn't want to listen to Peter Fitzgerald.

'It's not fair to read it if Harry isn't here,' she said. She looked as though she were going to start crying again. Father gave her another hug and said, 'Fair enough. What about *The Wouldbegoods*?'

We all like E. Nesbit – even Julia – although the children get up to lots of mischief, which she doesn't approve of. And Father is very good at reading aloud, so we all cheered up a bit when he was reading.

Still, I couldn't help wondering if Mother and Father

were just putting on a brave face so Julia and I wouldn't be upset. I know grown-ups mean well when they do this, but the problem is that you never know whether they are doing it or not, so when they say everything is all right you don't know if you can really believe them. Mother and Father certainly seemed all right that evening, but when Julia had measles eight years ago and almost died, they behaved in just the same way, and I only found out how worried Mother really was at the time because I ran into her room without knocking and saw her crying.

Anyway, I tried not to think about Harry and just listened to the adventures of the Bastables, and it almost worked. Good stories can be very distracting when one is worried. The Bastables seemed to work on Julia too, because by the time she went up to bed she seemed quite normal. Mother went up with her, and while Father was putting the book back in the shelf I took a quick look at the telegram, which Mother had left on a table near the fireplace. It said:

HARRY GOT SICK AT MATCH. COULDN'T TRAVEL. SLIGHT FEVER PROBABLY BILIOUS FLU BUT TOOK HIM HOME ANYWAY. WILL WIRE IF NEWS. PIERS.

The telegram proved that Mother and Father hadn't

just been putting on a brave face. I must confess that when I saw that I felt so relieved I almost started crying myself. And I was very relieved I could just go back to hating (well, sort of hating) Harry again.

But when I followed Julia up to bed a little later, I could hear sobbing coming through the door. And even though she is extremely annoying and smug, and even though I didn't think Harry was going to die (after all, we've all had some sort of stomach complaint at some stage), I hurried in and found her kneeling next to her bed, her shoulders heaving. I crouched down and put my arms around her.

'Oh Julia,' I said. 'You ridiculous goose.' But I didn't say it in a nasty way. 'Harry'll be all right. He's just staying up there because he couldn't get on a train home if he was being sick. Imagine having to share a carriage with someone who was sicking up everywhere.' And I made a being-sick noise (which was very realistic, I really am a born actress). But Julia didn't laugh or even tell me to stop being disgusting. She just wiped away her tears and sniffed some more.

'Why don't you say a decade of the rosary for him?' I said. And because I am quite a noble big sister really, I said, 'I'll pray with you.' Even though I just wanted to say my normal prayers as quickly as possible and go to bed. Anyway, Julia nodded and got her rosary beads out of their little box which she keeps on the table next to her bed, and we said a decade of the rosary for him.

Though I must confess that while we were muttering through all the Hail Marys I kept thinking, 'If Harry is away for a few days, then I can steal his alarm clock.' I hope that isn't a terrible sin. I have a feeling it must be. It's bad enough to be thinking of anything else when you're meant to be praying, but it's much worse to be thinking of stealing something from your sick brother. That must make me a terrible sister. But, after all, Uncle Piers seemed sure that Harry was fine. Anyway, the next time I go to confession I will say that I thought of unsuitable things during the rosary and see what the priest says.

The next day there was no news of Harry by the time I left for school, but Mother said that was to be expected and that Uncle Piers would only be in touch if there was any change, so no news was really good news.

'And Harry might be back to full health already,' she said. 'He might arrive home this afternoon.' I couldn't help hoping he wouldn't. It would spoil my clock-stealing plan, for one.

On the way to school I told Nora what had happened. She immediately thought of the clock too.

'It's as though fate is smiling on us,' she said.

Though I did point out what Mother had said about

Harry's possible imminent return. We were discussing how long bilious 'flu would last when we arrived at school, but when we walked through the door we found the entire place in a state of chaos. Girls, nuns and teachers were running around all over the place and there were dirty wet footprints everywhere.

'What on earth is going on?' asked Nora, as we watched Mother Antoninas hurry past, the bottom six inches of her habit sodden with water.

'There's Professor Shields,' I said. 'She must know. Excuse me, Professor Shields!'

Professor Shields was carrying a large pile of books and looked very harassed, but she said, 'What is it, Mollie?' in quite a polite voice.

'What's going on?' I asked. 'Is everything all right?'

Professor Shields sighed.

'You know about the plumbing work that's been going on?' she said. A lock of her hair had come loose and she pushed it behind her ear. You know something bad has happened when Professor Shields's hair isn't perfect. In fact, she looked much more dishevelled than usual. Even her academic gown was askew.

We knew all about the plumbing. Some men are doing something convoluted to the pipes; there has been a lot of banging and one of the lavatories was closed last week.

'Well, the workmen have damaged the pipes by

accident,' said Professor Shields. 'So we have floods in this part of the school and no water at all in others. And it's most inconvenient, especially with the exams coming up.'

'But what's going to happen to our lessons?' asked Nora.

'We might have to send all you day girls home,' said Professor Shields, and we tried not to look too excited. 'Don't pretend you're not thrilled,' she added. 'I know I would be if I were you.' She seemed much more human now that a crisis had struck the school.

Anyway, she told us we'd better go to our classrooms for now, so Nora and I hurried down the music corridor, where we met Stella and some of the other boarders, who were all hanging around the Middles noticeboard.

'It happened first thing this morning,' said Stella. 'Daisy went to the lav and it wouldn't flush. And then a few other girls tried to go and we discovered there was no water at all.'

I have never been so glad to be a day girl. Our house may be noisy but at least the lavatory is in working order.

'And none of us could wash properly,' said Daisy. 'We just had to sort of rub ourselves down with our dry flannels. I feel awfully grubby.'

What a horrible thought. I thought fondly of the nice jug of warm water that Maggie brings me every morning.

'I hope this doesn't go on for much longer,' said Stella. 'I feel quite grey with dirt.'

But I hoped it would last for a while (though I also hoped they could arrange something so the girls could wash – we had to spend ages honestly assuring Stella that she didn't actually look grubby at all). Because if the school closed down, then Nora and I would have more time to spend on our ... activities. I didn't have time to say anything to her, though, because the second bell rang and we all had to hurry off to class.

It was a strange sort of day. The teachers were all very distracted, and we couldn't use some of the classrooms because the pipes had leaked all over them. During our big break we were all called into the Hall and were told that because of the unusual circumstances, at the end of lessons today the school would be closed until the following Monday, as it would take until Friday to repair the burst pipes and fix the damage they had caused.

'But let none of you think that this is a holiday,' said Mother Antoninas sternly. 'We expect all of you to devote the rest of the week to your studies. After all, many of you will have your summer exams on Tuesday.'

Those boarders who couldn't go home for just a few days (which was most of them) would be taken out for educational outings and to study in the library of one of the other Dominican convents so as to leave the school (and its water system) as free as possible before we all returned next week to take our summer exams.

Nora and I were in an excellent mood as we walked down the library corridor with Stella at the end of lessons. Stella was carrying her knitting bag, which looked even bulkier than usual.

'What on earth have you got in there, Stella?' I said. 'That can't be just knitting.'

'I found Grace's big study notebook,' said Stella. 'She left it behind after historical geography. I'll give it to her in the cloakroom.'

'It's very noble of you to look after it,' I said. 'I'd have been tempted to drop it down the lavatory.'

'Oh come on, Mollie, you know you wouldn't have done that,' said Stella. Which was true. Probably.

'Well, I'd have considered it,' I said.

'Who cares about Grace and her silly notebook?' said Nora. 'We have a whole week of freedom. Well, practically.'

'Not quite freedom,' I said. 'You know our mothers will make us work.'

'Well, we'll have some freedom,' said Nora. And then she stared at me. 'I say, Mollie. We could do it.'

'Do what?' I said stupidly. Then I stared back at her. 'You mean ... the painting?'

Nora nodded.

'It's perfect,' she said. 'Now we've got time to do the preparations, and I bet Harry won't be back for a few days so you can take his clock. And if the worst comes to the worst and it all goes horribly wrong and we get arrested, we won't have to miss school that day.'

'You're right,' I said, though of course I was very much hoping we wouldn't get arrested. 'It's perfect.' I looked at Stella. 'And don't try and talk us out of it, Stella, because we're going to do it. Even if we do have to go to jail.'

And that was when a voice behind us said, 'Go to jail?!' in horrified tones.

We whirled around (Stella's extra-heavy knitting bag whacked me in the leg) to see Grace, Gertie and May. Gertie was smirking, Grace looked like she was going to burst into (pretend) tears of horror and May looked slightly uncomfortable.

'Why are you talking about going to jail?' said Grace. 'What are you planning?'

'Nothing,' I said.

'Oh Mollie, don't tell lies, you know it's a sin,' said Grace, sadly. 'I heard you say something about preparations, and telling Stella not to talk you out of it.'

'You shouldn't have been eavesdropping,' said Nora.

'It's for your own good,' said Grace. She reached out and tried to take Nora's hand, though Nora snatched it away. 'I can't let you get into trouble, Nora. What would

Aunt Catherine say if she knew you were planning to do something …' Grace paused for effect before saying, in a very dramatic voice, 'illegal!'

'She won't know anything,' said Nora, in steely tones, 'if you don't tell her. Because we're not going to be arrested.'

'But you might be,' said Grace. 'Oh Nora, it's not something to do with that suffragette nonsense, is it?'

And there she had us. Neither Nora nor I could deny our commitment the cause now that we'd been asked a direct question. It would be almost (I did say almost) like St Peter denying Our Lord. So we would just have to brazen it out.

'What if it is?' I said. 'It's nothing to do with you. And like Nora said, we're not going to be arrested.'

Gertie sniggered.

'Oh yes,' she said. 'Because you're such master criminals. That's why you're talking about your stupid plans at the top of your voice in the library corridor.'

She actually had a point there, not that I was going to admit it to her.

Grace shook her head.

'I can't let you do this, whatever it is,' she said. 'I must save you from yourselves. I'm sorry, Nora, but this time I really do have to tell Aunt Catherine that you're planning to break the law.'

I must say that Nora was marvellous. I knew that she was scared of what Grace might say to her mother (I know I was), but she hid it wonderfully.

'You have no proof,' she said. 'Do your worst!' She sounded like Peter Fitzgerald facing the jewel thieves. But it still looked as though Grace was going to call her bluff.

'I don't have to prove it,' she said. 'I just have to tell your mother and let her tackle you about it. And I know perfectly well you won't deny your stupid cause, or whatever you call it, if somebody asks you directly.' She was right.

Stella had been looking on in horror throughout this whole thing, but finally she spoke.

'I can't believe you're being such a … such a rotten beast about this, Grace,' she said, her voice trembling with emotion.

'Oh be quiet, Stella,' snapped Grace, dropping her sweet and concerned façade.

'What difference does it make what Nora and Mollie do for their cause?' cried Stella. 'It's got nothing to do with you.'

'Nora is my cousin!' cried Grace. 'And they're not going to give the Middle Grade Cup to someone who's related to a … a … a criminal!'

And there we had it. I might have known there was a

specific reason Grace had been going on at me and Nora about everything from passing notes in class to being suffragettes. It was all about that ridiculous cup and her chances of winning it. She didn't want us – or rather Nora – to do anything in public that could damage her family in the teachers' eyes. I was so angry I couldn't say a word.

But Stella could.

'The summer exams aren't until next week,' she said, her voice still a little bit wobbly. 'You don't know how you're going to do in them. Maybe you won't win the cup – especially if you don't have this.'

And she reached into her bag and took out Grace's study notebook. Grace gasped. Honestly, she actually gasped, like someone in a play.

'My notebook!' she cried.

'Swear on ... on your mother's life that you won't tell anyone about Nora and Mollie,' said Stella, her voice sounding much more steady now, 'or I will run down this corridor right now and drop this notebook in the lavatory. And you know I can run faster than you.'

Grace made a grab for the book, but Nora and I jumped in front of her to block her way.

'You're a pack of wicked blackmailers,' said Grace.

And then May spoke for the first time. 'Oh, don't talk rot, Grace,' she said. 'You were going to tell on them.'

Grace looked like a mouse had roared at her. Well, two mice, if you counted Stella as a mouse. Which I never would again. I know I've said she was a bit wet and white-mouse-ish in the past, but really, Frances, she was like a lioness that afternoon. It was glorious. Especially when Grace said, 'All right then. I promise. On my mother's life. But I hate you all.'

'It's perfectly mutual,' said Nora, which was a little like kicking someone when she was down. But I couldn't really blame her.

Stella handed over the notebook.

'And if you dare break your vow and say anything about Mollie and Nora,' she said, 'I will steal this notebook and burn it.'

It was all very dramatic. I really believed her when she said it, though now it's all over I can't actually imagine her stealing and burning anything. Anyway, Grace and Gertie didn't say another word. They just stalked down the corridor, but May looked back at us and said, 'Sorry' before hurrying after them.

Nora and I turned to Stella.

'You saved our lives!' I cried.

'Well, not literally,' said Nora. 'But you really did save us, Stella. Thanks awfully.'

'Yes, thank you, thank you,' I said.

Stella blushed (so it isn't just me who goes red).

'I just did what any friend would have done,' she said. 'Just because I'm not going to go out and paint slogans or chain myself to the post office doesn't mean I'm not on your side.'

'We know,' I said.

'And that's why,' Stella went on, 'I made you these.' And she reached into her knitting bag again and started to untangle what looked like a large moss-green bundle.

'The complicated scarves!' I said. 'Oh, you shouldn't have. Not for us.'

'They're not just ordinary complicated scarves,' said Stella, who had managed to separate the tangled woollen loops. 'Look.' She pointed to the ends, where a lacy pattern was knitted in white and orange wool. 'They're the I.W.F.L. colours. Green, white and orange.'

'Stella!' gasped Nora. 'They're the most wonderful scarves I've ever seen.'

Stella blushed again.

'There's more,' she said. And she held up the scarf so we could look more closely. It took a moment before I could see it, but when I did I said, 'Oh, Stella!' I almost felt tearful.

The main part of each scarf was knitted in plain garter stitch. But towards the end Stella had used purl stitches to create letters that looked as if they had been stamped into the surface of the scarf. And those letters made the words VOTES FOR WOMEN. You could only see it if you looked very carefully, but the message was there.

'How did you do it?' breathed Nora in wonder.

'I worked out the letters on a grid,' said Stella. 'There was some squared paper in the library. It was quite easy really.'

'You're a genius,' I said, and I meant it. I wrapped my scarf around my neck, and Nora did the same. 'I will wear it always,' I said.

'Well, it's a bit hot to wear it now,' said Stella, 'but the message will still be there in autumn. And if you've won votes for women by then, it can be a celebration slogan.'

Just then an imposing figure turned onto the corridor. It was Mother Antoninas and she looked very surprised to see us.

'What are you day girls still doing here?' she said. 'The last bell rang ten minutes ago.'

'Sorry, Mother Antoninas,' we said humbly.

'And why are you wearing those scarves?' she said. 'The temperature's well into the seventies.'

'I made them,' said Stella quickly. 'They're presents.'

Mother Antoninas's stern features softened, just a tiny bit.

'I see,' she said. 'Well, that's very nice of you, Miss Donovan, but your friends will get heat stroke if they bundle themselves up in scarves now. Even pretty ones

like that.' She reached out and held up the lacy end of
Nora's scarf. 'Very good lacework,' she said. 'Sister Therese
has certainly taught you well.' And then something
seemed to catch her eye. She leaned over and looked
at the scarf very closely, and my stomach tied itself in
a knot. Mother Antoninas may not have had Professor
Shields's terrifying eagle eye but she was very observant
in her own way. And when she stood up straight again,
she didn't look at any of us but said, 'You know, girls, that
at this school we hope that we are educating you to be of
service – to God, to your parents, to your husbands and
families when you have them.'

'Yes, Mother Antoninas,' we murmured.

'And we also encourage you to be independent, and to
think for yourselves, and to serve the wider community,'
Mother Antoninas went on. 'And some people would
say that part of serving the community is having a say in
how the country is run.'

She looked at us for a moment but didn't say anything.

'Now run along,' she said briskly. 'Your mothers will
be wondering where you are.'

'Mine won't. I'm usually a bit late home,' I said,
without thinking.

Mother Antoninas raised an eyebrow (Is this
something all grown-ups can do? I hope I learn how to
do it soon).

'I don't think you should say any more, Miss Carberry,'
she said. 'Now off you go. And you,' she looked at Stella,
'should be getting ready for the boarders' afternoon walk.
Come on.'

And she walked back towards the main body of the
school, with Stella trotting at her heels. Nora and I walked
as fast as we could down the corridor, into the entrance
hall and out the door. Only then did we dare talk.

'Well!' said Nora.

'She did mean …' I said. 'Didn't she?'

'I think so,' said Nora. 'Heavens, I feel quite dizzy.'

'You'd better not faint or anything,' I said. 'We've got
to make plans. I mean, we've definitely got to do the
painting after all that.'

As we walked down Drumcondra Road, we decided
just what we would do. Nora would be in charge of
providing the paint, as previously discussed. I would have
to ensure that we got up early by stealing Harry's clock,
waking Nora by throwing stones at her window. I had
serious doubts about the last part.

'I'm not very good at throwing stones,' I said. 'Not in a
specific direction, I mean. I'm not even good at throwing
balls, and they're actually meant to be thrown.'

'Well, it's not as though you'll have to hit a tiny target,'
said Nora. 'My window's quite large.'

'Yes, and so's your parents' window, right next to it,' I

said. 'What if I hit that instead?'

'You won't,' said Nora confidently.

'What if I hit your window and it doesn't wake you up?' I said. 'Or if I hit it too hard and it breaks?'

'It won't,' said Nora. She stopped walking and turned to me. 'You do want to do this, don't you?'

'Of course I do,' I said. 'I'm the one who introduced you to the cause, remember?'

'Well then,' said Nora. 'We know we're taking a frightful risk, but we have to be brave. And we have to believe it will work.'

'I suppose we do,' I said.

Nora said she would get the paint that afternoon, while I would wait until Wednesday evening to swipe Harry's alarm clock. We decided that the clock, being inside the house, would be more likely to be missed, so we thought I should take it at the last minute. If by any chance Harry had returned home by then and we had no alarm, we would just have to stay awake all night (I was privately rather worried about my ability to do this).

'What if someone catches us while we're doing all these preparations?' I said nervously.

'What if they do?' said Nora. 'There's nothing wrong with having some paint or alarm clocks. We could be using them for perfectly innocent reasons. We can just make excuses.'

And as it turned out, we didn't have to. That afternoon, Nora waited until her mother was out visiting a friend and Agnes was busy collecting the laundry so that nobody would notice her going into the shed. Then she sneaked the pot of paint out of the shed (it was at the back of the top shelf, so we thought the chances of Mr. O'Shaughnessy noticing that it had been used were pretty small). She ran back into the house and hid the pot under her winter jumpers in her chest of drawers, where nobody was likely to look at this time of year.

Meanwhile, there was news about Harry. Uncle Piers, who is clearly much more extravagant than his sister ever is (all those telegrams must have cost a pretty penny), sent another wire that read:

HARRY MUCH IMPROVED. NO FEVER BUT STILL BILIOUS. STAYING UNTIL SUNDAY TO RECOVER. PIERS

'Well, that is a relief, isn't it, Julia?' said Mother after she'd read it aloud to both of us.

'See?' I said to Julia. 'I told you he wasn't dying.' But I was happy to see her small face look less miserable. And a little bit pleased to have confirmation that Harry was going to be all right.

About half an hour later, another telegram arrived, this time a completely unnecessary one from Harry himself, who obviously had persuaded extravagant Uncle Piers to pay for it seeing as he certainly doesn't get enough pocket money to pay for all this wiring.

DO NOT WORRY MOTHER. HAVE UNCLE'S AENEID AND JIM'S OLD GEOMETRY BOOKS. AM WORKING HARD FOR EXAMS ON SICKBED. HARRY.

I'm not sure I'd have bothered getting someone to dig out my cousin's old schoolbooks if I was in bed with bilious flu. For a moment, I actually felt sorry for Harry, having to study in between getting sick, though a part of me thought he deserved it for all those times he threw socks at me and said rude things.

Anyway, I had to do some studying myself. As predicted, because it was officially a school week both my mother and Nora's made it clear as soon as they heard about the pipes that we weren't to think of this as a holiday. We would have to stay home and work on our studies or, as my mother put it, 'make yourself useful'. So I spent most of Wednesday doing my Latin translation and trying to remember history dates. But Nora and I did manage to meet up for a short walk 'to get some fresh air' on Wednesday afternoon, and I told her that Harry was still safely out of the way for a few days.

'Fate really is in our favour,' said Nora. 'What time

should we set the clock for?'

I had already been thinking about that.

'Half past four,' I said. 'So we can get back long before the servants wake up.'

'That'll be lots of time,' said Nora.

Neither of us said anything for a moment. I thought of what it would be like to creep through the deserted streets, and what might happen if a policeman caught us, and a shiver ran down my spine.

'You do really want to do this, don't you?' I said.

'Of course I do,' said Nora. 'We can't keep going around in circles like this. I was asking you this the other day.'

'I know,' I said. 'But it's just that I started all of this. And I don't want you to feel that I've, you know, dragged you along into something.'

Nora looked affronted.

'You've done nothing of the kind,' she said. 'I'll admit that if it weren't for you, I might never have thought much about the cause. But once I started thinking about it, I made my own mind up. And my mind says we should paint that postbox tomorrow.'

I felt much braver and more enthusiastic on my way home. But not everything went smoothly. I had been taking it for granted that I'd be able to swipe the alarm clock from Harry's bedside table without any problems, so it was a shock when I went into his room that evening and couldn't see it anywhere. For a terrible moment I wondered if he could have taken it with him to Dundalk (but why would he have done that? Especially when he thought he was going for the day). Then I looked closer and saw that it had fallen off the table and got wedged between the table and the headboard. It must have got knocked back there while he was packing his sports kit. That was quite reassuring, because it showed me that Maggie or Mother wouldn't notice it was missing if, by any strange chance, they should decide to enter the room over the next twenty-four hours.

I grabbed the clock and quietly slipped out of the room. My heart was beating like mad. Sneaking things out of rooms is terribly nerve-racking, I don't know how burglars and people like that do it. I knocked on the door of my room just to make sure Julia wasn't in there praying or something (I wouldn't put it past her, even though it was two in the afternoon), but luckily the room was empty, so I was able to quickly set the alarm for half past four and wrap it up in two woolly cardigans. Then I shoved the alarm clock bundle under my pillow next to my nightie. I hoped that the cardigans and the pillow would muffle the sound of the alarm enough so that Julia wouldn't wake up too.

The rest of the evening wasn't much easier on my poor nerves. It was another Peter Fitzgerald night

(Father has promised he'll let Harry read the bits he's missed when he returns home), and Peter found himself sharing a train carriage with one of the dangerous jewel thief gang. The jewel thief person didn't recognise Peter because Peter has grown an enormous beard, but Peter was still, understandably, quite worried about being found out and was convinced that his fear was visible on his features, despite the beard. I couldn't help wondering if the same was true for me – and I don't even have a beard to hide behind. And I think I must have been right to worry about my anxiety showing on my face, because halfway through the chapter, at a particularly exciting moment, Father stopped reading and said, 'Mollie, are you quite all right? You look very pale.'

'I hope you're not coming down with Harry's ailment,' said Mother.

'I'm fine,' I said, and tried very hard to look normal. I don't think it worked, though, because both Father and Mother kept looking over at me in a concerned way all the way through the chapter. When Father finished reading (The member of the gang had seen through Peter Fitzgerald's bearded disguise and he – Peter F, I mean, not the jewel thief person – had been forced to escape the carriage and crawl along the roof of the moving train. It was almost thrilling enough to distract me from my nerves, but not quite), he turned to me and said, 'I think Mollie needs to go to bed early. She looks worn out.'

'I don't know why,' said Julia. 'It's not like she's done anything strenuous today.'

'I do actually feel a bit tired,' I said. 'Maybe I will go to bed.'

Everyone looked surprised to hear this, because usually I try to avoid going to bed for as long as possible, but of course tonight was different. Going to bed before Julia meant that I was able to put on my nightdress over my clothes (which would save dressing time the next day). I had read about people doing this in books, but it is surprisingly uncomfortable in real life. For one thing, my clothes seem to have lots of layers, and so are terribly bulky when worn under a nightie. For another, it was extremely hot, too hot to actually get under the covers straight away after I'd said my prayers. When I was saying them I added a special extra bit asking Him to look after me and Nora during our painting, though I did wonder if this was all right. I mean, should one ask God to help you break the law, even if it's for a good cause? Especially after I'd been thinking about stealing a clock during that rosary the other night. I can't imagine God was very pleased with me at the moment.

When I'd finally finished my prayers, I just sat on the bed and tried to read the end of *Jane Eyre* until I heard

Julia at the door. Then I leapt under the sheets and blankets and hoped she wouldn't be able to tell how much I was wearing under there. Of course, she guessed something was up.

'Are you sure you're not coming down with something?' she said. 'You look very red in the face.'

'I'm fine,' I said, although I wasn't.

'I'll pray for you if you like,' she said, in her most saintly voice. 'You don't look very well.'

'Thank you very much,' I said sincerely, which was so unlike me that Julia gave me a very suspicious look. But she was obviously quite tired herself, because a few minutes later she had said all her prayers and got into bed, the light was turned out and she was snoring in a very loud and unsaintly manner.

Of course, as luck would have it, when I eventually closed my eyes I couldn't get to sleep, and not just because I was boiling hot and Julia was making the sort of snuffling noises that I can only describe as ungodly. I kept worrying about the alarm not going off, and then I started worrying about it going off too loudly and waking up Julia. And then I worried that I wouldn't be able to wake up Nora, or that I'd throw a stone through her parents' bedroom window.

It felt as though I were lying awake all night, but I must have dropped off at some stage because I started having a very odd dream about wearing a false beard while travelling on a train with Mrs. Sheehy-Skeffington and Peter Fitzgerald. Peter Fitzgerald had just accused me of stealing a Votes for Women posterboard when I was woken up by something rumbling and shaking under my pillow. The cardigans and the pillow had done a pretty good job of muffling the sound, but it was only now that I realised how difficult it was going to be to turn the alarm off without removing all the muffling materials. And if I removed them now, Julia would definitely wake up.

There was no time to think too much about it. I shoved my hand desperately into the bundle and fumbled around with the knobs and switches. And somehow, to my great relief, I hit the right thingamabob. The alarm stopped vibrating just as Julia rolled over and made a worryingly awake-sounding snort. I held my breath for what felt like a very long time, and then Julia let out a proper snore and I knew the danger had passed – for now. I hid the bundle under my pillow, pulled off my nightie and slipped out of the room. Then I went to the bathroom and splashed cold water on my face in the hope that it would wake me up a bit. Which it sort of did.

My shoes were in the hall, so I tip toed down the stairs in my stocking feet and put them on. The next challenge was getting out of the house. What if Father's keys weren't on the hall stand? Climbing out a window would be easy, but it was going to be a lot harder to get back in. But fortune was smiling on me once again, because there on the stand were the keys on their ring with the leather fob. I checked the clock in the hall. It was twenty to five. I had an hour and a half to meet Nora, go to our target, do the deed and get back to the house before Maggie got up. It was absolutely loads of time, as long as everything went well. But there were, I knew, so many things that could go wrong.

I turned the key in the front door's lock, unhooked the heavy chain and pulled it open as gently as I could. Please, I thought, PLEASE don't squeak today. But it did. Very loudly. I froze, expecting to hear the sound of Father or Maggie leaping out of bed and coming down to investigate. But nothing happened, and after a minute or so I went out and closed the door behind me. It only made a little squeak that time, thank heaven.

The sky was starting to get light, and there wasn't a person to be seen as I ran down the road to Nora's house. It felt quite odd and a little bit frightening being out at that early, lonely hour. It was only when I got to the Cantwells' redbrick villa that I wondered if I should have gathered some stones in advance. I couldn't see any lying about the place, and I was wondering if I could throw my shoe at the window without either breaking the window or the shoe when I noticed that one of Nora's neighbours had a sort of gravelly patch between the bay window and the railings. I grabbed some of the gravel and threw it up at Nora's window as accurately as I could.

It rattled against the glass so loudly that I was sure it would crack, but a moment later the curtains parted and Nora peered down at me through the crack and waved. She was wearing her nightie, but she must have had her clothes on underneath, because just a minute later she slipped out of the front door holding a little bag.

'Did you have any trouble getting out?' I asked.

'I told you my parents are very sound sleepers,' said Nora. 'What about you?'

I told her about the alarm and the noisy door, but we agreed it could have been worse.

'Imagine if Julia had woken up,' said Nora.

I shuddered at the thought. Actually, I shuddered a bit from the cold too.

'I should have brought one of the cardigans I used to wrap the clock,' I said. 'Or Stella's scarf. I didn't realise it was so cold at this time of the morning.'

'The walk will warm us up,' said Nora. 'And so will running,' she added, 'if we get spotted by a policeman.'

I looked around nervously, but there wasn't a

policeman in sight. Or anyone else, for that matter. It was so quiet that every time we spoke, even in a whisper, it seemed to boom through the streets, so we didn't say much. But when we reached the main road, we started to see delivery lorries and carts. Just before we reached the North Circular Road a lorry full of coal passed us. The driver gave us an amused look and called out, 'Are you right there, girls?' as he drove by.

'Come on,' I said. 'Let's hurry up.'

We quickened our pace and it wasn't long before we were at the postbox at the corner of Nelson Street and Eccles Street.

'Right,' said Nora. 'Here we are.'

But neither of us moved.

'Do you have the paint?' I whispered.

Nora nodded and held up the small pot. I looked around. The street was deserted.

'Come on, then,' I said.

Nora unscrewed the lid and dipped in the brush.

'Do you want to go first?' she said. 'After all, it was your idea to get involved in all this in the first place.'

I shook my head.

'We're both in it as much as each other,' I said. 'You write the first bit and I'll write the last few words.'

Nora gave one nervous look behind us, and then she wrote VOTES FOR on the pillar box in big letters.

'There,' she said. 'Now it's your turn. Quickly, in case anyone comes.'

She passed me the brush. I took a deep breath. All our playing around with songs, even the chalking, were nothing in comparison to this. Now we were breaking the law. Now we were – what had Frank said? – defacing public property. Now we were really standing up for the cause.

Good.

I dipped the brush in the pot and wrote IRISH WOMEN! in even bigger letters.

We both stared at the postbox for a moment, then at each other.

'Come on,' I whispered. 'Let's go.'

And, after throwing the paint pot and the brush behind some railings, we shot off down the road as fast as our legs could carry us. Which, as I have pointed out, is quite fast indeed, at least for short distances. But it wasn't long before we got out of breath.

'Stop, stop,' I wheezed, drawing to a halt. 'I can't go on.'

'Neither can I,' said Nora. She was panting too.

We leaned against the wall. Then Nora looked at me, and I looked at her, and we both started laughing (though not too loudly, in case we woke anyone up).

'We did it!' I said. 'We really, truly did it!'

'We're militants,' said Nora. 'Like Mrs. Pankhurst.

Except nobody has carried us off to prison.'

'Yet,' I said. And that sobered us up a bit, but only for a moment. Now that the immediate danger of discovery had passed, we felt giddy and bubbly, like soda water. We started laughing again.

'Oh, it hurts,' said Nora. 'I still can't breathe properly.'

And we tried to pull ourselves together. It had got much brighter and more people were starting to appear: servants and delivery men and even a few rather ragged-looking children. A Boland's bread van went past, the driver glancing at us with mild curiosity. He – and everyone else – was probably wondering what two girls dressed like us were doing out at this hour of the morning.

'We'd better get home,' I said.

And off we went. We decided it was safe to start walking normally again. After all, we were far enough away from the postbox that even if someone noticed us and asked us what we were doing roaming around in the wee hours, no one would connect us with the vandalism. But just in case anyone had spotted our daring deed and was following us, we took a sort of roundabout route home.

When we reached the corner where Nora turns off, and were quite sure no one had followed us there, I asked, 'Do you think it will get in the papers?'

'It might,' said Nora. 'I mean, it's not just chalk, it's actual paint.'

Just then, the church bells started to ring out.

'Six o'clock!' I cried. 'Maggie will be up soon.'

And, after agreeing to meet up later, we each ran home. Luckily, the door decided to behave itself and opened silently when I let myself in. I knew it was much more likely that a noise would wake someone now, at a time that was much closer to their normal waking up time, than when I left the house. I tiptoed down the hall and went into the kitchen to make a cup of tea, but of course the range and the fire weren't properly lit, and I didn't want to risk making a mess with either of them by trying to stoke them up, so I couldn't boil a kettle. I cut a slice of bread and got some butter and milk from the cold press, and was sitting at the table eating the bread and butter and drinking the milk when Maggie came in, yawning and rubbing the sleep from her eyes.

'Good morning, Maggie,' I said.

Poor Maggie nearly jumped out of her skin.

'What are you doing here?' she said.

'I woke up early and couldn't get back to sleep,' I said. 'The sun always wakes me up early at this time of year.' Both of which statements were perfectly true.

Soon Maggie had laid the fire and stoked the range. I asked if I could help, but she just looked at me and said I'd be less trouble sitting at the table. I was still feeling fizzy with excitement about what we'd done, so fizzy that I almost told Maggie about it. But I knew it wouldn't be fair to burden her with the knowledge of what me and Nora had done, even though she might approve of it (and I had a feeling she would).

I ate more bread and butter and tried not to think of the poor suffragette hunger strikers in England, and soon Maggie had made the tea. She gave me another shrewd look over the pot.

'What have you been up to?' she said. And then she sighed and said, 'Actually, don't tell me. I'm better off not knowing.' Then she leaned over and lifted the end of one of my plaits.

'Is that paint in your hair?' she asked.

It was as if the earth had stopped turning. I stared at her for what seemed like ages and didn't say anything, but she didn't ask any more questions. She just said, 'Honestly, I don't know how a nice girl like you ends up covered in muck', got a clean dish cloth and wiped my plait with it.

'There you go,' she said. 'Now, off you go and do something useful. I've got shoes to clean and breakfast to make.'

So I went. I sat in the sitting room and tried to read the last few pages of *Jane Eyre*, but I couldn't concentrate.

I can't imagine ever being able to concentrate on anything properly again; I've felt so jangled over the last few days. It was quite a relief when the rest of the family all started to come down for breakfast, even though they were all so surprised to see me there before them that I felt quite insulted.

'I just woke up early because of the sunlight,' I said. 'It *is* the middle of summer, you know.'

'I just wish it had been so easy to get you out of bed during term time,' said Mother.

And then Julia said she was going to start getting up at six and going to Mass every day, and Mother said that was very nice but who would take her, and that drew everyone's attention away from me. Which was a good thing, as the fizzy feeling had entirely evaporated by now, and instead I was gripped by a terrible fear. What if someone had seen us? What if they'd tracked us down? If I had managed to get paint in my hair without either me or Nora noticing, what other clues might we have left behind? I became completely terrified that I'd dropped a hanky or something (even though my hankies are all plain white with some flowers embroidered on them, rather than my initials or any other features that would identify the owner, so even if I had dropped one no one would figure out that it was mine). I was so worried about it I had to go out and check the pockets of my coat to make sure that my hanky was still there (which it was. It was also still plain white with a pansy embroidered in one corner).

I felt all nervous and fidgety for the rest of the morning. At around eleven Mother told me to walk Julia to Christina's house, so I did, but that wasn't very distracting. As soon as we left the house, Julia turned to me and asked, 'What's wrong with you?'

'Nothing,' I said. 'Now shut up and keep walking.'

Julia gave me her most annoyingly pious look, the sort of look that says, 'you are being very rude but because I am such a good and saintly person I am not going to say anything about it.'

'I know there's something,' she said. 'If there's anything troubling your conscience, you really should go to confession, or at least talk to one of the nuns about it.'

I took a deep breath and tried to stay calm.

'My conscience is perfectly clear,' I said, honestly. 'I haven't done anything wrong.'

'Are you sure?' said Julia.

I clenched my fists. I knew that if I lost my temper I was perfectly capable of letting the truth slip out in the heat of rage.

'Quite sure,' I said. 'Now come on, stop dawdling.'

Luckily, we had reached Christina's house so Julia went in (probably to do some praying for my guilty soul), and

I walked slowly home, running through the morning's events for a millionth time. By the time I got home I had reassured myself that we hadn't left any clues behind. I still felt a bit fidgety, but I didn't feel scared.

And then, at about two o'clock, when Phyllis and I were both sitting in the drawing room – her reading a novel in a half-hearted sort of way, me trying to read my French textbook – and Mother was playing some not-very-relaxing Beethoven on the piano, it happened. There was a loud knocking on the door and when Maggie answered it, Mabel ran in, looking very flushed and excited, and announced, 'Phyllis, I need to talk to you.'

'Well, really, Mabel,' said Mother. 'What's all this about?'

Mabel went even more red and said, 'I'm terribly sorry, Mrs. Carberry, but I do need to speak to Phyllis urgently.'

'Come on,' said Phyllis. 'Sorry, Mother.'

They went up to Phyllis's room.

'The sooner that girl is married the better,' said Mother. 'She seems a very flighty young lady.'

But I barely heard her because I was absolutely burning to know what Mabel was telling Phyllis. I knew she wouldn't have rushed around here in such a state if something important hadn't happened. I even considered sneaking up and listening outside the door, but I know that is the sort of behaviour that is unworthy of a suffragette. And a suffragette is what I officially am. Besides, I knew if it was general I.W.F.L. news Phyllis would tell me sooner or later. And I was right. After about half an hour Mabel and Phyllis came back into the drawing room. Phyllis's eyes were bright and she looked as if she could barely suppress her excitement.

'I'm very sorry about bursting in like that,' said Mabel. 'It won't happen again.'

'Well, it's all right, Mabel,' said Mother. 'But I do think you should try to calm yourself. It can't be good for your digestion, all this rushing about the place.'

'No, Mrs. Carberry,' said Mabel humbly. 'Goodbye.'

When she was gone Mother said, 'Is Mabel's engagement still on?'

'What?' said Phyllis. 'Oh yes. It's quite all right. She just wanted to tell me that, um, that they're going to Paris for a honeymoon.'

'Paris!' said Mother. 'Good Lord, how grand. Your father and I went to Killarney, and very lucky we thought ourselves too.'

And before she could go into a reverie about the good old days of the nineteenth century, I gave Phyllis a meaningful look and said, 'Phyllis, will you help me find that ribbon I was looking for? I can't find it anywhere.'

'What?' said Phyllis. I stared at her even more

meaningfully and raised my eyebrows (both of them, sadly, although I tried to just raise one) until she said, 'Oh, all right.'

We went up to Phyllis's room and closed the door.

'What did Mabel want?' I asked.

'Ssh, not so loud,' said Phyllis. She took a deep breath. 'It's happened. Militant action has begun.'

An extraordinary feeling washed over me. I felt hot and cold at the same time, and my stomach seemed to tie itself in knots.

'What sort of action?' I said, or rather croaked. Because suddenly my mouth had become very dry. Somehow I hadn't expected the news of what we'd done to the postbox to get around so quickly. Now that it had, it all felt a bit overwhelming.

'Mrs. Sheehy-Skeffington and Mrs. Palmer and some of the other ladies have broken lots of windows,' said Phyllis. 'In the GPO, and Government Buildings, and lots of other places.'

For a moment I wasn't sure if I was hearing things correctly.

'What?' I said.

'They've all been arrested,' said Phyllis. She was almost trembling with excitement. 'I didn't know they were planning it. Well, of course, none of us did.'

'I don't believe it,' I said. I was stunned. How could

we have predicted that we would commit our daring deed on the very morning that our movement's leaders would spring into militant action? It wasn't as if they were basing their activities on Harry's absence and Eccles Street's burst water pipes (At least, it would be very odd if they were).

'Isn't it wonderful?' said Phyllis. 'They're such heroines. Everyone will know how serious the movement is now.'

'Did they do anything else?' I asked. 'Besides smash windows I mean.'

'Isn't that enough?' said Phyllis. 'It's more than any of the rest of us have done.'

'Of course it's enough,' I said quickly. 'I was just wondering.'

'Well, as far as I know, that was it,' said Phyllis. 'I only wish I could have done something too, but obviously they couldn't have told just anyone that they were planning it – not mere rank-and-file members like me and Kathleen and Mabel.'

'Yes, of course,' I said.

'I must go and tell Kathleen,' said Phyllis. 'Mabel hasn't had a chance to call on her, although of course her aunt might have heard and told her already. In fact, everyone will know soon, it'll be in the evening papers.'

A few minutes later, she was gone, practically skipping up the road on her way to Kathleen's house. She looked so happy, but I didn't really know what I felt, apart from slightly stunned. I wanted to rush off to tell Nora the news, but Mother still wanted me to make myself useful. By which she now apparently meant helping her trim my last summer's hat to 'make it look presentable' (I think it looked perfectly presentable as it was, but Mother says it looked like an old rag, which is a bit harsh if you ask me).

Unsurprisingly, measuring bits of ribbon wasn't enough to stop my thoughts whirring around like a top. I was comparing the length of the new ribbon to the old one when a horrible thought struck me. What if Mrs. Sheehy-Skeffington and the other window-breakers got blamed for what we had done? What if our postbox painting meant extra time was added to their prison sentences? I felt sick at the thought, and must have looked it too because Mother suddenly said, 'Are you all right, Mollie? You've gone very pale. I really think you must have Harry's flu.'

'I'm all right,' I said, untruthfully. 'Mother, may I go to see Nora later? I want to ask her something about school.'

'Out again?' said Mother. 'You spend far too much time gallivanting.'

'Oh, Mother, you sound like Aunt Josephine,' I said. Mother looked horrified. I suppose it was quite a terrible insult. She took a deep breath and then said, 'Well, I suppose you can call over to her for an hour, as long as it's all right with Mrs. Cantwell.'

'It always is,' I said. I started to get up from my seat, but Mother reached over and gently pushed me back down again.

'When you've finished helping with this hat,' she said. Which was fair enough, I suppose. Fifteen minutes later, I was knocking on Nora's front door. Agnes went off to fetch her and she came bouncing down the stairs.

'Is that a new hat?' she asked.

'It's last summer's,' I said. 'I just helped Mother trim it.' And I glanced around to make sure nobody was within earshot. Agnes had gone back to the kitchen, but I didn't want to risk Mrs. Cantwell overhearing.

'I have news,' I whispered. 'Important news about ... you know what. Let's go to your room.'

Nora looked a bit like I must have looked this morning. When we were in her room she said, 'Did someone see us?'

'No,' I said. 'It's bigger than that.' And I told her what I'd learned, and how worried I was that the ladies would get blamed for our slogan-painting.

'Well, if that happens,' said Nora bravely, 'we'll just have to own up.'

'I know,' I said. 'We can't let them be punished for

what we did. Besides, some people would argue that we should own up to painting it anyway. I mean, that we should have the courage of our convictions.'

'Well, I'm not sure about that,' said Nora.

'Neither am I, really,' I agreed. 'But I am sure about the other part. We can't let them be blamed for something they didn't do, even if they approve of us doing it. If you see what I mean.'

Nora nodded to show that she did.

'When will we know?' said Nora. 'What exactly they're being blamed for, I mean.'

'It might be in the newspaper,' I said. 'Tonight or tomorrow.'

We looked at each other nervously.

'You're not regretting doing it, are you?' I asked.

Nora seemed to pull herself together.

'No,' she said firmly. 'Never. It's the best thing we ever did.'

And when she said that, I knew that it was true. All our lives we've just done ordinary things. We've gone to school and read books and climbed trees and played games and had enemies (Grace) and friends (Stella) and annoying big brothers (you know who). But nothing we'd done before had been like this. None of it had been bigger than ourselves, bigger than everyone we knew. Standing up for women – standing up not just for what we want our lives to be like when we grow up, but for everyone else too – was bigger than ourselves. And even though we'd only painted something on a postbox, which doesn't seem like much in the greater scheme of things, other people would see that postbox and know that there were people out there who thought votes for women was important. What we'd done wasn't nearly as meaningful or brave as what Mrs. Sheehy-Skeffington and the others had done. But it was a big step for us. I was very glad we'd done it. And if I had to, I would go to the police and tell them so.

I couldn't stay at Nora's for too long – we hoped her father might come home early with an evening paper, but he was working late. When I left, we arranged to meet first thing tomorrow.

'We'll definitely know what's happened by then,' I said. 'Even if I have to run out and buy a newspaper with my own money.'

'Do you actually have any money of your own at the moment?' asked Nora. 'You're not terribly good at saving.'

'I have two and six left in my money box,' I said indignantly.

Nora apologised for doubting me and said she would try and buy a paper too.

I was so nervy and fidgety when I got home that

Mother asked again if I was all right.

'I'm fine,' I said. 'I've just been studying too hard.'

Mother let out a very undignified snort of laughter at this.

'Really?' she said. 'Well, I hope we see the results of this in your summer exams.'

When Mother left the room, I asked Phyllis if she'd had any more news about the prisoners but she hadn't. None of her friends had called around and Father hadn't brought home an evening newspaper.

'And I don't think I'll hear anything more until tomorrow,' she said. 'I told Mother I wanted to call around to Kathleen later and she said she needed me to stay at home and help her sort out old sheets. And I didn't want to kick up too much of a fuss now because I know there might be a lot to do over the next week.'

So there was nothing we could do but wait until the next day. Even the latest installment of Peter Fitzgerald's adventures couldn't distract me, although they were frightfully dramatic (He is now being pursued across an Arabian desert by the leader of the gang of jewel thieves). When I went to bed, I couldn't sleep for ages, and when I finally did fall asleep, I had terrible dreams about being chased by policemen while covered in paint.

I felt exhausted the next morning, as if I really had been chased all night. When I came down to breakfast

Phyllis didn't look as if she'd got much sleep either. But when the meal was over, she gave me a meaningful look as she left the dining room. I followed her up to her room. There was a copy of today's newspaper lying on her bed.

'Page six,' she said.

I grabbed it and hurriedly turned the pages. And there it was, halfway down the page, under a piece about the inquiry into the sinking of the *Titanic*. I read it aloud: '"In North Dublin Police Court yesterday Hilda Webb, Maud Lloyd, Marjorie Hasler, and Kathleen Houston were charged with having, in furtherance of the suffragette movement, smashed the windows of the Custom House, Post Office and Local Marine Board Office between five and six o'clock that morning." I thought you said Mrs. Sheehy-Skeffington was arrested too?'

'Different police court,' said Phyllis. 'Keep reading.'

I looked further down the report and there it was. '"In the Southern Court Margaret Palmer, Jane Murphy, Hanna Sheehy-Skeffington and Margaret Murphy were charged with having, with a like object, broken the windows of the Land Commission and Ship Street Military Barracks."' I kept reading. 'They've all been admitted to bail,' I said. 'What does that mean?'

'It means they're free, for now,' said Phyllis. 'They've been let out until the trial.'

I looked at the report again. 'It just says they're being charged with breaking windows,' I said.

'Yes, of course,' said Phyllis. 'They didn't do anything else. Anything else illegal, that is. '

I felt relief rush through me. So they weren't being accused of painting the postboxes, and me and Nora hadn't got them into more trouble.

'Now, I really must go and see Kathleen,' said Phyllis. 'Mother can't possibly want me to help her around the house now.'

And off she went. I sighed and went down to the dining room to work on my Latin, but I'd only got one verse into Ovid's 'Last Night in Rome' when there was a knock on the door, and a moment later Nora hurried into the room.

'Maggie told me you were in here,' she said. 'Did you see? They haven't been charged.'

'I know,' I said. 'I'm so relieved.'

'Me too,' said Nora. 'And I met Kathleen and Phyllis on my way over, and they were so excited they deigned to talk to me. Apparently, they – the arrested ladies, I mean – are going to talk at a Phoenix Park meeting tomorrow.'

We looked at each other.

'We must go,' I said.

'Of course we must,' said Nora. 'I mean, we're fellow militants.'

And we looked at each other and felt very proud.

'I sort of feel we should sing the song,' I said.

'Better not,' said Nora. 'Someone might hear. But I will hum it on my way home.'

Just then, there was a very loud knock on the front door. Nora and I looked at each other.

'It couldn't be ...' My voice trailed off.

'The police? Of course not. How could it be?' said Nora. But she didn't sound as confident as I hoped.

And then I heard the door open and Harry's voice booming, 'I'm home!'

Nora and I both sagged with relief.

'I've never been so glad to hear that horrible voice,' I said.

'Me too,' said Nora. 'I thought you said he wasn't back until Sunday?'

'He's not meant to be,' I said. 'Maybe Uncle Piers has sent him back because he's so awful.'

Sadly, this was not the case, as I found out when Nora and I went downstairs. Harry had returned because just as he recovered my cousin Margaret had arrived home from France and promptly come down with scarlet fever. Which is of course very serious, not that Harry seemed to care about that.

'I'm sure she'll be perfectly fine,' he said. 'And besides, I did have to get away from all those germs, especially after being sick myself.'

'But, Harry, why didn't you send a telegram?' asked Mother, once she'd made sure Harry hadn't had any direct contact with Margaret and so wasn't riddled with scarlet fever germs. 'It's not like Piers to just pack you off without a word.'

Harry looked slightly shame-faced, which is extremely unusual for him.

'Well, actually, Uncle Piers did give me the money to send one yesterday afternoon, but I thought it was an awful waste when I was going to see you so soon,' he said. 'So, um, I spent it on things to eat on the train.'

Mother was very annoyed and told him he would have to pay back Uncle Piers with his own money. I can't pretend I didn't enjoy seeing him get into trouble. It happens so rarely, after all.

'Can I go over to Frank's house?' asked Harry, after he'd solemnly promised to send Uncle Piers the money he'd essentially stolen. 'I haven't seen him since I got sick on his feet.'

Poor Frank. Anyone getting sick on your feet would be bad enough, but Harry! You'd have to burn your shoes afterwards.

'Harry, don't say such disgusting things,' said Mother. 'All right, you can go, but you must be back here for supper.'

And, just like that, things were back to normal. If I'd just admitted to spending telegram money on sweets

I would definitely not have been allowed go round to Nora's house straight afterwards.

Sunday

This letter is getting longer and longer, but I must tell you about the meeting yesterday. First of all, it was surprisingly easy to get away because Mother suddenly decided that I looked 'peaky' and needed some fresh air. I almost pointed out that the reason I looked peaky (I'm not sure I did, anyway – I think I looked pale and interesting) was because I'd been stuck indoors for most of the last few days, but I didn't want to antagonise her in case she changed her mind. Anyway, I asked if I could go for a walk in the park with Nora and she said I could.

'Maybe you can take Julia too,' she added.

My heart sank.

'Oh Mother, please don't make us,' I said. 'She'll just keep telling me I need to join that sodality in school and that I don't concentrate enough on my prayers at Mass.'

From the expression on Mother's face I wondered, not for the first time, whether she wanted me to take Julia out for a walk so that Mother herself didn't have to put up with her going on about how the rest of us weren't praying enough (when really we all say lots of prayers every single day. Even Harry says his prayers every night, not that it seems to do him much good). She took a deep breath.

'All right,' she said. 'Phyllis was talking about going for a walk in the park too. Maybe you can go with her.'

'Thanks, Mother,' I said, and ran out before she could change her mind. I wanted to tell Nora straight away. I do wish we could have a telephone. Imagine if I could just ring up and talk to Nora whenever I wanted. I suppose I could send her a telegram, but even if I could afford it (and I can't), her house is on the way to the post office so it would defeat the purpose to walk past it in order to send her a message. Grace says her family have a telephone at home but I don't believe her.

For once, Phyllis and Kathleen didn't mind me and Nora tagging along, if only because they still felt guilty about the fact that we had had to sit in a hall the other week while they were enjoying the meeting.

'Phyll told me I had your ticket,' said Kathleen. 'Sorry about that. I must say I was impressed you wanted to come at all.'

'Thanks very much,' I said, and tried very hard to stop myself staring at her new hat, which had what looked like an enormous cotton cabbage leaf and a felt carrot attached to the band. I obviously wasn't trying hard enough because Kathleen said, 'Do you like my new hat?

It's a commemoration of the time we were attacked by those dreadful Ancient Order chaps.'

'It's very impressive,' I said, and for once I wasn't lying. I mean, it's not every day you see a girl with a felt carrot on her hat. That said, Nora and I did make sure we kept a bit of a distance between us when we got off the tram at the park, especially when small boys started shouting things like, 'Miss, you've left your dinner on your head!'

'Ignore them, Kathleen,' said Phyllis. 'They're just jealous.' Which was a blatant lie, but Kathleen didn't seem to mind. I suppose she's used to people saying rude things about her hats. It actually makes me admire her for continuing to wear them in the face of ridicule. I'd have probably started wearing ordinary hats by now.

It was a very hot afternoon and by the time we reached the park I was utterly parched. Phyllis and Kathleen had promised to take us for tea and buns afterwards 'to reward you for being so stoical about missing the Antient meeting' but the tearooms seemed a very long way away as we made our way to the place where the ladies would be speaking. When we were almost at the spot, we saw a couple of policemen.

'Maybe they think there's going to be more stone throwing,' said Nora.

'Well it wouldn't do much good throwing stones here,' said Kathleen. 'There aren't any windows to smash in this part of the park.'

We had almost reached the lorry from which the
women would be making their speeches. A very large
crowd had gathered, some of whom looked a bit rowdy.
Two more policemen stood nearby, observing the scene.
We could see Mr. Sheehy-Skeffington and some of the
I.W.F.L. ladies looking slightly uncomfortable at the front
of the crowd. Phyllis turned to me and Nora.

'I think you girls should stand back,' she said. 'This
might get a bit ... raucous. I have a horrible feeling the
Hibernians are here.'

'We're not afraid of that,' said Nora indignantly.

'Well, I'm afraid of having to explain to my mother –
and Mrs. Cantwell – why the pair of you are covered in
cabbage leaves or worse, bruises,' said Phyllis. 'So go on.'

And she looked so stern that we did what she said,
though we grumbled as we moved towards the back of
the crowd. The ground was a little higher there so we
had a decent view down towards the lorry. We did get a
few odd looks from the men.

'Here to see the fun, girls?' said one man with a
very red face. 'Don't worry, I'll protect you if they start
throwing any more of those stones.'

But we didn't have to answer him because there was a
sort of commotion at the front of the crowd.

'What's going on?' I asked Nora. This was one of those

times when her being taller than me made a difference.

'They're after Mr. Sheehy-Skeffington,' she said. 'I think Phyllis was right, it is those Ancient Order people.'

Most of the crowd were quiet and well behaved, but quite a few people at the front were shouting now, and it seemed like Mr. Sheehy-Skeffington was their target.

'Cut his whiskers off,' shouted one lout. 'He's no man!'

'Oh dear,' I said. I felt very sorry for Mr. Sheehy-Skeffington. The crowd were rude fools. Imagine telling someone he wasn't a man just because he supported women's rights!

'Put some breeches on him!' shouted another man in the crowd.

'No!' bellowed another. 'We should take off his breeches and give him a skirt!'

There was more jostling and pushing at the front of the crowd. The men around us started to move forward to try and see what was happening. One of them looked at us.

'You kiddies should get out of here,' he said. But we ignored him.

'Where are those policemen?' I said to Nora. 'They were here a few minutes ago.'

Nora looked back. 'They're over there,' she said. 'But they're not doing anything.'

Nora and I made our way further up the slope where

we could both get a better view of the terrible scene. It looked like the rowdy troublemakers were trying to stop the ladies getting to the lorry, and Mr. Sheehy-Skeffington and the ladies were trying to push them back, with little success. Finally, Mrs. Sheehy-Skeffington made her way through and mounted the make-shift stage. She looked scornfully at the crowd.

'What kind of law have we,' she cried, 'that allows women to be mobbed while the police are looking on?'

This seemed to strike some sort of chord with the policemen, as well it might. A few minutes later, four of them, three constables and an inspector, were at the front of the crowd, pushing back the louts who had been attacking the suffragettes.

'Be quiet, boys,' said the Inspector.

But the rowdies just laughed and made rude remarks. They stopped pushing and shoving, though. For a while, at least.

That was when the orange sellers arrived. There are always fruit sellers in the park at the weekends, but these ones had discovered a new way of selling their wares.

'Suffra-gate oranges!' cried one woman. 'Two suffra-gate oranges a penny!'

'They're not saying the right word,' said Nora. 'People might get confused.'

So we went over to one of the orange sellers.

'I'm sorry,' said Nora, 'but you're calling the name wrong.'

The orange-selling woman stared at us.

'What in the name of goodness is it then?' she asked.

'Suffragette,' I said. 'Can we have two oranges, please?'

I handed over a penny. The woman gave us the oranges, and we thanked her and went back to our vantage point. We hadn't even reached it when she started calling out, 'Two more suffra-gate oranges a penny!'

'Well!' I said. 'She's not even trying. And we bought oranges and everything.'

They were nice fresh oranges, though. We started to peel them as Mrs. Cousins, another of the window smashers, got up on the lorry and started addressing the crowd. She read a long statement about how women had a definite right to the vote, but the goons at the front kept shouting.

'Go home and mind the baby!' shouted a man standing near us. Some people – or rather men – laughed and cheered, but quite a lot of others told him to shush. Nora and I glared at him (and you know how good Nora is at glaring), but he just laughed at us.

'This is no place for little girls like you,' he said, but we ignored him. We have become very good at ignoring rude and ignorant men.

Then Mrs. Cousins introduced Mrs. Palmer, who got up on the lorry. The rowdies jeered even louder and some even booed when they realised this was another one of the women that had been arrested on Thursday.

'Have you any bricks with you?' shouted one 'wit'.

'No, I used them all up,' cried Mrs. Palmer, and the crowd laughed again, though it was a different sort of laughter this time. They were laughing with Mrs. Palmer, not at her.

Mrs. Palmer went on to tell us that we were fortunate enough to be addressed by two criminals that day – herself and Mrs. Sheehy-Skeffington. Some men in front of us started talking very loudly then so we couldn't hear exactly what she said next, but we heard the words Mountjoy Jail. Which is where the brave window-smashers will doubtless soon be languishing.

'The proper place to have you for life!' shouted another man at the front of the crowd, and some of his pals cheered, but Mrs. Palmer was undaunted by their rudeness. It was inspiring, but it was also horrible. She had been so brave, and these awful men were just laughing at her and spoiling the meeting for all the well-behaved people who wanted to listen. Luckily, most of the crowd wanted to listen, and she ignored the louts and kept talking, all about why they had broken the windows ('to assert our rights to vote and to bring our claims prominently under the notice of Government') and how she believes that the Irish people will not want Home Rule if it excludes women.

This just made the rowdies at the front laugh even more. Their laughter made me feel a bit sick. I had thought what we did on Thursday was very brave, but I realised those awful men would just laugh at us for doing it if they knew.

'You won't get a vote for smashing glass!' shouted one man.

It was very discouraging. At least, I would have thought so, but Mrs. Palmer didn't seem to be bothered by their rudeness. She just introduced Mrs. Sheehy-Skeffington, who climbed back on the lorry.

'Ladies and gentlemen,' she cried. 'And police notetakers,' she added, glancing at the policemen that were still standing near the front. The whole crowd laughed, even some of the rowdies.

'Well,' Mrs. Sheehy-Skeffington went on, 'as far as quantity goes, this is the biggest meeting we've ever held in the park.'

The rowdies booed and some people cheered. In fact, from now on you can just take it for granted that this happened almost every time the women spoke.

'You all know the way we did it,' said Mrs. S.-S. (I can't keep writing out her name, it's just too long). 'And now people want to know why we did it.'

'Why did you do it in the dark hours of the morning?' shouted one man.

'Yeah,' yelled another. 'You should have been out in broad daylight.'

'I don't consider half past five on a June morning dark,' said Mrs. S.-S.

'You thought there'd be no policemen about,' yelled another man.

'This is a very serious matter,' said Mrs. S.-S., trying to ignore them. 'Before this day week, a good many of the women who are here now will be in prison.'

'Hear, hear!' shouted the rowdies.

I hated every one of them.

Mrs. S.-S. told them that if she didn't believe that militancy was the only way to change things 'when all constitutional means have failed', she wouldn't have bothered. But, as she pointed out, 'Home Rule – which will be granted one of these days – was the result of militancy. If my father hadn't gone to jail in his time for the cause of Home Rule, I might not be imbued with a militant spirit. I'm very glad it is hereditary in the female line as well as the male. And I'm ready to go jail for my cause – namely, Parliamentary votes for women.'

Nora and I cheered and clapped as loudly as we could, though our cheers were almost drowned out by the

Ancient Order of Hibernians and their chums, yelling things like, 'All right then, twelve months hard labour' and 'Go home and mind the baby!'

Mrs. S.-S. went on to talk about Wolfe Tone and Robert Emmet and other Irish heroes, and said 'I wonder do the Irish Party realise that if they had the women of Ireland with them, they could make a very good thing of Home Rule. But if they don't have the women of Ireland with them, the Home Rule bill might go through, but it will be a terrible fiasco.'

After that, the rowdies started booing so loudly we couldn't hear anything Mrs. S.-S. was saying for a while.

But after a while it subsided long enough for us to hear her say, 'A cause that can produce women who are ready to face imprisonment for the sake of their rights is not likely to die. You must remember that militants do not hurt *people*. Window-breaking is a historic method of protest against the Government. And we did not break shop windows; we only broke the Government windows.' She was trying to explain that they made sure to act at a time when there were no clerks inside who might be injured when an absolutely extraordinary noise was heard coming from the front of the crowd, drowning out all of her words. It was a sort of squeaking instrument, playing a very unpleasant tune.

'What on earth is that?' said Nora.

It was difficult to make it out, even from the raised ground. We jumped up and down until finally a man took pity on us and said, 'It's a melodeon.'

I don't know whether melodeons always sound like that but this one was hideous. And it went on for ages and ages. We were wondering if the women would have to give up the meeting altogether because no one could hear a word Mrs. S.-S. was saying, but eventually the melodeon-player gave up and she was able to continue her speech. She talked about how Mr. Asquith, the Prime Minister, was coming to Dublin soon and how the suffragettes were determined to let him know that they thought.

'He wouldn't dare address a meeting of the Irish people at the Phoenix Park!' she cried. Then she talked about how soon she would be going to jail, 'a place where I won't be able to tell if the sky is blue or grey', but that the cause of the suffragettes 'will prosper as a result of our militancy!'

Some people laughed, but quite a few cheered too. Then there were questions from the crowd. Some of the questions were actually quite polite. One man asked whether it wasn't irresponsible to smash things, and Mrs. S.-S. pointed out that if the law held women to be the same as lunatics, it wasn't surprising if they adopted irresponsible methods. And, she said, more and more women were joining the fight.

'A few years ago we had only three hundred suffragettes in Dublin,' she cried. 'And now we have a thousand!'

And she sounded so brave and optimistic that even if I hadn't already been devoted to the cause, I really do think it would have won me over. Quite a lot of the men clapped. And then some more started asking questions (most of which we couldn't hear because we were too far back), and the ladies answered them, and that was the end of the meeting.

We made our way through the crowd to Phyllis and Kathleen, who were part of a number of women sort of guarding the speakers as they made their way towards the park gates, with the policemen taking the lead. Phyllis spotted us as we approached.

'Go and wait for us in the tearooms,' she cried. I suppose she was afraid we might be caught up in more roughness – which looked likely as some of the rowdies jostled around them. She kept going towards the gates and I was wondering whether we should join them anyway – surely the men would be less likely to attack the speakers if there were young girls there too – when a familiar voice said, 'I thought that was you. Were you there for the speeches?'

I turned around and there was Frank. He was even

taller than I remembered him being. His fair hair was, as usual, falling over one eye and he looked as though he'd been running around (which it turned out he had).

'Haven't I met you before?' he said to Nora. He held out his hand. 'I'm Frank Nugent, Harry's friend. You're Nora, aren't you?'

'How do you do?' said Nora, very politely – for her.

'What are you doing here?' I said. I felt quite flustered, especially as this was the first time Frank and Nora had met since she discovered I had told him about our suffrage activities.

'I was playing football on the playing fields,' said Frank. 'I came over to listen to the speeches on my way out. I must say, the suffragettes were fine, weren't they?'

'What we could hear of them,' said Nora.

'It wasn't the most receptive crowd,' said Frank dryly. He looked over at the men that were still jeering the suffragettes and their guards. Then he took a deep breath and shouted, 'Votes for women!'

Some of the men looked over him and made rude gestures.

'Charming,' he said. 'Are you going home now?'

'We're going to the tearooms,' I said. 'We're meeting my sister there.' I pointed towards the crowd escorting the speakers. 'She's over there.'

'Ah,' said Frank. 'May I walk you there?'

'You should come in and have tea with us,' said Nora, extremely boldly.

Frank himself looked a bit taken aback, though not in a bad way.

'I wish I could,' he said, 'but I told my parents I'd be home at the usual post-footer time. Another day, perhaps?'

And now Nora looked as if she was starting to blush.

Anyway, we walked to the tearooms. Frank asked how Harry was.

'He looked a bit feeble when he called over to my house,' he said.

'There's nothing wrong with him,' I said. 'I think it was all a ruse to get out of school.'

But Frank said no, Harry really had been very sick and there was no way he could have gone home on the train with the rest of the team.

'Well, there's definitely nothing wrong with him now,' I said.

'He really isn't that bad, you know,' said Frank, laughing. 'Though I will admit that as a brother he leaves something to be desired.'

'He definitely wouldn't approve of that meeting,' I said, gesturing back towards the site of all the drama.

'You're probably right,' said Frank. 'Oh well, maybe you'll convert him in the end.'

'I doubt it,' I said. We were nearly at the tearooms. 'What did you think of, you know, the window smashing?'

And he said he was impressed by the suffragette leaders' deeds.

'Really?' asked Nora, surprised.

'Well, I'm not sure I always approve of breaking windows and that sort of thing,' he said. 'But it was very brave. And it's certainly getting people's attention.'

'Not always in a good way,' I said, thinking of the rude men in the crowd.

'True,' said Frank. He smiled at me. 'I half expected to hear you had been smashing windows yourself, after all your chalking.'

Now both Nora and I definitely went bright red. For a moment I wondered if we could ever tell Frank the truth, but I knew that probably wasn't a good idea. The fewer people that knew about it, the better. So I laughed (I don't think it was very convincing) and said, 'Oh, we're not going to do anything like that.'

'No,' said Nora. 'Chalking is enough for us.'

We had reached the tearooms.

'Well, Mollie, I suppose I'll see you soon,' said Frank. 'You can tell me more about your crusading.'

'Yes,' I said. Even if I couldn't tell him about the postbox painting, I could tell him about missing the meeting, I thought. In fact, I was sure there were lots of things we could talk about.

'Goodbye, Nora,' said Frank. 'It was very nice to meet you.'

'Goodbye,' said Nora, smiling back at him.

'Goodbye Mollie,' he said. 'If you need me to catch any more terrible dogs for you, do let me know.'

And with a cheery wave, he strode away towards the North Circular Road gate. I do hope I see him again soon. Though hopefully without Barnaby having anything to do with it.

'Well!' said Nora.

'Oh Nora,' I said. 'Don't go on about Romeo and Juliet again, it's quite ridiculous.'

'All right, I won't,' said Nora. 'But,' she added in her grandest voice, 'I give you my blessing.'

I thumped her arm but I couldn't help laughing because she is very funny when she talks like a duchess. And then Kathleen and Phyllis returned, looking very hot and out of breath.

'Well, they've gone off on a tram,' said Kathleen. 'And those louts seem to have given up quickly, for once. For a minute I thought they were going to break the windows.'

'Now, let's have some tea,' said Phyllis. 'And then I'd better get you two home. Don't you have exams this week?'

And so when we had finished some decent buns, we got two trams home. After all the excitement of this week, I ended it studying French verbs and Latin poetry, and of course writing this letter to you. And there I suppose I should end the letter, because this coming week will be devoted to exams and I really don't think I can write anything interesting about them.

I do hope you have found everything else interesting – I always worry that my letters are too long, even though you always say you prefer long letters to short ones. Anyway, I will put this in the post on my way to school tomorrow. I hope all is well with you and that your own exams haven't been too awful. And just think, soon it will be the holidays, and who knows what will happen then?

Best love,
Mollie.

P.S.

Monday

I know this letter is even longer than usual (which is
saying something), but I'm glad I forgot to post it this
morning because something has happened that makes
me realise how much things have changed in the last
few months. And not just for me, or for Nora. Things are
changing in general.

But I'll start at the beginning. It seemed very strange
to be back at school today, when so much had happened
since we were last there. I wish they could have just let
us go on holidays early. I mean, our summer exams aren't
that important, surely? Though I suppose they can't just
abandon the Inter. Cert. and Matric. girls (Their exams
don't start for another week or so).

Anyway, there was nothing we could do about it. Just
as there seems to be nothing we can do about Grace
(unfortunately).

'I saw those suffragettes of yours were making trouble
last week,' she said snootily, when me and Nora were
hanging up our hats in the cloak room. She's more or
less given up on her pretend niceness now. 'I think it's
disgraceful, ladies throwing stones like little boys.'

'We wouldn't expect you to understand,' said Nora haughtily.

'I'm quite glad I don't,' said Grace. 'A lot of grubby nonsense.'

And then the bell rang for our first lesson – which was historical geography, one of my very least favourite subjects. It was very hot, and the classrooms seemed even stuffier and smellier than ever. In fact, as the morning went on, I found myself feeling strangely flat and depressed. Just a few days ago, we'd been brave suffragettes – or at least we'd felt like them. But now we were back in school with exams starting tomorrow, while our leaders were probably going to prison in a few days. And what difference had it made, really? None to those rude men in the crowd. And certainly none to Grace.

What were we doing at all? That was what I thought as a bluebottle buzzed relentlessly against the glaring classroom window. What was the point of it? Did it really make a difference if two girls tried to go to meetings and annoyed their classmates and chalked slogans and even painted something on a postbox? Did anyone notice? And if they did notice us, would they just laugh and jeer like those awful men on Sunday? I mean, if people could laugh at such brave ladies (and Mr. Sheehy-Skeffington), would anything ever change? We hadn't even managed to change people we know. After all, Grace was still being

Grace, only worse. Harry was still being Harry.

And me and Nora didn't even have the courage of our convictions. If we were real suffragettes, I thought, we wouldn't have got rid of the paint and run home. We would have proudly stayed at the scene of the crime and got arrested. They'd have dragged us off to prison shouting 'Votes for Women!' And maybe we'd have got to talk at the meeting on Saturday instead of just standing there eating 'suffra-gate oranges' like good little girls. I sighed.

'Are you quite all right, Miss Carberry?" asked Professor Costello.

I sat bolt upright.

'Yes, Professor Costello,' I said. 'I'm sorry.'

Professor Costello gave me a stern look and then went on talking about the Boyne valley or some such nonsense. I slumped back down in my seat and tried to ignore Grace, whom I could see looking smugly at me from the next desk. And so the morning wore slowly and hotly on.

And then, at break time, it happened. Nora was telling Stella about everything that happened last week, and I left them to go to the lavatory. It was blessedly cool in there, and after I'd washed my hands I leaned my head against the looking glass over the sink for a moment. And in the reflection, out of the corner of my eye, I saw

some pink lettering. I turned around and there it was.
Someone had written VOTES FOR WOMEN NOW!
in large letters of pink chalk on the door of the lavatory
cubicle.

Nora must have done it, I thought, or maybe even
Stella. Though it's strange neither of them told me they
were planning to chalk something at school. I made
my way back to the refectory and when I was pushing
open the big door at the end of the corridor I saw that
someone had scratched VOTES FOR WOMEN into the
corner of one of the panes of glass in the door. I was very
impressed – scratching into glass is a lot more difficult
to get rid of than chalk, or even paint – but again, it did
seem strange that Nora and Stella hadn't mentioned it.
Still, seeing it cheered me up a bit. When I got back to
the refectory the two of them were sitting in a corner
drinking their milk and eating buns.

'Nora's been telling me about how you managed the
postbox,' said Stella eagerly. 'You *are* brave. Well done.'

'I told her we should have worn our scarves,' said
Nora. 'I never knew it was so cold at that hour of the
morning.'

'Which one of you did it?' I said.

'Did what?' asked Stella.

'One of you must have,' I said. 'Was it you, Nora?'

'My dear Mollie,' said Nora, 'I haven't the foggiest idea

what you're talking about.'

'Have you had a touch of the sun?' said Stella in a worried voice. 'Maybe Mother Antoninas was right about the scarf giving you sun stroke last week.'

'In the loo!' I said. 'The pink chalk. And on the window of the door.'

Nora looked a bit worried now.

'I think she has had a touch of the sun,' she said.

'No I haven't,' I said, crossly. And I told them what I'd seen in the lavatory and on the door.

'It wasn't me. I don't think I have the nerve,' said Stella. 'Yet,' she added quickly.

'It wasn't me either,' said Nora. 'I wouldn't have done it without telling you.'

The three of us looked at each other, our eyes wide.

'You know what that means,' said Nora. 'It was someone else. Or two someone elses.'

'Someone we don't know,' I said. 'I mean, we must know at least one of the people who did it, because the chalk was in the Middles lav, but we don't know who exactly it was.'

'But who could it be?' said Stella.

We looked around the classroom, at Maisie and May and Johanna and Daisy and all the others. Inside at least one of those girls – maybe even two, or three, or five, or ten of them – beat the heart of a suffragette. Me and Nora and Stella – we weren't alone. And maybe everything we'd been doing really had made a difference here. Maybe our ideas were spreading out. Like the bilious 'flu or a cold. Only good, of course. Maybe someone had heard us going on about suffragettes and started thinking for the first time about why it was important for women to get the vote, like I had done after I heard the speaker at the Custom House. And just like Frank, I remembered suddenly, had only started thinking about it after I talked to him. Maybe someone had always felt it was important but had thought she was alone until she heard us. And maybe it was nothing to do with us, maybe someone in our class just happened to believe that women should have a say in how the world was run. It didn't matter. What mattered was that there were lots of us who cared and were also willing to do something about it. Well, at least four of us: me, Nora, Stella and the mystery chalker/glass-scratcher. But that is four more girls than there were last year, or even a few months ago. And that has to be a good thing.

Anyway, I didn't feel as glum after that. And of course I don't know what's going to happen next. But I'm glad that Stella made us suffragette scarves, and I'm glad that those brave ladies broke those windows, and I'm glad we painted that postbox, and I'm glad that mysterious suffragette schoolgirl wrote Votes for Women in the lav and on the window. I do think that what happened this week brought us one step closer to getting the vote. It might take months, or even years, but we're going to win this fight. I know we are.

And won't Grace and Aunt Josephine and Harry be absolutely sick as pigs when we do?

Best love, and votes for women!
Mollie

A NOTE ABOUT THIS BOOK

Hanna Sheehy-Skeffington and the other militant suffragette activists mentioned in the book were all real people. Mollie, Nora and their friends, families and teachers are all products of my imagination.

The school the girls attend, however, is real, and I went there. Dominican College was founded in Eccles Street in 1883 and moved up the road to Griffith Avenue in Drumcondra over a century later in 1984. I entered the school four years later, though it wasn't until the twenty-first century that I discovered Hanna Sheehy-Skeffington had been a pupil and a teacher at the school over a hundred years earlier.

One of Sheehy-Skeffington's students, feminist activist and educator Louise Gavan Duffy, went to Eccles Street in 1907. She later wrote that 'it was a very exciting place for me in a very new life: there were crowds of girls from all parts of Ireland – there were whiffs of politics – we had lectures from some very fine women, to whom we owed more than we knew, and who, as well as giving us outstanding teaching in their subjects, let in for us a little outside air.'

While I was researching the book, the school's archivist Sister Catherine Gibson very kindly allowed me to look at the old Eccles Street yearbooks, *The Lanthorn*. As well as providing me with details about the routine of the school and the subjects the girls studied there, pictures of some of the rooms and inspiration for the names of all of the characters in *The Making of Mollie* (apart from the male ones, who are all named after my relatives), the yearbooks also included fascinating and often very funny articles by the girls themselves. These were full of contemporary schoolgirl slang. If you're wondering if Irish girls around 1912 really did use the word 'kid' for a child or use expressions like 'I say' and 'frightfully', I can assure you that they did!

No Surrender by Constance Maud, the book that inspires Mollie and Nora, is a real book. It was first published in 1911 and was reissued by Persephone Books in 2011. You can find more about it at www.persephonebooks.co.uk

While Mollie and Nora's adventures are fictitious, they take place against a backdrop of real events. The parade attended by Phyllis which was disrupted by the Ancient Order of Hibernians took place in the spring of 1912, and the Dublin police protected the suffragettes from the violent mob. Dublin suffragettes really did share information about all the cafés, restaurants and shops that would allow suffragettes to use their toilets, and they also chalked slogans and information about suffrage meetings all over the city. The scene in which a passerby thinks Mollie and Nora are praying is based on a real incident which was reported in a Dublin newspaper!

The big suffrage meeting in the Antient Concert Rooms that Mollie and Nora fail to get into took place on the 1 June 1912 and was a big success (Louise Gavan Duffy was one of the speakers). The I. W. F. L. held meetings in the Phoenix Park every weekend and outside the Custom House every Wednesday. There are some descriptions of these meetings in the I.W.F.L magazine *The Irish Citizen* (which was launched on May 25th 1912), though these reports are not very detailed.

Most of the suffrage meetings I describe in the book are wholly imaginary apart from the very last one, which took place just a few days after the I.W.F.L. women were arrested for breaking windows. That scene in the book is based very closely on the *Irish Times* report of the meeting which appeared on 17 June 1912. All the speeches and the heckles are direct quotations. The same report includes the story of the melodeon and the women selling 'suffragate oranges'. The report says that a young suffragette politely corrected the women's pronunciation, though her advice was ignored – it didn't give the name of the young activist, so I thought Nora could do it!

And finally, according to the *Irish Citizen's* report of the suffragettes' appearance in the police court on the day they broke windows all over the city, the court was told that on the same morning, the words 'VOTES FOR IRISH WOMEN' had been painted on several postboxes across the city, 'for which the police were not able to produce a single culprit'.

www.obrien.ie